'In *The Fetish* are collected forty-one of Alberto Moravia's
stories of Italian life. They are short, clear, realistic vignettes . . .
The central quality here is Moravia's gift for recreating the harsh
disillusionment of lovers; but that special clarity and realism
of description, catching so well a variety of locales and social
settings, is an important element of their concentrated success.
There is a stark exactness about the psychological description
and the description of external reality'
Punch

'Quick and stabbing tales . . . Signor Moravia pulls off the
miracle of completeness on a postage stamp . . . packs an
immense control, with little specious tidying up, his tales are
instantaneous'
Sunday Times

D0267493

Also by Alberto Moravia in Panther Books

Alberto Moravia

The Fetish
and other stories

Translated by Angus Davidson

Panther

Granada Publishing Limited
Published in 1976 by Panther Books Ltd
Frogmore, St Albans, Herts AL2 2NF

L'Automa first published in Italy 1963
This translation first published in Great Britain
by Secker & Warburg 1964
Copyright © Casa Editrice Valentino Bompiani 1963
Translation copyright © Martin Secker & Warburg Ltd 1964
Made and printed in Great Britain by
Richard Clay (The Chaucer Press) Ltd
Bungay, Suffolk
Set in Linotype Times

Contents

Scatter-brains

Signora Cecilia was very like some kind of exotic bird with a tiny body and an enormous, fantastic head. Thin and small (apart from her big head), pale and nervous under her bright make-up, her round eyes made larger by eye-shadow, she appeared to be perpetually traversed by an extremely high-tension electric current which inspired her movements, and even more her conversation, with an irrepressible, over-excited, feverish agitation. As Signora Cecilia herself expressed it, she was absolutely incapable of concentration; or, in other words, of following, just for a few minutes, the development even of the most obvious idea or the description even of the simplest fact. Like horse-flies round a horse that is already irritable and exhausted, associations of thought allowed her no peace: piling up ceaselessly in her over-worked mind, they forced her, against her will, to cut short a subject of conversation she had scarcely begun and launch forth into a second one long before she had even skimmed, still less explored, the first. Usually, oppressed by the tumultuous speed and loquacity of her own mind, Signora Cecilia went chasing after them for as long as she could with her talkative tongue which, it must be admitted, was exceedingly fluent; until, at a certain moment, unable to extricate herself from the muddle, she would take her head between her hands and sorrowfully exclaim: 'Oh, my head, my poor head!' It was her way of, as they say, cutting the Gordian knot. The person she was talking to would, naturally, be left gaping and would give up all idea, for the moment, of getting any further.

That day, Signora Cecilia had something of the greatest importance to relate to a friend of hers, Sofia. The latter, like her, was a very young and pretty married woman. And she too was a scatter-brain of the highest degree. But whereas Cecilia's giddiness came from having too many things to say, Sofia's proceeded from the opposite cause:

from having nothing to say because astonishment, at every moment, emptied her head and completely took away all power of speech. She was perpetually astonished, and escaped one astonishment only to fall into another. Cecilia, therefore, was scatter-brained from too great an abundance of things to say; Sofia, from an absolute lack of them.

On the telephone, after greeting her friend, Cecilia expressed herself in the following manner: 'My dear, my darling, there's something of the greatest importance that I must tell you.... No, no, not on the telephone.... It's a very delicate matter, too ... Come along at once.... You can't? You haven't got the car? Oh, these cars, always under repair....' – and here there followed a long and confused discourse on the troubles of motor-cars – 'I'll send you mine, shall I? ... You'll come in yours? Then it's not broken down? ... Oh, I'm sorry, I understood it was broken down.... Oh, my head, my poor head! Anyhow, come along, come at once, don't waste a single moment.'

So Sofia came. It was early in the afternoon; but Cecilia, notwithstanding her haste to tell her friend of this highly important thing, could not refrain from keeping her waiting almost three quarters of an hour. She had bought, that very morning, a house-coat of absolutely stunning cut and colour, and she wanted to make her appearance in this new and most original garment which was calculated to produce a flattering astonishment in her friend. And indeed, as Cecilia at last came running in with arms out-stretched and an embarrassed expression on her face, exclaiming: 'My dear, my darling, you've been waiting, I know; forgive me, tell me quickly that you forgive me!', Sofia, at the sight of the house-coat – which was truly beautiful and original beyond all description – all at once forgot the highly important thing she had come to hear and, rising to her feet, started walking round and round her friend, full of praises for her elegance. Meanwhile Cecilia, fussy and bewildered, bent over the little tea-table, pouring the tea feverishly into the cups and adding sugar with the tongs: 'D'you like it strong or weak? ... How much sugar? Two lumps?

Three? Oh my goodness, I've put in five ... My head, my poor head! So you like my house-coat, then ... thanks, you're too kind.... Now just imagine, Iole had already sold it to that Signora Pallotta or Pallottola, whatever her name is ... that ghastly parakeet ... and so I said to her: "You tell her that *I've* taken it" ... Iole, naturally, answered: "But I can't lose a customer" ... So I retorted: "Never mind, tell her *I've* taken it; that woman's such a snob she'll be pleased that I've deigned to recognize her existence, even if only to deprive her of a house-coat" ... And so I took the house-coat, and as well as the house-coat I ordered a Dior model – you know, for the party they're giving at the Grand Hotel on Shrove Tuesday.'

Poor Sofia, by this time, had already three things to think about: the house-coat, what Cecilia had said to the dress-maker, and the party at the Grand Hotel. And so once again she forgot the highly important thing that Cecilia was going to tell her, and fastened upon the last of these three novelties – the party. She herself had already, as they say, 'turned down' this party, thinking it to be one of the usual ill-frequented dances that are given in hotels for charity. But on hearing that Cecilia, always a most fastidious person, was going to it, she was filled with astonishment and for a moment quite incapable of thought or speech, as though the ground had suddenly opened beneath her feet. She then asked her friend for explanations; and the latter immediately let loose a flood of comments and criticisms, from which her listener gathered two pieces of news which plunged her once again into her usual dizzy astonishment: at the ball, so it seemed, a royal personage from the Middle East would be making an appearance, an Arab prince or a Shah; and at the ball, also, a prize would be awarded to the most elegant woman in Rome. At this juncture, while Sofia was still vainly seeking to collect her wits, Cecilia smote herself violently on the forehead and exclaimed: 'But there was something I had to tell you!'

'Yes indeed, that's true. Well?'

'Well, it's gone out of my mind.... I simply can't

remember what it was.'

'Make an effort...'

'Impossible ... I've completely forgotten ... I have too
many things to think of – this house-coat, this ball, the
Shah, the most elegant woman in Rome.... But how silly!
It's no use having a competition: everyone knows that the
most elegant woman in Rome is Giovanna.'

Now it must be admitted that Cecilia had thrown out this
name – a quite improbable one – because she was convinced that in reality she herself was the most elegant
woman in Rome, and she hoped that Sofia would tell her
so. But Sofia was too astonished to grasp this subtlety and
all she did was to show indignation: Giovanna the most
elegant woman in Rome? Why, she had no taste, and
besides, she wasn't even young....

Cecilia interrupted her. 'I know for certain that she went
to see a specialist at Lausanne.... He cut the skin underneath her hair and pulled the whole of her face upwards....
He did the same with her bust.... She's all sewn up, from
head to foot, like a football.'

Sofia's astonishment now spread from Giovanna's person
to the prodigies of facial surgery. They spoke of doctors
and operations and then, somehow or other, from doctors
they went on to dentists, and from dentists to the teeth –
probably false because too beautiful – of someone called
Clarice, and from Clarice's teeth to Clarice's fur coat,
which had cost, so it seemed, not less than five million lire,
and from this price to the fashion in fur coats which that
year were being worn long and full, in the 'Raglan' style. It
was now evening, and the manservant exchanged the tea-
tray for a cocktail shaker and two glasses. When he had left
the room, Cecilia suddenly stopped shaking the iced drink
and exclaimed: 'One moment ... wait ... It's on the tip of
my tongue.'

'What? Tell me...'

'That thing I was going to speak to you about ... that
important thing .... Wait a moment, help me...'

'But how can I? I don't know...'

'Wait ... Oh, devil take it, I almost had it.... But no, it's no use.... My head, my poor head!'

They started chattering again. To tell the truth, the subject this time was as serious as it could well be: the merits or demerits of the long drawers, in the 1890 style, which the French dressmakers were intending to launch that same year to take the place of the now old-fashioned 'rompers'. Cecilia doggedly supported the long drawers. Sofia, no less doggedly, championed the short ones – why, she herself did not know; possibly, if she had gone deeply into the matter, she might have discovered that she liked short drawers merely because Cecilia preferred long ones. Pure spirit of contradiction, in fact; and actually – as in those duels in ancient tragedies in which the duellists end up by exchanging swords – Sofia all at once found herself supporting long drawers while Cecilia defended the short ones. The two friends simultaneously burst out laughing, and then Sofia looked at her wrist-watch and jumped to her feet, exclaiming: 'Why, it's getting very late! Roberto's expecting me: we're going out to dinner.... Thank you, my dear; it's been a really delightful afternoon.... Good-bye, my dear ... let's telephone...' They walked through into the entrance-hall, where the first thing they did was to embrace and kiss several times. Then they started chattering again about the dinner to which Sofia had been invited; and there is no knowing how far this conversation would have taken them if Cecilia, suddenly, had not cried: 'At last!'

'At last what?'

'I've remembered what I had to tell you – that important thing. But my dear, it's extremely simple: your husband is Ninon's lover.'

Now Sofia had been married for barely two months. Her astonishment, this time, was enormous and legitimate. Turning pale, she said: 'It's not possible.'

'But of course it is.' Cecilia with a speed equal to the importance of the subject, related how Roberto, Sofia's husband, had been seen, by a reliable person, in a car with Ninon, in a lonely place, in the act of kissing her. Carried away by her own impetuosity, Cecilia added that the thing did not surprise her. Ninon was full of lovers, she had even had a child by Fabrizio.... Sofia was now in the position of one who, in order to assuage the pain of a tooth by pulling it out, uses the rudimentary method of a thread tied to a door and a punch on the head from an obliging friend. Her initial astonishment at her husband's unfaithfulness was driven out by her succeeding astonishment at the affair of Ninon's child. 'You don't say so!' she exclaimed; 'a child by Fabrizio!' Cecila knew all about it: the clinic at Florence where Ninon had gone to have the baby, the sex of the child, its weight, its name. While she was speaking of all this, the front door opened and in came Orazio, Cecilia's husband, a brusque man, of few words and abrupt manners. Without more ado, he simply showed poor Sofia to the door. The two ladies threw each other a last kiss as the door closed; and then Sofia, thoroughly exhausted by the excessive astonishments of the afternoon, went downstairs, got into her car and lay back in her seat with eyes closed.

Later, at home, her husband asked her how she had spent the afternoon. Sofia, who was decking herself out for dinner, was seated in front of the glass at her dressing-table. 'I went to see Cecilia,' she replied; 'a really quiet afternoon.... But the funny thing is that she told me something very important – and I've forgotten it. I simply cannot remember it.'

'Now, come on! What was it?'

'It's no use,' said Sofia, in a decisive, almost irritated tone of voice. 'I've forgotten it, and it's useless for you, with your usual morbid curiosity, to try and find out what it was ... Don't torment me, please; I have a terrible headache.... I've forgotten it and there's nothing to be done about it.'

Appointment at the Beach

They left the car in a clearing amongst the undergrowth, in the shade of a pine-tree, and walked off through the sand-dunes towards the sea. She went ahead of her husband Sergio, running joyously over the burning sand, while Sergio followed her at a distance, carrying the lunch-basket and the beach-wraps. All at once she vanished behind the crest of a dune, and Sergio, following behind, was happy that she seemed so happy; he was sure that, when he reached the top of the dune, he would see her already splashing in the sea. But, when he looked over the top, he discovered that his wife had come to a halt and that the beach was not deserted, as he had hoped. A group of people – half-naked fishermen, from the look of them – amongst whom a man in military uniform stood out conspicuously, were standing still, in attitudes of embarrassment, in front of some branches stuck into the sand. Between the branches could be seen something white.

Sergio walked slowly over towards them and, when he came near the branches, asked his wife: 'What is it?'

'A dead man,' she replied, with a dissatisfied air.

Sergio looked: the branches, already withered by the heat of the sun, drooped their faded leaves over a long form wrapped in a sheet. He was reminded of Egyptian sarcophagi in a museum. The sheet did not mould the dead man's features, but indicated his outline, in simple lines, from his feet to his head: you could make out his knees, his arms folded over his chest, his chin thrown back. Outside the sheet nothing was to be seen but his hair, which was brown and glossy, young, still living. 'He was drowned about an hour ago,' said the man in uniform, a police inspector, taking off his cap and wiping the sweat from his brow; 'we don't know who he is; he had no papers.' Sergio, after a last glance at the corpse, went off with his wife towards the sea.

He watched her as she walked slowly into the shallow water with a discontented air, her arms dangling, her belly thrust forward to meet the little warm waves that seemed to be boiling beneath the blazing sun. It was their first bathe of the year, and Clara was white, with a cold, hard whiteness which, as Sergio knew, would soon turn violently red without ever changing to brown. She was not well-built, being narrow in the hips but with thick legs and slender in the shoulders but with a large head; nevertheless there was, in her figure, so much of her harsh, reserved, suspicious character that Sergio smiled with affection and rushed after her in order to catch her up. But as he ran over the sandy bottom, he tripped in a tangle of seaweed and fell on top of her, knocking her down. She got up at once and said rudely: 'I don't like horseplay in the water.' 'I'm sorry, I tripped,' said Sergio. 'Please don't do it again,' his wife admonished him. Sergio, somewhat mortified, watched her as she moved away from him. They had been married for only six months and their marriage was not happy. They did not get on well together; but Sergio attributed this intractable lack of understanding to the novelty of living together and hoped each day to dispel it.

They bathed together, in silence, wary and ill-humoured, beneath the burning sun, in the warm, shallow water that seemed like clear soup. Yet the coastline, seen from the sea, was beautiful: deserted as far as the eye could see, it stretched, in one direction, to the remote phantom of an ancient watch-tower, in the other it curved away below a rocky shore crowned with woods. The sultry air veiled the horizons in a cloud of sand and heat; the pine-woods above the yellow dunes melted into it as into a mist. 'Beautiful, isn't it?' said Sergio suddenly, breaking the silence. 'To me it looks horrible,' replied his wife gruffly. 'But it was you who wanted to come here.' 'Well, what of it? I made a mistake, that's all. . . . But that doesn't alter the fact that the place isn't beautiful at all.' Sergio, discouraged, was silent. He saw that, whatever he said, his wife would contradict him.

At last they came out of the sea and went to the place on the beach where they had left their little pile of clothes, only a very short distance from the corpse. The beach was now entirely deserted: there was nobody there but the two of them and the dead man underneath the branches. The fishermen and the police inspector had gone away, back over the sand-dunes.

Clara, with an expression of disgust, stood wiping her arms and legs. Sergio said: 'Couldn't we go a little further on? There's plenty of room.... Being so close to a dead person...'

Throwing down her towel, she answered: 'Dead people don't disgust me.'

'Only living ones,' Sergio ventured.

His wife answered him harshly: 'Why d'you always want to pick a quarrel? ... We've come to the beach, so let's enjoy it. But no, not at all; you always have to start arguments.... Now you're trying to make me say that *you* disgust me.'

'I should prefer you to say the opposite,' said Sergio desperately.

'Well, anyhow, it really is true: you do disgust me.... When you start contradicting me just for the sake of contradicting me, you disgust me more than any dead person .... Now are you content?'

Sergio, stunned by such a display of ill will, was silent. Clara stretched herself out, face downwards, and untied her brassière and her slip, burying her bare chest and belly in the burning sand. As soon as she was settled, she asked in an impatient voice: 'Why, what's the time?'

Why does she say: 'Why, what's the time?' instead of: 'What's the time?' thought Sergio, dimly surprised. 'It's eleven o'clock,' he replied. 'It's not possible,' was her immediate, violent reply. Sergio, without a word, simply placed his wrist, with the watch on it, in front of her eyes. 'All right, all right,' she said, in a voice that was almost sorrowful; and Sergio was again astonished.

The dead man under his shelter of branches nauseated

Sergio. He felt a secret longing to go over and pull away the sheet that enveloped his body. Beneath the shelter of branches it appeared to be hotter than elsewhere; you could see a slight trembling in the air, as though from the first exhalations of decay. Sergio thought of the green and gilt flies on corpses, in the war; and he shuddered with repugnance. All of a sudden he said angrily: 'Really, I should like to know why we have to stay close beside this dead man.'

From the hollow of her arm in which her face was hidden, his wife answered: 'Go away then, if you like. I'm staying here.... There's no one to watch beside him: I shall be here, at least.'

So there was nothing to be done. The sun beat down strongly and the glare from the sand was blinding. Sergio, deeply vexed, remained motionless for a little, then, unable to bear it any longer, he rose to his feet, ran across the beach and flung himself headlong into the water. The plunge refreshed him, although the water seemed to him even warmer than before. When he stood upright again, he saw that his wife had also risen and was circling warily round the branches that sheltered the dead man. Seen from a distance, he was attracted afresh by the figure of his wife; and all of a sudden he was amused by the idea of giving her a little display of gallantry. Why is our marriage going so badly? he thought. Why is it? I'll go over to her now and start flirting with her as though she were a girl I had only just met.... Surely, by this evening, I shall have made a conquest of her. He smiled with amusement at his plan and came slowly out of the water. His wife, after wandering for some time around the dead man, had gone back to lie face downwards again beside their pile of clothes. Sergio stretched out beside her and, putting his arm round her waist, whispered: 'Give me a kiss.'

'Why, what's the matter with you?' replied his wife, without raising her head; 'are you crazy?'

'Come, come, can't I even ask you for a kiss?'

'No, not now and not here.'

'Aren't we husband and wife, then?'

'But we're in public, here. And anyhow, you should have some respect for the dead.'

'Oh, hell,' said Sergio, 'didn't I ask you to come away?'

'I'm not going away,' she answered, in a voice that was full of grief but with no anger left in it; 'you go ... I'll stay here.'

Sergio lay down flat and remained so, in the sun, for about twenty minutes, in silence. Then he looked at his watch and saw that it was half past twelve. 'How about having something to eat?' he suggested with forced gaiety, reaching for the lunch-basket.

'But it's not time yet,' cried his wife from inside the hollow of her arm, this time in a voice full of tears. Sergio, as before, said nothing, but placed his wrist in front of her eyes. She looked at his watch and said: 'You eat, then. I'm not hungry.'

Sergio opened a packet, took out a roll with a *salame* filling and began eating with a good appetite. At that moment a little procession appeared on the crest of the dune. First came the police inspector, then two men who seemed to be carrying a stretcher, then a few women and men and finally a number of children. The procession started coming down the dune, over the sandy slope, moving in the direction of the dead man. 'They're coming to fetch him,' said Sergio, his mouth full of bread and sausage; rising, he also went off towards the corpse. His wife, in great haste, re-tied her brassière and slip, jumped to her feet and ran after him.

The little procession, having arrived in front of the shelter of boughs, halted; the men with the stretcher, which had been improvised out of two branches and a blanket, put it down on the ground. The inspector, hot and bored, gave his orders: 'Come on, then! Throw away those boughs! Then lift him up, two of you by the legs and two by the arms, and put him on the stretcher.... Come on, get on with it!' 'Shall we take off the sheet?' 'No, leave him covered.'

Sergio, his curiosity aroused, stood watching the scene, still holding in his hand the half-eaten roll and vaguely conscious of its unseemliness: but it was too late to put it back in the basket and too soon to swallow it in a single mouthful. His wife, who was hovering uneasily round the stretcher-bearers, went up suddenly to one of them and asked in a harsh voice: 'I say, can you tell us who he is?'

The man, who was violently pulling out the boughs that had been stuck in the sand, answered without turning round: 'We don't know; he hadn't any papers.'

'But how did he get here?'

'There's his motor-bike ... up there in the bushes.'

'A ton-up boy,' Sergio could not help saying, in irritation at his wife's attitude.

'Don't be a fool,' she said loudly. One of the bearers heard the abusive remark and turned in surprise to look at them. 'Come on, get on with it!' said the inspector. The four men, two at each end, lifted the white bundle and placed it on the stretcher. But, as they did so, the dead man's head fell back, releasing itself from the sheet, and Sergio saw his face – dark, with fine features but rather commonplace, and of about his own age. His wife ran back towards the pile of clothes and threw herself face downwards on the sand, sobbing.

The procession moved off towards the dune in the same order in which it had arrived: first the inspector, then the bearers with the stretcher, then the varied cortège of fishermen, women and children. Sergio, still holding the roll, went over to his wife who was weeping with her face in the sand and said: 'Why, Clara, I quite understand that it upset you ... but, after all, he was only a stranger.'

Then, from the hollow of her arm, came her despairing voice. 'You never understand anything ... you never will understand anything.... He wasn't a stranger.'

'What ...?'

'We loved one another.... This morning I made an appointment with him here ... and now he's dead.'

Too Rich

When they were on the motorway, the woman said to him, in an insinuating, off-hand manner, as though she were making him an immoral proposal: 'Why don't you drive now? I'm tired of it.' At the same time the enormous American car slowed down and came to a stop on the verge of the road. Lorenzo was startled: 'What? *Me* drive? But I don't know this car.' She answered impatiently: 'It's perfectly simple.... When you want to change gear you press on the accelerator. This is the brake; you only have to touch it and the car stops.' 'Let's try, then,' said Lorenzo, looking at her. She was sitting sideways now, turned towards him, one leg curled back on the seat. She was thin, elegant, yet with something puppet-like about her, due perhaps to her too tight black trousers. A multicoloured head-scarf, knotted on her flat bosom, did duty as a blouse; her face, above her long, sinewy neck, was triangular, her features simple and even coarse though somewhat meagre, and shaded by a straw hat secured by a band at the back of her neck. It occurred to Lorenzo that she looked rather like the long, flat car, which was black outside and red inside; or rather, that she was its logical human accessory, as much in harmony with it as the chromium-plated fins on the boot or the stylized eagle on the bonnet. 'Let's change places, then,' said she, smiling. And, without leaving the car, she started clambering over Lorenzo's legs – it looked as though she were trying, intentionally, to sit on his knee for a moment – and moved over to the far side. Lorenzo, in turn, slipped across behind the steering-wheel, put the car into gear and pressed the accelerator. At once the big car, with its seven yards of rigid, black-painted metal, moved off, light as a bird, with a powerful and silent forward thrust. Then, as the hand of the speedometer moved from sixty to seventy miles an hour and then to eighty, the woman said: 'It's perfectly easy, even a bit boring, don't you think?'

'Yes, it's perfectly easy,' Lorenzo replied.

She added, in a self-satisfied, childish tone: 'If my husband knew that I've taken his beloved car and that I've made you drive it, into the bargain, I should be in trouble.'

'Why, is he jealous?'

'Of his car? Yes, terribly jealous.'

'No, about you?'

'About me? Much less.'

Lorenzo now realized that the car was going faster than he intended. It ran very smoothly, it is true; but it was a smoothness charged with hidden fury, like that of some sly beast with fearsome muscles. A slight pressure on the accelerator, and the car would hurl itself over the asphalt of the road with impatient voracity, as though eager to suck it in. Lorenzo was accustomed to his own small car, which was harsh and ungracious, but docile; whereas this one got out of hand at the slightest provocation. 'And now explain to me,' he said, 'why you woke me up this morning and wanted to go out with me.'

She shrugged her shoulders. 'Boredom,' she said. 'I felt so depressed. When I woke up, I looked out of the window at the swimming-pool. It was just after dawn; an enormous red and green indiarubber frog was floating on the water. Then I thought of you as the only person I wanted to see, and I telephoned you.'

'You did quite right. But alas, things are just as I told you the first day we met: there can never be anything between us.'

'I'm not asking anything from you,' she replied, in an imperious voice that seemed to contradict what she was saying; 'only to be friends.'

'Friendship between you and me is not possible,' Lorenzo answered slowly; 'nor is the other thing possible.'

'But why?'

'Why is it impossible? I might answer: because you have a husband. But that wouldn't be true. The truth is something different: it's because you're too rich.'

She said quickly: 'What importance has that?'

'A very great importance. Money always has importance. In your case, because you have so much of it. In my case, because I have very little.'

'Try to forget it.'

'That's not possible. You're too rich. What does your husband's estate amount to? People say he's a multi-millionaire. My earnings, on the other hand, are on an infinitely more modest scale. You see the difference?'

'I don't see anything.'

Lorenzo went on: 'This car – how much is it worth? Seven million lire, they say – one million per yard. On your finger you have a sapphire – more millions. And your villa on the Via Cassia? Apart from anything else, that swimming-pool which filled you with such an acute sense of boredom cost two million, so I undertand. Again, you have a house in Paris and one in London as well as in Rome. For holidays you go to Venice, Cannes, Majorca. How much does a life like that cost?'

'A great deal,' she said petulantly.

'A very great deal, indeed. And what should *I* do, so as to be with you? Run around after you? And how could I afford that?'

'I could stay in Rome.'

'You have to go where your husband goes. But it's not just a question of that. The money's not only all round you, it's also inside you.'

'Inside me there's nothing but an enormous boredom,' she exclaimed with sincerity.

'And what d'you think this boredom is? Money, nothing else but money.'

'I don't understand you now.'

He stopped the car again on the verge of the road close to a little pine-wood. These pines, with their slender red trunks that looked as pliable as rushes and their green crowns shimmering in the blue air, formed a suitable background for the long, low, glittering car. And the car was a suitable setting for the beautiful woman dressed in the latest fashion. Lorenzo said to himself that the landscape arranged itself in an altogether too docile manner round the woman and the car, and he had an almost spiteful feeling against the servility of nature. A coloured illustration from an American magazine, he thought. She was looking at him imploringly, now. 'Don't let's talk any more about money, if you don't mind.'

'What should we talk about?'

'About us two.'

'We've already done that.'

'We two,' she said emphatically, 'are made for one another. D'you know when I realized that? Yesterday evening, while we were dancing. You said so many things to me, which I didn't understand but which gave me pleasure all the same. You talked to me as no one had ever talked to me before. Thank you.'

Lorenzo blushed right up to his ears. The truth of the matter was that, the evening before, in a night club, he had got slightly drunk, enough anyhow to make him talk too much. He answered vehemently: 'Forget that nonsense.'

'Why? It wasn't nonsense.' As she said this she put out her hand, seeking his. Lorenzo said hurriedly: 'Well, let's go.' The car moved off suddenly, as though on a rush of air. After a moment, as its speed increased, she cried: 'Anyhow, I'm happy now, I'm no longer bored. Isn't that already a good deal?' The car rushed like lightning up a slight rise and an immense plain came into view. In the distance, beyond the green band of pine-wood, the sea sparkled. The car leapt forward, in a kind of rage, on to the downward slope.

Lorenzo now saw, at no great distance, a lorry which was moving fast although laden with dressed stones. Behind the lorry was a small, cheap car, battered and dusty, with a quantity of household goods tied on its roof, full of women and children. Suddenly, at the entrance to a house under construction, the lorry slowed down, stopped almost, in order to enter the building site. The little car slowed down too. Lorenzo remembered his companion's remark: 'This

is the brake; you only have to touch it and the car stops';
and he pressed down the pedal slightly. But the car did not
slow down; on the contrary, to his terror, he saw that the
huge bonnet, like a beast of prey anxious to escape notice,
continued its silent advance towards the little car which,
very soon, it would devastate. Then he pushed the brake-
pedal down as far as it would go, violently, and this time,
with a deafening screech, the car stopped. By this time the
bonnet was barely two feet from the little car. Lorenzo,
white in the face, lay back in his seat. His companion did
not appear to have noticed anything. 'Why, what's the
matter?' she inquired.

'The matter is that the brake doesn't work and I was on
the point of killing that whole family.'

The lorry had now entered the building site, the little car
moved on, and Lorenzo, in turn, pressed the accelerator.
But immediately afterwards, when he touched the brake, he
felt that it was loose and offered no resistance. At the same
time he noticed a smell of burning, which seemed to come
from behind. He pressed the brake again, but felt that it did
not grip. The car came to a stop, by force of inertia, a little
farther on. Lorenzo jumped out immediately.

Thick blue smoke was pouring from one of the rear
wheels. Lorenzo touched the wheel: it was on fire. When he
looked up, he saw the woman's face leaning out close to his
own, with an expression on it that alarmed him. 'What's
happening?' she asked.

She made an ugly grimace of anger and fear. 'Why, what
have you done? Now the wheel's burning. The car may
catch fire.'

'I had to press hard on the brake, otherwise ...'

'It's going to catch fire. And what will my husband say?
Why, what have you done? What have you done?'

'I braked so as not to run into the car in front of me,
that's what I've done.'

'It would have been almost better if you *had* run into it.
What have you done? Now it's going to catch fire. What
have you done?'

Without taking any further notice of him she suddenly ran, in her fear and agitation, into the middle of the road and began waving her arms at every car that passed. Standing on the wide expanse of blinding asphalt she looked, in her tight black trousers, more than ever like a graceful, bewildered puppet. Lorenzo looked down at the wheel: smoke continued to pour from it, thick and blue; and he felt an intense dislike for the great sly machine. 'Let it catch fire in earnest,' he thought. He looked again at the woman gesticulating in the middle of the road and realized all of a sudden that, for some reason which he could not at the moment explain, this accident ended their relationship. This thought restored his serenity; slowly he walked over and sat down on the kerbstone, at some distance from the car.

The woman went on waving her arms in the road; cars slowed down, their drivers looked at the smoke still coming from the wheel and then drove on again. Lorenzo took a cigarette from his pocket, lit it and began smoking with his head lowered. The woman turned, saw that he was smoking and cried, in a voice of uncontrolled irritation: 'Why don't you *do* something? Anyone would think you were *pleased*.'

There was a shrill screech of brakes. Lorenzo looked up and saw a small, open, flame-red car come to a stop; its driver, a bald young man with a pale face almost hidden behind an enormous pair of green- glasses, smiled and started talking to the woman. Lorenzo did not hear what the young man was saying, but he judged from his expression that he and the woman knew each other.

The red car slid gently to the edge of the road, stopped, and the young man got out. Everything then happened just as if Lorenzo had not been there. The young man went to the car, examined the wheel, then opened the boot, took out the jack, placed it under the car and started it working. The woman, meanwhile, stood behind him, anxious but already relieved and full of gratitude. The young man took off the wheel and rolled it away towards the ditch. Smoke was still coming from it, just as thick as before. Lorenzo watched the young man as he stood for a moment observing this persistent smoke; then he heard him say, in a well-controlled voice: 'You know what we'll do? I'll take you in my car and we'll go back to Rome and inform the garage.'

She answered impatiently: 'I'm going home. The chauffeur will see about informing the garage and all the rest of it. Take me home.'

Lorenzo got up from the kerbstone and went over to them. She introduced the two men without looking at him, in a hurried, evasive tone. The young man shook Lorenzo's hand and said: 'I'm sorry, I've only room for one in my car.'

'Never mind, never mind.'

He watched the two of them as they got into the red car, which turned in a half-circle across the road and started off with a roar. Then he went over to the other car, and after examining, for a moment, the smoke which was still coming from it, looked round. The picture had changed now, he reflected. Bereft of a wheel, supported crookedly on the jack, the great luxurious car now looked like a piece of scrap-iron. And there were no pine-trees to provide a setting for its violent forms and glittering paint-work, nothing but the wide asphalt road, with a bristling barbed-wire fence running along the ditch. Beyond the fence, in the midst of burnt-up, yellow fields, could be seen the ruins of an old farm-house. Lorenzo threw away his cigarette and started off slowly in the direction of the sea.

The Escape

As they came close to the island, the outboard engine began spluttering and then stopped; the husband rose to his feet to re-start it. His wife looked at the confused mass of buildings piled up on top of the highest part of the island and finally asked: 'What's that castle?' Her husband, busy with the engine, answered without looking up: 'It's not a castle, it's a prison.' She noticed then that, above the towering buttresses, a grey wall rose against the sky with three rows of windows that appeared to be walled up. 'The windows are blocked up,' she said; 'why is that?' 'They're *bocca di lupo* windows.' 'What does that mean?' 'It means,' replied her husband with a touch of impatience, 'that anyone inside the cells sees nothing but a little piece of sky, very high up.' 'And why?' Her husband inserted the lanyard into the engine and gave a vigorous jerk; but the engine, after a few revolutions, stopped once more. 'Why? To prevent the prisoners making signals, I imagine.' The woman asked again: 'And who is there in the prison?' To her husband this seemed a particularly irritating question, owing no doubt to its quality of obviousness. He half straightened up holding the lanyard, and said: 'It's full of nice, honest people on holiday – original sort of people who prefer prison to a good hotel.' 'Now you're teasing me,' she said. 'But Laura, who would you expect to be there? Murderers, thieves, criminals of the worst kind.' She turned away from the direction of the island, crouching on the seat with her arms encircling her legs, offended.

The memory of an encounter of the previous year had come back to her. She had gone to the island by steamer with her husband, and had seen, coming out of a cabin and going ashore with the other passengers, a young man between two guards, his wrists handcuffed, with a handsome though arrogant face, very pale and with black curls en-

circling his forehead and temples. At the time she had not
asked who the young man might be, although she had
guessed; it had seemed to her that there was a tacit understanding between herself, her husband and the other passengers to take no notice of him and even to pretend to be
unaware of his presence. Yet he had remained in her
memory, owing perhaps to the contrast between his good
looks and the chains with which he was laden. Now, thinking back, she regretted she had not asked for information:
perhaps the young man had been condemned for life; but
she was sure that it could not be for any of those hateful
crimes that give rise to feelings of scorn; clearly he must
have been sentenced for some crime of passion ordained, as
they say, by fate. Suddenly she said: 'Whenever you're
behind an engine, whether it's the engine of the car or the
engine of this boat, you become unreasonable.' Her husband did not reply; but, having again inserted the lanyard,
he gave it an even more violent jerk. The engine started up,
the boat purred away again over the calm water, leaving
behind it a tenuous track that looked like a piece of white,
evanescent lace upon the shot silk of the sea.

And now the boat, having passed beyond the rocky fort-
ress, moved across in front of the island's harbour. The sun
had not yet come into view on this side, and the red, yellow
and white houses along the quayside were still plunged in
the subdued half-light of early morning and looked as if
uninhabited. The boat left the harbour behind and rounded
a promontory. Neither the prison nor the harbour could
now be seen, only a white, slanting shore crowned with
frolicsome vines and rising higher and higher in the distance. They went on for some way parallel with the shore,
then the engine started spluttering again and stopped. The
woman, annoyed, turned her back on her husband and
looked towards the shore; and she took no notice of the
stifled curse he uttered as he rose to his feet again to restart
the engine. He made several attempts, while she continued,
obstinately, to turn her back upon him; finally the boat
started off in the direction of a little beach shut in between

two high rocks, but, when they arrived at a short distance from the shore, it stopped again. The woman heard her husband say, in a tone of irritation: 'I don't know what's the matter ... there must be something broken: what we need is a mechanic'; and, without turning round, she answered: 'Let's go back to the harbour; you'll find a mechanic there.' 'And what happens if we get stuck out at sea? No, I must get out here and go to the village.' She said nothing; she was accustomed to leaving matters of this kind to her husband; and besides, it did not in fact matter to her in the least that the engine refused to work. This indifference, which seemed to be proclaimed by her bent, bare back, exasperated her husband. 'To you it doesn't matter in the least, does it?' he said. 'It's *I* who will have to take that walk to the village.'

She shrugged her shoulders, very slightly, imagining that her husband would not notice. But her husband saw her and said, with the utmost irritation: 'And don't just shrug your shoulders.' 'I didn't shrug my shoulders.' 'Yes, you did. For some time now I haven't liked the way you've been behaving.' 'Oh, leave me in peace, you idiot.' She realized that her eyes were full of tears, for some reason that she could not explain; and she twisted herself yet further towards the shore, as though she were trying to see something. And she did in fact see a man in blue trousers and a white shirt coming quickly down a path from the top of the slope towards the beach. It was, however, a very brief glimpse; once he had reached the beach, the man vanished, as if by enchantment. She wondered whether she ought to tell her husband of her strange vision, and then decided not to do so; but at the same time she realized that she had a guilty feeling – why, she did not know.

Her husband meanwhile had cast anchor, as she knew from the sound of the tackle and the plop in the water; then he said: 'Well, shall we get out?' Mechanically she put her legs over the side of the boat and let herself slip into the water up to her knees, until she touched the sandy bottom with her feet. As she came out on to the black, damp shingle of the beach, she noticed, in the wall of rock on her right, a dark cave that appeared to be deep; and she was suddenly sure that the man of whom she had caught a glimpse on the path was inside it. But she said nothing and again felt a touch of remorse. Her husband had now caught up with her; he took her arm and murmured: 'Forgive me.' '*You* must forgive *me*,' she replied with a lively feeling of hypocrisy, turning and giving him a smacking kiss on the cheek. Meanwhile she was thinking: 'If only he would go away ... if only he'd leave me alone.' Her husband, his serenity quite recovered, said: 'You don't mind waiting for me? I'll go straight there and back; it'll take about an hour.' 'Why, of course not,' she answered; 'and it's so beautiful here.' Her husband went off, climbing the path up the slope. Then she went and sat down on the beach, at some distance from the water, in such a position that she could watch the cave without attracting attention.

For some time she remained motionless, sitting on the shingle, looking at the sea; then, almost imperceptibly, she turned her head in the direction of the cave and was surprised that her husband had failed to notice it: and as she had guessed, the man was there, sitting on the ground inside the cave, his blue-trousered legs bent, his hands clasped round his knees. The upper part of his body and his head were not visible, partly owing to the deep shadow, partly because of a rock which jutted out across the opening. She looked at the hands intertwined over his knees, and all at once she was certain that he must be the young man whom she had seen in chains a year before; those were his hands, she recognized them, the hands which she had then seen loaded with chains. She wondered whether she should speak to him and decided, with a certainty that surprised her, not to do so. Something, she reflected, had started between them from the moment when she had seen him coming down the path and had not informed her husband, something that had happened in silence, that would continue in silence and would end in silence. Meanwhile the minutes were passing, the man did not move, and the impenetrable shadow that enveloped his face seemed to her to be the actual shadow, the mysterious, almost sacred shadow, of the misfortune which separated them and prevented them from communicating. She was aware, nevertheless, that the man's immobility troubled her, as if there existed between them a kind of challenge as to which of them should be the first to move and betray his own feelings. Almost against her will, she suddenly made a gesture which seemed to her to give a name to her troubled feelings; she knew that she had pretty ears, round and small, so she raised her hand and threw back her hair in such a way that the man could see one of them. But the man did not move; and she had a feeling of unreality, of irresponsibility, at the thought of having allowed herself to go so far as to flirt with a convict.

She started gazing at the sea again, profoundly troubled now, more by her own feelings than by the presence of the man. She was now coldly determined to entice him out of the cave, at all costs, even if he came out in order to attack or kill her. She recalled that there were a few objects of value in her bag, and slowly she drew them out – a gold cigarette-case with a ruby in the clasp, a lighter, also of gold, with which she lit a cigarette. Finally, as though she were impatient, she fumbled again, found her watch and looked at the time. The watch, also, was of gold, and she put it down on the shingle beside the cigarette-case and the lighter – a little heap of gold which, she thought, should be tempting to him. But she remembered having imagined that the man had been sentenced for a crime of passion, and she bit her lips; he would not allow himself to be enticed by gold, something else was needed.

Her heart was beating very fast, she gasped for breath, she felt a deep blush mounting in waves to her cheeks: she raised her hand to her shoulder, grasped the shoulder-strap of her costume between two fingers and pulled it slowly down over her arm, until one breast was almost completely uncovered. Then she cast a wild glance in the direction of the cave: the man was still there, silent, motionless, his face invisible. She lowered her eyes to the useless little heap of gold on the shingle, and thence back again to the sea. Her gaze wandered at first to the horizon; then, moving closer, showed her the boat anchored in the dark, still water, a short distance from the shore; and at last she understood what it was that the man was looking at, greedily, anxiously, from the deep shadow of the cave.

Slowly, lazily she rose to her feet and gently stretched herself, clasping her two hands at the back of her neck and throwing back her head. Then she moved down towards the water, saying to herself: 'Good-bye.' She did not go towards the boat but, walking on the sandy bottom, the water rising gradually over her body with an uncomfortable tickling sensation, she made her way towards the extreme end of the little bay, to the place where, by rounding the rocky point, it was possible to reach the adjoining bay. When the water came up to her throat, she threw herself forward and started swimming, drawing farther and farther away from the boat. She went round the rock, put her feet on the bottom and, finally, turned. It was no more than five minutes since she had looked back; but the man was already in the boat; bending down, with his back turned to her, he was busying himself with the engine. He was evidently an expert with outboard motorboats; almost at once the engine started up and the boat went off, describing a semicircle; but, by a chance which seemed to her disastrous, everything happened without her being able to see his face. She stayed where she was, the water up to her chin, speechless, feeling that this silence was the final act of complicity between them. And now a thought tormented her: 'If the engine breaks down again, he'll think I wanted to entice him into a trap.' At last she came slowly out of the sea and made her way to the point on the beach where she had left her bag.

The sun had come into view behind the cliff and shone brightly upon the damp shingle, upon the little heap of gold which the man had not touched, and upon the blue expanse of the sea. She sat down beside her bag and with her eyes followed the outboard motorboat which appeared to be aiming straight towards the open sea. To the right of the beach, from beyond the promontory, there suddenly appeared a launch with three men on board. The motorboat went farther and farther into the distance, changing shape and growing smaller as it went; nevertheless she could clearly distinguish the man sitting in the stern, his hand on the tiller. Then, all of a sudden, it stopped, at the point where the smooth, almost transparent sea became ruffled and purplish blue. It had stopped and the man had risen and was now bending again over the engine. Meanwhile the launch was making resolutely for the motorboat. The woman saw what was going to happen and watched resignedly. The man remained standing for some time, intent on the engine, while the distance between the launch and the motorboat visibly lessened; then he appeared to give up, sat down again in the stern and remained motionless. The launch was now close to the motorboat, now it was touching it. The woman still watched: between the man and the three men in the launch, in the midst of the deserted sea glittering in the sunshine, a leisurely, peaceful conversation seemed to be taking place, as though they were trippers who had met by chance and knew each other. Anyhow, she reflected, the sunshine, the distance, the immensity of the sea and sky made this meeting insignificant, incomprehensible, remote. Then the man stood up, and she saw him move from the motorboat to the launch. She lowered her eyes and looked at her watch: almost an hour had gone by and soon her husband would be returning.

Small and Jealous

The pine-wood was deserted, lapped in a blue, smoky haze in which the red rays of the sun, already low, seemed to be entrapped, incapable, as it were, of penetrating to the undergrowth; nothing was to be seen on the road but three cars, standing empty beside thick tangles of briars and shrubs. Silvio stopped the car at the edge of the road and said: 'Three empty cars and nobody visible.... At this moment, in this wood, there are at least three couples all saying the same things to each other and making love more or less in the same manner. We shall be the fourth.' He intended that his companion should understand, from his ironical tone, that he thought exactly the opposite; but she smiled confidently. He reflected that with her it was necessary to speak clearly and brutally: she was not intelligent, and this, furthermore, was the least of her defects. But how was one to say to her: from today we shall not go on seeing each other? Silvio opened the door and looked at her as she got out: short but slim, with a brief, narrow skirt and a huge leather coat; a large head, with bulging black hair; a pale face, olive-complexioned, passionate. He recalled the summary description of her which one of his friends had given, the first time he had seen her: 'Small and jealous'; and he sighed as he reflected how true it was. But he also realized that he could now look at her coldly and objectively, with an eye that was devoid of feeling. Before, when he still loved her, he reflected, he used to contemplate her without really seeing her; now he saw her, as one sees any ordinary object, without contemplating her. He felt heartened by this thought, which confirmed him in his wish to part from her. And he followed her along a path through the pine-trees.

She walked in front of him with a self-confident step, almost running towards the place in the woods, still unknown to both of them, where they would lie down on the grass and would be, as he had foreseen, the fourth couple to do the same thing at the same moment. Even this resoluteness on her part, he thought, once used to excite him, as being an unusual feature in a woman; now, on the other hand, it seemed to him yet another sign of her stupidity. Without speaking they walked along the path which turned and twisted through the thick undergrowth, and finally came out into a wide, sunlit clearing scattered all over with blackened and trampled litter. 'Last summer's litter,' he remarked, baffled; 'you certainly won't want to sit down here, amongst all this filth.'

She shrugged her shoulders: 'It's all the same to me.' 'Not to me,' Silvio replied sharply. An idea had now occurred to him which pleased him, on account, perhaps, of its cruelty. In the past, their search for a suitable place in this same pine-wood had usually been long and careful: such a place had to be almost level, shady in the summer, sunny at other seasons, shut in by undergrowth from indiscreet eyes, neither damp nor too dry and dusty. It was an agreeable search, owing to the anticipation and tacit understanding which they brought to it. Now, he thought, he would act in the opposite way: he would reject, one after another, all the places she suggested to him, until she became aware that he did not want any place at all and that there was no longer any understanding between them. Rather like the oak-tree from which Bertoldo, in the story, was to be hanged, he thought; the oak-tree was never found for the good reason that it was Bertoldo who had to choose it. Pleased with his sudden inspiration, he followed her, whistling as he went.

'You seem cheerful,' she said, half turning and speaking with a shade of uneasiness in her tone, as though she were jealous of his cheerfulness. 'Yes,' replied Silvio, 'it's a lovely day today.'

'For me too.'

'Why?'

'Oh, you know, because we're together. And why, for you?'

'Guess.'

'How can I possibly know?'

'Guess.'

Now, again, they were in a clearing: protected, without any litter, open to the sun. Silvio noticed, however, that it was on a slight slope and that there were stones on the ground. 'Let's sit down here,' his companion suggested.

'Here? But can't you see that it's on a slope, so that as soon as we sit down we shall feel ourselves sliding away?'

'All right, let's look for another place.'

She started walking on again, and said: 'Now let's see whether I can guess the reason why, for you, this is a lovely day. You must tell me whether I'm hot or cold.' This was a game they often played. She stooped down, picked a blade of grass, put it in her mouth, and went on: 'Well then, for you this is a lovely day. The reason?'

'What next! You've got to guess.'

'But at least give me some indication.'

Silvio hesitated. 'Well, let's say it's because I'm on the point of setting myself free from something.'

'Setting yourself free from something? From the chill you had yesterday?'

'Cold, cold!'

'Why shouldn't we sit down here?' she asked, pointing to a patch of ground. It was a more or less level clearing, well enclosed on all sides by undergrowth. Silvio immediately shook his head. 'Don't you see how dusty it is? We should be covered with dust from head to foot when we got up again.'

'Ugh, how difficult you are today!' she said coquettishly. 'Well then, let's go on farther.'

So they went on. The pine-wood was now so thick that there were no paths. The low boughs of the undergrowth yielded with a fierce rustle to let them pass; thorns caught in their clothes; yellow autumn leaves, twitched from the branches, were left clinging to them.

'So you're on the point of setting yourself free from something,' she resumed. 'Let's see, then; is it an object or a person?'

'Try to guess.'

'An object?'

'Cold, cold.'

'A person?'

'Hot.'

'A person, then?' They had now reached a point where it appeared impossible to go any farther. The tangle of briars and bushes was so dense that the sun itself seemed to penetrate only in hesitant, mysterious fragments. as though its rays had been torn and shattered on the way. But a great, round bush had an opening at the bottom which revealed a spacious hollow, a kind of cave amidst the foliage. 'Let's creep in there,' she suggested; 'it's like a little room.'

'In there?' Silvio twisted his lips. 'We'd have to crawl along the ground and get dirty.'

'Not at all; look!' Impetuously she threw herself down on all fours, taking no notice of him as he stood watching her, and, walking on hands and knees, like an animal, penetrated into the recess; then she turned and called out to him, laughing: 'Come quick! It's lovely inside here.'

'No, no,' said Silvio in a peremptory tone, 'I'm not coming.... And will you please be so kind as to come out again at once?'

His voice must have sounded disagreeable to her, for the laughter died on her lips; without a word, she crawled out of the opening and stood up again. 'What's wrong with you today?' she asked.

'Nothing. Let's look for another place.'

She gave what seemed like a sigh; but she recovered herself quickly and said, as she started off in front of him: 'Well then, you want to set yourself free from some person. If I were in your place, I know who it would be.'

'Who?'

'Your housekeeper. I can't bear her. She always looks askance at me when I come to see you. If only because of that housekeeper, I should like us to get engaged. Then she'd have nothing to find fault with. Is it the housekeeper, then?'

'Cold.'

'Then it's Gildo.'

Gildo was Silvio's best friend. She was jealous of him, as she was of all the people she had found in his life at the time they had first met. Silvio said roughly: 'Cold again. And you needn't even hope for that.'

'I'm not hoping for anything,' she replied; 'he's not a good friend to me, that's all.'

'Cold, cold, cold as ice.'

'Very well,' she said, annoyed; 'then is it by any chance your mother?'

His mother, also, was one of the people of whom she was jealous, either because she did not look with a friendly eye upon their relationship, or for the simple reason that Silvio was fond of her. 'Cold, of course,' he said. 'Don't you think you're going a bit too far?'

'Why? Your mother can't bear me and I can't bear her.'

'All right, but anyhow – cold.'

'Are you quite sure?'

Silvio looked at her and suddenly felt almost sorry for her. None of his own immediate circle liked her; and now he too was turning against her. He started, on hearing her announce triumphantly: 'This is the ideal place.'

It was, indeed, a clearing to which there could be no objection – level, full of sunshine, carpeted with pine-needles, shut in by the undergrowth. 'I'm not moving a step farther than here,' she said, in a voice that was at the same time bellicose and mournful. Silvio noticed this unusual tone and did not dare to protest. His eyes wandered over the clearing, then he looked up at the bushes which surrounded it. 'But we're right up against the road,' he exclaimed. He crossed over to the bushes: the road, in fact, ran along only a step away from them, deserted as far as the eye could reach and already invaded by the blue mist of sunset. She replied in the same strange voice, both melancholy and aggressive: 'I don't mind in the least. I'm staying here.' As she said this, she lay down, awkwardly, remaining for a moment with her legs in the air and then

regaining her equilibrium with difficulty. Silvio saw that he
could not go on refusing, so he too sat down, saying: 'All
the same, I don't like this place; we're too close to the
road.'

She made no answer. She took his hand and, looking him
in the eyes, asked in a clear voice: 'It's *me* that you want to
free yourself from, isn't it?'

Silvio realized that he must give her an answer, but he
had not the courage and sought to gain time. He, in turn,
asked: 'What makes you think that?'

'A short time ago, in the car, I said: What a beautiful
day; I should like to die on a day like this. And you
murmured between your teeth: I wish you would. You
thought I hadn't heard; but I've got very sharp ears.'

Silvio was so disconcerted that he found nothing to say.
She continued firmly: 'You actually desire my death. It's
sad, that. Don't you think that, this being so, we'd better
part?'

Silvio raised his eyes towards her as if he hoped to discover a pretext for the answer he had to give. He expected
to see a face that was sorrowful, pathetic, unbearable; he
was surprised to find, instead, that she looked calm and
resigned. She truly loved him, he reflected, even to the point
of being willing to lose him. Then he noticed a detail: like
the pine-wood beneath the rays of the sun, so, as his eyes
moved gradually upwards, her face at the same time became animated. There was a faint smile on her lips, her best,
her most seductive smile, a smile that he loved because,
perhaps, it was ambiguous and a little cruel; her cheeks,
usually pale, seemed to redden slightly; her eyes, which
were large and lack-lustre, seemed to become clearer and
more luminous. Suddenly it occurred to him that, for
himself at least, it was even more important to be loved
than to love. And that his decision was perhaps merely
a point of pride; after which he would be left alone
with his mother, his friends, his housekeeper and all the
people, in short, who hated this woman, but who could not

take her place. At last he declared slowly: 'The things you're saying are absurd ... I don't want to leave you.'

'Truly?'

'Really and truly.'

The Fetish

Immediately after the wedding they had gone to live in a penthouse flat in the Parioli district of Rome which Livio's father-in-law had made over to his daughter as a dowry. The flat was almost empty, except for such pieces of furniture as were indispensable; but the bride declared she was in no hurry: she wished to furnish it in her own way. And so, in a leisurely manner, she started to acquire, here and there, furniture, fittings, ornaments and pictures, all in a very 'modern' taste which to Livio, convinced that she was following the fashion rather than a reasoned preference, seemed at the same time both conceited and snobbish. The fetish was discovered by his wife in the back shop of a rather special kind of antique-dealer, an elderly American who had set up a small shop in order to liquidate the stuff he had accumulated, in a villa belonging to him, during twenty years of travel all over the world. It – the fetish – was a cylinder of grey stone of the most ordinary kind, as tall as a man but much broader, terminating in a head shaped like a pointed cone, with strongly stylized features: all that was indicated was the arches of the eyebrows, the septum of the nose, and the chin. At each side of the cylinder, where the junctions of the arms should have been, two round bosses, like two buttons, were carved in the stone. The figure, rough and imprecise though evilly expressive, at once aroused extreme antipathy in Livio. He did not admit it to himself, but the reason for this antipathy lay, in truth, in his wife's infatuation for the fetish – one infatuation amongst many that he disapproved of because he did not understand it.

Livio took to calling the figure 'The Martian'; it did in fact somewhat resemble the clumsy puppets by which the illustrators of comic papers usually represent those imaginary celestial creatures. 'I'm not going to kiss you good morning today,' he would say; 'the Martian is watching us.'

'The Martian seems more than usually ill-humoured today; d'you see how sulky he looks?' 'Last night I went into the bathroom and what did I see? The Martian brushing his teeth.' 'Don Giovanni had the statue of the Commendatore, I have the Martian. That's an idea: why don't we invite him to supper?'

This last remark, contrary to what was usual, elicited a response. They were eating in the living-room, right in front of the fetish, which appeared to be watching them intently from its half-dark corner. 'I'm almost inclined,' she said, 'to take you at your word and leave you to finish eating with *him*.'

She spoke calmly, pronouncing each syllable distinctly, her head lowered. But with so obvious a hostility that Livio had almost a feeling of fear. Nevertheless, carried away by his own joke, he persisted: 'The first thing to do is to see whether he'll accept the invitation.'

'In fact,' she went on, as though she had not heard him, 'I'll leave you anyhow. Enjoy your meal.' She put down her napkin on the table, rose and left the room.

Livio remained seated, and tried for a little to imagine how the fetish would manage to leave its corner, roll on its circular base up to the table, and then sit down and eat. A few days before he had been to a performance of *Don Giovanni* at the Opera; and the coincidence amused him. But what sort of a voice would the fetish have? In what language would it speak? To what Papuan or Polynesian hell would it drag him down at the end of the supper-party?

These fancies, however, did not suffice to distract him from his wife's gesture. He hoped it was a piece of momentary ill-humour, he expected to see her reappear in the doorway; but nothing happened. Now, after his previous amusement, the idea of the fetish coming to dine with him disgusted him. And the fetish itself, looking at him from its dark corner, filled him with embarrassment. Finally he called out in a loud voice: 'Alina!'; but no one answered, the flat seemed empty. The maid had come in with the dishes on a tray. Livio told her to put it down on the table, then rose and went out.

The bedroom was at the far end of the passage; the door was ajar; Livio pushed it and went in. This room, too, contained no furniture apart from the bed and two chairs. There was a suitcase on the bed, open. His wife, standing in front of the wide-open wall-cupboard, was taking a dress off its hanger.

For a moment Livio was dumbfounded, not knowing what to say. Then he realized that his wife was on the point of leaving him, two months after their wedding; and an icy chill ran up his spine. 'Why, Alina,' he said, 'what in the world are you doing?'

At the sound of his voice she at once let go of the coat-hanger and sat down on the bed. Livio also sat down, put his arm round her waist and murmured: 'But why, Alina, why? What's come over you?'

He expected a conciliatory reply but, when he looked at her, he saw that he was mistaken. His wife's face, round, massive, of a livid pallor in which her pale blue eyes stood out conspicuously, was darkened by a settled hostility. 'What has come over me,' she said, 'is that you make jokes about everything and that I can't stand your jokes any longer.'

'But it's my nature; I like making jokes – and what's the harm in it?'

'There may not be any harm in it, but I can't stand it any longer.'

'But why, my love?'

'Don't call me "my love". You never talk seriously, you have to be witty about everything, you always have to show that you're superior to everything.'

'Come, come, Alina, don't you think you're exaggerating?'

'I'm not exaggerating at all. Every time you make a joke, I feel my heart sink. One would think ...'

'What would one think?'

'One would think that, since you can't bring yourself up to the level of certain things, you try, by means of sarcasm, to bring them down to *your* level. Besides, it's not only that...'

'What is it, then?'

'You even make jokes at moments when no man would make jokes. During our honeymoon you said something that I shall remember all my life.'

'What was that?'

'That I shall never tell you.'

Silence followed. Livio was still clasping her round the waist, as he sat beside her. Then, as he looked at her, he realized, with the feeling that he was making an important discovery, that it was the first time since they had come to know each other that he had spoken to her seriously, in a sincere, affectionate way, without hiding behind a mask of jokes. He reflected that it had needed nothing less than a threat of abandonment to induce him to change his tone, and suddenly he felt remorseful. 'Now, Alina,' he said, 'let's consider what it is that has really happened. You bought that fetish, which I didn't like, and brought it home. Why did I begin to make jokes about the fetish? Not, certainly, because it's ugly or ridiculous or clumsy; there are already plenty of clumsy, ugly, ridiculous things in this flat. No, it was because you became infatuated with it to such a degree...'

His wife sat listening to him with an attentiveness that seemed to emanate from the whole of her compact, heavy body and become concentrated in the small, fleshy ear which peeped out from beneath her black hair. All of a sudden she clapped her hands and turned towards Livio: 'You said it, you've said it, once and for all.'

'What d'you mean?'

'You can't endure what you call my infatuations.'

'No, of course not; and so...?'

'But don't you realize that what you call my infatuations are my feelings, my affections, myself, in fact?'

'Have you then a feeling, an affection for that stone puppet?'

'I might have – who knows? I have – or rather I had –

a feeling for you, certainly. And you've treated it as an infatuation, you've thrown your icy shower-bath of jokes over
it.'

'When have I ever done that?'

'I've already told you, during our honeymoon.'

'I made jokes about your feeling for me during our
honeymoon?'

'Yes, in Venice, to be precise in the hotel room, the first
night. And you didn't make jokes only about my feeling but
also about my physical appearance, and just at a moment
when no man – and mind, I say this with utmost seriousness
– when no man would have dared to do so.'

'I made jokes about your physical appearance?'

'Yes, about one detail of my appearance.'

Livio suddenly blushed up to his ears, although he was
quite unable to recall having made a joke on that occasion.
At last he said: 'It may be true, but I don't remember.
Anyhow I should like to know what the joke was. It may
have been an innocent thing, like the remark I made about
your fetish this evening.'

'Certainly it was an innocent thing, inasmuch as you
weren't conscious of it. However, it had the same effect on
me as if you had put a piece of ice down my neck. It was
our first night after our wedding and you didn't realize that
I hated you.'

'You hated me?'

'Yes, with all my soul.'

'And do you hate me now?'

'Now – I don't know.'

Livio again remained silent, looking intently at her. Then
suddenly he had the feeling that he was face to face with a
complete stranger, about whom he knew nothing, neither
past nor present, neither feelings nor thoughts. This feeling
of estrangement had arisen from her remark: 'You didn't
realize that I hated you.' And indeed he had not realized
that he was holding in his arms a woman who hated him.
About that night he remembered everything, even the wind
that from time to time caused the curtain to swell out

slightly over the window wide-open on to the Lagoon; but not her hatred. Moreover, if he had not been aware of so important a feeling, how many other things had escaped his notice, how much of her had remained unknown to him? But it was clear by now that his wife did not intend to leave; that the suitcase open on the bed formed part of a kind of ritual of matrimonial dispute; that he himself must now initiate the reconciliation, however strange and unknown she might seem to him. With an effort, he took her hand and said: 'You must forgive me. I am what is generally called an impious man.'

'What does impious mean?'

'The opposite of pious. A man for whom sacred things do not exist. But from now onwards I shall try and mend my ways, I promise you.'

His wife looked at him, she contemplated him, in fact, with her pale blue, rather sullen eyes; as one looks at a singular and incomprehensible object. Finally she said, quite simply: 'Well, go on back, I'll be with you in a moment'; and, leaning forward, she gave him a smacking kiss on the cheek.

Livio would have liked to say something but he could not find anything to say. He rose, went back into the living-room and sat down again at the table. He took a cutlet from the tray, put it on his plate and prepared to start eating. Then he dropped his knife and fork and looked in front of him.

The fetish, as before, was right opposite him; its brow low above its eyes like a vizor, it seemed to be staring at him with a menacing, demanding air. As though it wished to say to him: 'This is only the beginning. There will be all too many other things about which you will have to stop making jokes.'

Livio remembered Don Giovanni and reflected that he at least had had the consolation of being punished for mocking at the principles of a recognized and respected religion. But he himself had to pay respect to an unconsecrated world, without hell and without paradise, a world that was mute and absurd, like the stone fetish.

A rustling sound made him start. His wife had come back and was now seated opposite to him again. Livio noticed that, in perspective, his wife's face appeared to be closely coupled with the stupid, ferocious face of the fetish. And he shuddered anxiously.

The Automaton

After he had finished dressing, Guido went and looked at himself in the wardrobe mirror and had, as usual, a feeling of dissatisfaction. He was, in fact, wearing clothes that were entirely new and of the best quality – a new jacket of herring-bone cloth, new grey flannel trousers, a new tie with bright-coloured stripes, new red woollen socks, and new wash-leather shoes; and yet he failed to achieve elegance, he looked like a lay figure in the window of a multiple store.

Guido left the bedroom, the untidiness of which irritated him, and went into the living-room. Here all was clean and tidy and gleaming; he felt calm again, in spite of the fact that, ever since he had woken up that morning, he had been tormented by a suspicion of having forgotten something: an appointment? a telephone call? a bill to pay? a festive anniversary? Finally he shook his head and went over to the record-player in the corner beside the fireplace. The record-player, of American make, was automatic; that is, when you pressed an external knob, the arm with the stylus rose by itself, moved across, lowered itself and came to rest at the edge of the disc. Guido took a disc of light music at random from the holder, inserted it and pressed the knob. Then an unexpected thing happened: the arm raised itself, moved across, but did not lower itself; instead, it went on moving across in what seemed a thoughtful sort of manner, and finally, instead of at the edge, came to rest at the centre of the disc. There was a crackling, scraping sound, the arm darted back across the disc, lifted itself up again and with a loud click went back to its original position.

Guido took off the disc and examined it in the light by the window: it was ruined; deep scratches could be seen in several places. For once the automatic device had failed to work. Guido, considerably disconcerted, put on another record, but the arm raised and lowered itself without any further errors. As he listened to the music, he wondered what could have been the reason for the record-player's strange behaviour, but he was aware that the probable technical explanation did not satisfy him. At that moment his wife came in.

She was leading by the hand their two children, Piero and Lucia, both of them under five years old, both of them with fine, sensitive faces, particularly Piero who strongly resembled a photograph of Guido at the same age. She said to the two children: 'Run and give Papa a kiss,' and she herself remained in the middle of the room while they, obedient and affectionate, ran over and climbed on their father's knee. Guido, in turn, embraced them; and as he did so, he looked over their curly heads at his wife and noticed, as though he were seeing her for the first time, that she was tall, thin and flat, dried up and drained of vitality by her two confinements, devoid, now, of any kind of feminine charm. He noticed also that she wore glasses and that her nose was slightly red; that she was wearing a blue, full skirt and a sweater of a darker blue. It seemed to him all at once that all these details must have a significance of their own, rather like the details of picture-puzzles that can be explained by one single word; but his wife did not give him time to find it. 'Come along, let's go,' she said: 'it's getting late already, and if we wait any longer there's a danger of our finding the roads crammed with cars.' 'Let's go,' repeated Guido; and he followed his wife, who had again taken the children by the hand.

The flat was on the ground floor of a new building in the Parioli district; its entrance door opened on to a minute garden with cement paths, beds of tulips and little trees cut to the shape of globes and cones. The family crossed this garden and came out into a narrow street flanked with new buildings and encumbered with rows of cars along the pavements. Guido was now again asking himself what he had forgotten that morning, and, still with this thought in mind, helped his wife and children into the car, put it into gear and started off. They went quickly down on to the Via

Flaminia, crossed the bridge and turned along the Lungo-tevere. The goal of their expedition was the Lake of Albano. It was Sunday and a beautiful day, as his wife observed, sitting at the back with the little girl; it was a pity, it was really a pity that they could not have a picnic, but it had rained recently and the ground was still damp. To this, Guido made no answer. His wife went on talking volubly and sensibly, addressing herself now to her husband and now to the two children. Guido, for his part, concentrated his whole attention on the road which, crowded as it was, and with people on Sunday outings into the bargain, demanded more prudence and skill than usual.

After a long stretch of the Via Appia Antica, Guido turned into the Via Appia Pignatelli and thence into the Via Appia Nuova. He kept up a regular speed, not driving very fast even when the road in front of him was clear. His eyes, meanwhile, took note of a quantity of things which seemed interesting but whose significance escaped him – the glitter on the chromium plating of a big black car in front of them, the immaculate whiteness, speckled with points of light, of a cylindrical petrol-tank half hidden amongst the budding trees of spring, the lime-washed brilliancy of houses, the silvery gleam of an aeroplane as it came down diagonally across the sky to land at the Ciampino airport, a sudden flash from a window struck by a ray of sunshine, the chalky tinge of the warning lines painted on the trunks of the plane-trees along the road. All these white, gleaming, flashing things contrasted stridently with a big black cloud which had spread over the sky and threatened to spoil the fine day; the landscape, too, of a bright, tender, almost milky green, was out of harmony against the dark, stormy background. Once again Guido wondered what could be the significance of this contrast, but he could find no solution: and yet he was sure that there was one. His wife, behind him, was talking to the little girl; the little boy, who was sitting beside him, had knelt up on the seat with his hands on the back of it and was taking part in the conversation between his mother and sister. The fresh, shrill voices of the children asking questions, the calm voice of the mother answering them, also concealed some meaning or other, he was sure; but Guido, as with all the other things that he noticed one by one, failed to discover it, although he was convinced that it was there.

Then the children stopped talking and in the silence that followed Guido's wife seemed to become conscious of his silence and asked him: 'What's the matter? Are you in a bad humour?'

'No, I'm not in a bad humour.'

'You're not in a good humour either, are you?'

'I'm in a middling humour, my usual sort of humour.'

'That's just what I value most in you, your middling humour, as you call it; but I had the impression that you were in a bad humour.'

'Why d'you like my middling humour?'

'I don't know, it gives me a feeling of security. The feeling of being with a man in whom one can have complete confidence.'

'And that man is *me*?'

'Yes, you'; his wife spoke quietly, objectively, as if about a third person. 'I have confidence in you because I know that you're a good husband and a good father. I know that with you there can't be any surprises; that you always do the right thing. This confidence makes me happy.'

'You're happy with me?'

'Well, yes'; his wife appeared to reflect for a moment, scrupulously; 'yes, I am happy, I can say without any doubt that I'm happy. You've given me everything I wanted, a home, children, a comfortable, secure life. Are you glad I'm happy with you?' She leant forward and gave him a light, affectionate caress on the back of the neck. Guido replied: 'Yes, I'm glad.'

They had left the Via Appia Nuova now for the Via dei Laghi and were moving between green fields in which could be seen, here and there, the little quivering white and pink clouds of fruit-trees in blossom. Then there was a yellow mimosa beside a blue house; and then some Judas trees whose branches were thick with wine-red flowers. 'I wasn't in a bad humour,' said Guido; 'I was merely thinking about something that happened a short time ago.'

'What was that?'

He told her about the record and about the failure of the mechanism of the record-player, and concluded: 'The record's ruined now. But above all I can't find any explanation of why in the world the record-player failed to work.'

His wife said jokingly: 'Obviously machines sometimes get fed up with being machines and want to prove that they're not.'

'Yes indeed, it may be that.'

The little boy, who was still kneeling on the seat beside Guido, suddenly asked his mother whether they were going to have strawberries to eat that day. His mother explained that there were no strawberries at that time of the year; strawberries were fruit and spring was the season of flowers, as he could see for himself if he looked at the countryside. Guido listened for a few moments to his wife's discourse and then made a last, feebler attempt to remember what he was convinced he had forgotten that morning, but he could find no solution. A business appointment, possibly, for the next day, which was Monday: in any case, at his office everything was written down in the appointments book and it would be easy to make certain of it.

By now they had come on to the road that runs round the Lake of Albano which, nevertheless, was not yet visible, being hidden by the gardens of the numerous villas. Then, at a bend in the road, the lake began gradually to appear: first the precipitous slopes, covered in dark, thick furry green, then, far below, as though at the bottom of a funnel, the motionless, sombre lake in which the high banks and the cloudy sky were reflected with uneven shadows. Guido cast a hasty glance at the lake and again had the feeling of a significance concealed behind numerous, scattered details. The road, now, was uphill, and he changed gear from

fourth to third. At the top of the hill could be seen a belvedere outlined against the sky, beyond which, supposedly,
there would be a sheer drop of several hundreds of feet.

Suddenly Guido felt as if he were coming out of a long
tunnel into the open, emerging from a close, stagnant
atmosphere into the clear, light air. And in company with
this sensation there came to him a precise thought – to
drive the car at full speed into the void beyond the top of
the hill, to hurl himself, together with his wife and children,
into the lake. The car would take a leap of eight or nine
hundred feet and fall straight into the lake; death would be
instantaneous. Guido wondered whether this thought was
inspired by some kind of hatred for his family and realized
that this was not so. On the contrary, it seemed to him that
he had never loved them so much as at this moment when
he desired to destroy them. But was it then truly a thought,
or was it a temptation? It was a temptation, an almost
irresistible temptation, of a deathly, tenacious, consuming
sweetness, such as might inspire the kind of compassion
that is unwilling to remain impotent.

The car swerved to the right until it grazed the verge of
the road as it went rapidly up the hill towards the belvedere. But as it passed the highest point, Guido found himself
faced by a small meadow that he had not foreseen; the
precipice had been left behind and now the moment had
passed: to plunge into the void would have been a natural
thing, to go back in order to do so would be a crime. He
stopped the car, put on the hand-brake and sat still. He had
no particular feeling; merely it seemed to him that he had
left the clear, light air and gone back into an atmosphere of
closeness and stagnation. His wife, as she got out of the car,
said: 'Well done, it was a good idea to stop; we'll go and
have a look at the lake.'

When they were standing, all four of them, at the edge of
the belvedere and leaning forward, hand in hand, to gaze
at the lake, Guido remembered, all of a sudden, what it was
that he had forgotten: that this Sunday was the anni-

versary of their wedding-day; they had spoken of it the evening before, after the children had been put to bed; and the expedition had been, in fact, planned to celebrate the occasion.

The Bill

As soon as he arrived, Claudio, leaving his suitcase at the hotel, ventured out on a first walk. He had never been on the island, he knew no one there and at once felt a little intimidated by the air of complicity, of blissfulness even, in all the people he ran into as he walked along. They were almost always couples, some of them young, some middle-aged, some elderly; men without women, like himself, were rare; solitary women were positively not to be seen. This fact struck him like a rebuke: he was alone, his last love-affair went back to a couple of years previously, and what had he come to do on the island? It seemed to him that all these couples, as they passed close to him, were saying: we're two and you're only one; we know where we're going and you don't; we have a purpose in life and you haven't. His shyness now was transformed into panic; in order to recover himself, Claudio went into a bar and ordered a cup of coffee of which he felt no need.

There too there was a couple – he, a thin, fair-haired young man with a sharp face and a clear, inflexible look in his eye; she, a very dark girl who looked attractive to Claudio. The young man, leaning forward with his foot on the brass bar at the counter, was playing idly, as he chattered, with some keys or some other metal object; and Claudio, when he had drunk his coffee, went over to the cash-desk to pay. There was a tinkling sound on the floor; Claudio, thinking that a coin had fallen from his pocket, stooped and put out his hand: a silver, five-hundred-lire piece was indeed lying there, two steps away from him. But the fair young man said in a calm voice: 'I'm sorry, but that coin is mine,' and Claudio, too late, became aware of his mistake. Blushing with an absurd kind of shame, he hurried out of the bar and made his way, at a run, towards the Passeggiata degli Oleandri, which was indicated in the guide-book as one of the most beautiful spots on the island.

There was no one on this 'Oleander Walk' which, shaded by thick-foliaged trees, wound sinuously all round the island, half-way up the coastal slope, with, on one side, a steep incline covered with pine-trees through which could be seen, here and there, the blue, shining expanse of the sea, and on the other, an uninterrupted row of gardens and villas; there was no one walking on the red brick paving beside the white- and pink-flowered oleanders that gave the path its name; and Claudio very soon felt reassured. At a bend in the path he saw in the distance a two-storeyed villa, white with green shutters and a small neo-classical porch with fluted pillars; he reflected that it must be an old house, to judge at least from its style, from the extraordinary size of the heavy-blossomed wistaria that covered its façade, and from its stained and peeling plaster. No sooner had he passed the villa than he heard an insistent voice calling: 'Signor Lorenzo, Signor Lorenzo!' This voice was pronouncing a name which was not his, but it seemed actually to be calling him, as he realized when he caught sight of a hand sticking out through a gate and making signs at him. He walked over and then saw, behind the bars of the gate, a stout, elderly lady with a red, puffy, downy face and intensely blue eyes. Looking down, he saw that she was holding back by the collar a magnificent Great Dane, dappled pink and grey, which was yelping and whining, possibly with pleasure. 'How are you, Signor Lorenzo?' said the lady. 'You see, Tiger recognizes you too, although he was only a puppy when you were here.... Come inside a moment. I'm so pleased to see you again.'

Claudio was on the point of informing the lady of her mistake when he was deterred by an instinct of fun and adventure: he was alone; he knew nobody; and possibly, with luck, thanks to her misapprehension, he might find companionship. Meanwhile the old lady had turned away and was leading him, with heavy, tired steps, into the porch and thence into an entrance-hall furnished with wicker seats and armchairs and so into a half-dark sitting-room. Here there were two armchairs and a stiff settee with embroideries on the backs, there were oil paintings of sea-pieces and bunches of flowers, openwork, bead-studded lampshades, vases, ash-trays, snuff-boxes, photographs and other knick-knacks on shelves, tables and cabinets. The lady now collapsed into an armchair and the dog stretched itself out at her feet. Still somewhat out of breath, she said: 'Here everything is just as it was when you left.... Well, well, nothing changes in my house, nothing has changed for years. But you too, d'you know that you haven't changed at all.'

'I haven't changed,' said Claudio, anxious to know when, according to the lady, he had been in that house before. 'I haven't changed because, after all, it isn't so very long ago.'

'Three years,' said the lady. 'A long time for me, who am old, but very little for you, who are young. But d'you know that, whenever she sees me, Elena asks me about you?'

So there was Elena too, thought Claudio, much pleased. A nice name, Elena; and she must be a pretty, young, attractive, likeable woman. 'Elena still remembers me?' he asked.

The lady threw him a glance which he did not understand. '*Remember* is not quite the right word. I think she has a longing for you.'

Better and better, Claudio could not help saying to himself: a longing; and therefore a possibility that, owing to the lady's mistake, he might be able to make Elena's acquaintance and take the place of the elusive Lorenzo. 'I too,' he said – and it seemed to him, to such an extent was he now absorbed in his role, that he was not altogether insincere – 'I too have a longing for her.'

'Instead of having a longing now,' said the lady, 'you'd have done better to come back then. You can have no idea of how sad Elena was at your going away. For some days she wouldn't come out of her room and she did nothing but weep. She didn't eat, she didn't sleep, I was afraid she would make herself ill. I should very much like to know why you were so unkind?'

'I wasn't unkind,' said Claudio haphazardly; 'it was more

than I could bear.'

She sighed and sat silent for a moment, lost in reverie. 'That may be so. And yet something must have happened that night. Next day Elena had a black eye, as if she had been beaten. But, Signor Lorenzo, don't you know that one doesn't hit women?'

Claudio felt suddenly ill at ease. So Lorenzo had hit his girl friend; whereas he himself had never touched a woman in his life. He answered in some confusion: 'Once again, it was more than I could bear.'

The lady seemed to be reflecting, her blue eyes gazing into emptiness. Then, in a strange tone of voice, no longer so very benevolent, in fact almost severe, she remarked: 'You ought to have realized that in running away like that you were not behaving well. If Elena had even been the type of little girl that could easily find someone to console herself with.... But Elena was a woman who had already reached an age when any love affair may be the last of her life. A widow, into the bargain, and with that dissolute son who gave her so much trouble. No, you didn't behave at all well.'

Claudio stirred uneasily in his armchair, cast a glance through the open window at the trees in the garden. So Elena was not young, in fact she was much older than Lorenzo, with a son already big enough for it to be possible to describe him as dissolute. Annoyed, he said: 'Perhaps it was just the difference in age between us that made me run away.'

The lady was now toying with a pair of spectacles attached to her belt by a ribbon; Claudio noticed that, possibly because of the relaxing of the muscles, the features of her face had become hard and hostile. Finally, with no cordiality left in her voice, she said: 'Signor Lorenzo, with regard to the difference in age, you should have thought of that before you started keeping company with Elena. The general impression, however, was that you came to an understanding with Elena not from love but from self-interest. Elena was rich, you hadn't a penny, and, as we all know, people don't go in for making subtle distinctions.'

Claudio saw that it was now up to him to defend the
despicable Lorenzo, for by defending him he would be
defending himself. He protested with a certain warmth: 'I
didn't go with Elena from self-interest. From the very
beginning I felt strongly attracted to her, and I stayed with
her until the attraction came to an end.'

The old woman shook her head. 'That is,' she said, 'until
you met that American woman who was quite as old as
Elena but possibly more generous, and with whom you
were seen leaving on the very day you deserted Elena.'

'I didn't leave with any American woman.'

'But you were seen.'

'That was pure chance. She was merely a person I happened to know.'

'A curious chance. Then explain to me about this other
chance.' She rose suddenly and, with her heavy, hesitant
step, went over to a desk near the window. Claudio
watched as she opened the desk, fumbled among some
papers in a drawer, took out a sheet and then returned to
her armchair. She fell back into the chair and placed the
sheet of paper on her knees. 'Tell me now,' she said,
'whether it was also pure chance that you left secretly, at
dawn, without paying your bill. Elena refused to pay it; she
said she had already spent enough on you, and I, in all
conscience, could not blame her. If I did not report you to
the authorities,' she concluded very disagreeably, 'it was
out of consideration for Elena, who seemed still to love
you. Was this unpaid bill just a matter of chance, too?'

She had now put on her glasses and, having unfolded the
sheet of paper, was looking at it. Then Claudio understood
– or at least thought he understood – that she was extremely short-sighted and had mistaken him for someone
else for this reason. For a moment he hoped, and at the
same time feared, that she would raise her eyes in his
direction and become aware of her mistake. But no; she
took off her glasses again and let them fall into her lap.
Claudio, at this point, wondered whether he ought not to

undeceive her and decided that it was no longer possible for him to do so. He ought to have done it at the moment when she had imagined that she recognized him; now, to the loss of the bill that he would not pay would be added the mockery of the ridiculous comedy he had been acting. Having settled the question of the recognition, he was faced with the problem of the bill. Should he pay it or not? If he refused to pay it, it might come about that the old woman would turn nasty and really report him, and then the comedy would come to light just the same but in a stranger and more sensational manner; if he paid it, he finally thought, he would be losing a little money, but he would be punishing himself for the calculated design with which he had assumed the role of Lorenzo. The old lady, in the meantime, was saying: 'It's the last week's bill. It's not a large amount, but of course you know that my daughter and I make our living out of these few rooms that we let, and for us even small sums are important.'

Claudio said firmly: 'Give me this bill. I'll pay it at once.'

'Here it is.'

Claudio took the bill and looked at it: it was in fact not a large amount; the punishment was a light one. He took out his pocket-book and handed the money to the old woman, who said immediately, as she received it: 'Of course, Signor Lorenzo, I never believed in the rumours about you. All the same, you did wrong to run away like that.'

'These things happen,' answered Lorenzo, rising to his feet.

'By the way, Signor Lorenzo,' said the old woman, who had now become agreeable again, 'when you ran away you left some things behind. I kept them; here they are.' She went to a cupboard at the far end of the room, opened it and took out a parcel which she handed to Claudio. 'I think it's a pair of drawers and two pairs of socks. They'll come in useful.'

His face darkening, Claudio accepted the parcel and

followed her out into the porch. 'You know what I think?' added the old woman. 'That you ought to go and see Elena. She's staying at the Pensione Sorriso. Go and find her, and you'll see how she'll welcome you.'

Claudio said he would do so, then said good-bye to her and went out. When he had walked only a few steps, the badly-tied newspaper parcel came undone and the drawers and socks, all crumpled and obviously not washed, fell to the ground. Claudio dropped the newspaper too, and continued on his way; but a voice warned him: 'Hey, look! you've dropped something.' It was a woman, speaking from behind one of the iron gates. With difficulty overcoming his disgust, Claudio bent down, picked up the drawers and socks with the tips of his fingers, wrapped them up in the newspaper again and walked on. Young, middle-aged and elderly couples were now coming towards him, passing close beside him, overtaking him; but he was conscious of looking at them without envy, in fact almost with repugnance. It was as though the imaginary experience which he had taken upon himself had satiated and disgusted him. Then he remembered the coin that did not belong to him, in the bar, which, soon after his arrival, he had stooped to pick up, receiving a cold reproof from the blond young man who was its owner; and he reflected that the same thing had happened to him with the old lady, except that in this case the coin was a false one into the bargain. At that moment he was walking past a green-painted municipal litter-bin fixed on a pole. He lifted the lid and threw the parcel into it.

The Triple Looking-Glass

The maid had gone out to do the shopping; his wife could not hear the bell because she was out on the roof-terrace with the baby; so Giovanni went to open the door himself, and was faced by two men in shirtsleeves carrying a wrapped-up object which looked like a screen. 'It's the mirror,' said one of the two men; 'where shall we put it?' Feeling very cheerful because he had slept well and also because it was Saturday and he did not have to go to his office, Giovanni led the two men in, whistling as he went, and showed them a corner in the bedroom, beside his wife's dressing-table. The men put down the mirror in the corner and went away. Giovanni tore the paper from the mirror, which was a triple one just like those in dressmakers' shops, and then looked at himself in it. And then his good humour vanished, for he became conscious of a fact of which he had never been ignorant but which, for some time, he had almost forgotten: not merely was his face unpleasing to him but it also appeared to him to be, in a disagreeable way, an entirely new face, with the result that he had difficulty in believing that so unpleasing a face could be his own.

Evidently, he thought, turning first in profile, then three-quarter-face, evidently he had a different idea of himself, a better, a flattering idea. But what idea? Thinking it over, he realized that in reality he did not have any idea of himself; it was simply that he did not want, on any account, to recognize himself in that unpleasing face. Gradually, slowly changing position, he again started looking at himself, as if hoping, by closer examination, to discover some likeable quality; but he became conscious that, the more he looked at himself, the more his aversion grew. His forehead was hard, compact and unsymmetrical, his nose undecided and ungainly in shape, his eye lacked intelligence, the expression of his mouth inspired disgust, his complexion was inclined to be red and shiny, and even less expressive features such as his ears and chin aroused in him a feeling of repulsion. Struck all of a sudden by an acute sense of unhappiness, Giovanni looked at himself again three or four times, then left the glass and went out on to the terrace.

They lived in a pent-house flat surrounded by roof-terraces from which one enjoyed a view of the Tiber, jade-coloured as it wound between low green banks, of the Ponte Milvio with its ancient golden stonework and of the white and yellow modern buildings lined up on the far shore. Half-closing his eyes in the luminous, pale sunshine of the fine spring day, Giovanni crossed the terrace, which looked like a garden owing to the numerous vases and boxes of flowers along the parapets, and went towards the corner where his wife was sitting reading beside the baby's cradle. Sitting down beside her, he said: 'The mirror has arrived. I took off the paper it was wrapped in.'

'The cheval-glass,' said his wife absent-mindedly, continuing to read.

'Strictly speaking,' said Giovanni, 'a cheval-glass is one of those antique mirrors, movable, and mounted on a stand. This is a triple looking-glass.'

'Well,' said his wife, '*I* call triple looking-glasses cheval-glasses.'

The scorching sunshine was conducive to silence. Giovanni, however, persisted. 'It's not very beautiful,' he said. 'It looks like a dressmaker's mirror.'

'That's just what it is,' his wife confirmed.

'I looked at myself,' Giovanni went on, hoping that his wife would reassure him, 'and, to tell the truth, I didn't like myself at all.'

But his wife appeared not to have heard him and said nothing. Giovanni, too, was silent; then he remembered that an elderly female relation had come to see them the day before, who had declared emphatically, as soon as she saw the boy, that he was the very image of his father. At the moment, this declaration had given him great pleasure; but now, thinking it over, he was aware of a feeling almost of terror at the idea that this, his first child, so dearly loved by him, might really resemble him. It was a strange kind of terror that seemed to go beyond the physical resemblance and hint at the child's destiny. At that moment there was a thin, clear wailing sound: the baby had woken up. His wife rose at once and hurried to the cradle. Giovanni also rose.

Once again he admired the extreme delicacy with which his wife inserted her two hands underneath the little wrapped-up body of the baby, lifted him from the cradle and then carried him in her arms to the chair near the parapet. She rested her foot on one of the flower-boxes and laid the baby in her lap, raising him to a sloping position with her left arm. Giovanni sat down beside her and gazed intently at the child who now, as soon as his mother had taken him from the cradle, had immediately quietened down. He was really a very beautiful baby; his fine, soft hair reminded one of the down on a coconut just torn from its husk; his brow was white and free from thought; his eyes looked out from pupils of a dark, limpid blue; his pink mouth wore a grave expression, between cheeks of remarkable firmness and rotundity. The baby clasped his foot with his hand and stared with ecstatic fixity at some unspecifiable point in the air in front of him. Almost without thinking, Giovanni said: 'I wonder which of us two he'll look like when he grows up.'

'He'll look like you,' his wife answered with assurance.

'I hope not,' said Giovanni sharply.

'Why not?'

'Because I don't like myself.'

His wife waved away a bee which had come buzzing close to the baby, then said in a good-natured way: 'I assure you there's nothing unpleasant about you. In fact, on the whole, everyone finds you very likeable.'

'Everyone, I dare say, but not myself.'

She leant over the baby and repeated in an affectionate and instructive tone of voice: 'Ma-ma ... Ma-ma ...' The baby, letting go of his foot, stretched out his hand eagerly towards his mother's face and almost succeeded in catching hold of her nose. Giovanni realized that his wife, wholly taken up with her baby, was not interested in his troubles. He went on, nevertheless: 'I dislike myself as I might dislike a stranger or someone one doesn't know. By which I mean that to the dislike is added the idea of strangeness. The first thing that came into my mind a short time ago, when I looked at myself in the mirror, was: how on earth is it possible that that man there is myself?'

'And yet,' said the wife with careless cruelty, 'it's not only possible, but it's certain.'

'That's why I hope my son won't resemble me.'

His wife lowered her face again towards the baby's hand, seeking its hesitant caress; then she raised her head, looked at her husband and started laughing: 'You know you're very funny. You're the only father in the world that doesn't want his son to look like him.'

Giovanni thought for a moment and was forced to admit, inwardly, that his wife was right. However, the fact remained: he felt an aversion for himself and a genuine fear that his son would resemble him. He said emphatically: 'The mere thought that in the future I might look on my son with the same dislike that I look upon myself makes me feel sick.'

'But why? Come on: be rational.'

'Dislikes aren't rational; otherwise they wouldn't exist. They're dislikes, and that's that.'

His wife put out her hand and gently tickled the chin of the baby, who at once smiled, but without altering the expression of gravity on his face. For a long time she sat contemplating this smile which she had provoked and won, with the look, almost, of a painter who pauses to gaze at the picture he is painting; then, in an excess of tenderness she bent over her son, kissing him and repeating with passionate determination: 'But *he*'s lovable, oh yes, yes, he's very very lovable, yes, he's very lovable indeed.' Finally, having given vent to her mother love, she seemed to remember her husband and said hurriedly: 'Why, why? You have a mania for self-destruction. Why do you dislike yourself? Now come on, let's make a joint examination of your personality. You're a good lawyer with a practice that's doing very well; as a man you're clever, gentlemanly, reliable, well-balanced, intelligent, cultivated; you're young, you're good-looking, you also come of a rich family, which is a further asset; you're esteemed and highly thought-of by your colleagues, you have lots of friends, you go in for several kinds of sport, you have a taste for beautiful things: what more do you want? Why in the world should you dislike yourself? I tell you, I should be really pleased for our son to resemble you in every point.'

His wife had spoken with so much energy that Giovanni suddenly felt doubtful. Supposing that he had made a mistake and that his wife was right? Then all at once he remembered having read in the paper that morning a matrimonial advertisement in which a man described himself with almost the same words as his wife had used about him; and he also remembered having thought, as he read this eulogy at so much a line: 'Goodness knows, I dare say he's really an odious type.' He said sourly: 'You've painted a very external, conventional portrait of me. If you'd gone a little deeper you would have seen that things aren't like that.'

With a touch of irritation, his wife answered: 'I see you like that because I love you. However deeply I dig I don't find anything else. Dig deeper yourself, seeing that you want to so much.'

Giovanni thought again, but found nothing. Shaking his head, he said: 'I don't know, I don't find anything. I feel that this dislike has a reason but I don't know what it is.'

His wife replied in an absent-minded and at the same time triumphant tone of voice: 'There, you see, you contradict yourself. You dislike yourself and at the same time you can't discover any defect in yourself, which is as much as to say that you consider yourself perfect. What are we to suppose?'

'I dislike myself,' answered Giovanni, 'as one dislikes certain people that one meets in the train, people about whom one knows nothing and whom one has nothing to reproach with, and yet one dislikes them. The fact that I have nothing to reproach myself with and that I find myself, as you say, perfect, merely proves that it is not a small or a large part of myself that I dislike, but the complete whole. In other words, if I looked at this alleged perfection from a correct point of view, it would be transformed into its opposite, into a complete imperfection.'

'And why don't you look at it from this correct point of view?'

Giovanni replied bitterly: 'Because there isn't one, or at any rate I don't know it.'

The baby had now gone to sleep again. His mother rose slowly to her feet, so as not to awaken him, and then went and deposited him, with cautious movements, in the cradle. She came back to her husband and, before sitting down, gave him a quick caress, saying: 'It's simply that you're not content with yourself, that's all. You'll get over it.'

Giovanni shook his head. 'No, it's not like that.'

'What is it, then?'

Giovanni thought intensely, trying for a moment to identify his own feeling precisely and to grasp its whole significance. Finally he said: 'It's as though there were some deception between me and myself; or as though I had been cheating myself in a fraudulent manner, continually, always. The dislike I feel for myself is like the antipathy one feels for someone who has pretended to us to be something that he was not, for interested, or anyhow obscure, motives. But I don't know what the deception is. I feel it, that's all; it's in the air, like a smell, but that's all I can say about it.'

Serenely, his wife answered: 'I understand. In you there must be two people, one who deceives and one who is deceived. I'm for the second one; he's the one I love.'

Family Life

They were a very united family, but the fact that the children were now grown-up, coupled with the increasingly straitened circumstances of the last few years, made it clear that a break-up was imminent. They all knew by now that the rooms which had remained unchanged since childhood – rooms once neat and cheerful, now lustreless and full of worn and broken furniture – would not see them during the coming winter: the two sons would be going to work in a town in the North, the younger daughter was to betake herself to England in order to gain a diploma as a nurse, and finally Leonora, the elder daughter, would be getting married. Immediately after the wedding the parents, who expected nothing else, would move into a smaller flat.

In the meantime, even in this atmosphere of removal and disintegration, the brothers and sisters continued to spend much of their time together, for in spite of the violent language and brusque manners that they affected amongst themselves they were devoted to one another, with a deep affection which was still the perfectly natural affection of childhood and which they knew was fated to come to an end as soon as they left home. At that time, Leonora's probable marriage to a rich young man from the provinces was the special object of their sarcasm. They called this marriage the 'cattle-market', alluding in this way to the fact that Leonora was not marrying for love but, as she herself admitted, for convenience. In any case neither Leonora nor her brothers and sister could have said precisely whether this marriage of interest really disgusted them. Economic necessity seemed to them, in an innocent way, to be a good justification; besides, they were all too young to be precisely conscious of what they felt.

The suitor, a young man called Moroni, although he had made a private declaration of his own feelings, had not yet brought himself to do this in an official manner. When, after lunch, the maid announced to the family as they were still sitting at table that Moroni was waiting in the drawing-room, Leonora at once rose excitedly to her feet; and her brothers and sister bombarded her with their usual sarcastic remarks: 'The fish is hooked; not surprising since you're the bait.' 'Get on with it: your job awaits you.'

'The good man has seen at last how he can make himself useful.'

'If he still doesn't make up his mind to it this time, call me and I'll take your place. I assure you I'd be quite willing. My goodness, with all that money!' This was spoken in the shrill, silvery voice of her sister.

'Oh, go to hell,' cried Leonora. Her mother, indifferent to this cynical babble to which she was accustomed, said: 'Leonora, you'd better put on your green dress.'

'Why? Or should I show myself naked in order to convince him?'

'What's that got to do with it? You look better in your green dress.'

Her father, sucking his pipe, his grey head enveloped in blue smoke, remarked pleasantly: 'Your mother's right, Leonora. Besides, you should always obey your parents, especially when they're wrong.'

'No, I'm not going to change,' Leonora said suddenly, in annoyance, as she went to the door. 'And you,' she added, turning to her brothers and sister who were still teasing her, 'don't be such idiots.'

But, once she was in the passage, she changed her mind and, instead of going straight to the drawing-room, went into her own room. There were endless patterns of little flowers on the wallpaper, on the curtains, on the bed, everywhere, but tarnished and worn: this coquettish room of her adolescence seemed to her, now that she was soon to leave it, even more dreary than usual. She took the green dress from the wardrobe and put it on in front of the looking-glass. She was fair, with a very slender, almost excessively supple figure, a long neck, a white face and enormous blue eyes; the green dress, as she was forced to admit to her annoyance, gave her a radiant look, as though it were woven of light. Pulling the folds of the dress with her nails over her hollow belly and bony hips, she hurried into the drawing-room.

This room, too, bore witness to the decline of the family – armchairs and sofas with dirty, threadbare arms, dusty lamp-shades, old-fashioned ornaments, junk and bric-à-brac. Moroni, who was sitting in one of these sordid armchairs, leapt to his feet and made as if to kiss her hand. Leonora pretended not to understand and kept her hand down; afterwards, when he did finally bend his head, glossy with brilliantine, over her hand, she put out her tongue at him, in order, perhaps, to give herself encouragement. Then they sat down; and Moroni began talking of what he had done during the two weeks that had passed since they had last seen each other.

While Moroni was speaking, Leonora started examining him relentlessly: he did not attract her, but she was always hoping to discover some quality in him which might at least partly justify the marriage. Moroni was not tall but rather massive, with a short neck and broad shoulders. His hair was thick and black, his eyes prominent, brown, bright but devoid of expression, his complexion muddy, his nose stumpy, crooked-looking from in front and aquiline in profile. It was his mouth, particularly, that Leonora disliked: thick but shapeless, it made one think of a full purse. And full, in fact, it was, of large, close-set teeth which overlapped and encroached upon each other, as though he had a double or triple row of teeth like a shark. 'No,' she thought, in final disillusionment, 'decidedly no; he looks quite frightful.'

Moroni opened the conversation in a very roundabout way. First of all, with excessive albeit sincere emphasis, he described the beauties of his native place: the sea, the orange-groves, the olive-groves, the climate, the rocks, the mountains. Leonora reflected that this enthusiasm for nature was, when all was said and done, a positive element. 'A good mark,' she said to herself. From nature Moroni went on to his own family, speaking with just as much emphasis, though of a different kind, more sentimental and more affectionate; telling her of his aged parents, of his sisters and brothers, and exalting their qualities with expressions of almost melting tenderness. Again Leonora said to herself: 'A good mark'; love of family was also a positive element.

After nature and his family, Moroni started to speak of himself. He applied to this subject the same emphasis, the same enthusiasm, and at this Leonora was less pleased. 'I warn you, I'm a martinet,' he said. 'I'm dictatorial, a lover of tradition and convention, attached to the old ideas and the old principles. I am, in short, full of prejudices; there's not a single one lacking in me. I am, into the bargain, rather violent and rather aggressive, jealous, exclusive, intransigent.' He spoke with great relish of his defects, as though they had been good qualities. Leonora wondered whether he did this in order to forestall criticism or because he thought they really were good qualities; but she was unable to decide which of the two hypotheses was the correct one. Moroni added: 'And everything turns out well for me, whatever I undertake. If I take it into my head to obtain something, I manage always to succeed in obtaining it, in the end.'

Leonora saw that Moroni was approaching the object of his visit, and she asked with feigned innocence: 'What, for instance?'

'Well, as an instance,' replied Moroni, 'I don't know. . . . It's happened in endless cases. For instance, the lawsuit that kept me in the country this time. It's a lawsuit brought against me by one of my employees. Note that the wrong is entirely on my side and the right entirely on his. But I have made up my mind to win the case just the same, and in fact I shall win it.'

'And how will you do that?'

'Perfectly simple: by paying witnesses in my favour. This is one case, but I could tell you of others as well.' Moroni went on talking, but Leonora, by this time, was scarcely listening to him. She had been tempted to exclaim: 'It's horrible, what you're telling me;' but she restrained herself in time. She was thinking now that this affair of the lawsuit was not one of those things that can be criticized for being the only negatives in a positive panorama. One could not correct Moroni on this one single point, she went on to think; it would have to be done from beginning to end, and that was clearly impossible. Convinced, she said to herself: 'He's a monster, I'm marrying a monster.' Meanwhile, Moroni, like a bird of prey narrowing the circles of its flight before hurling itself on its victim, was further remarking: 'And now, to give you another example, I've taken it into my head to obtain a certain thing and I know I shall succeed.'

'What thing is that?'

'To marry you.'

Leonora had a lively feeling of annoyance in face of this complacency on Moroni's part; and before she realized what she was saying, she asked: 'Are you really sure you'll succeed in this too?'

'Well, yes. It would be the first time in my life that I haven't succeeded in getting what I want.'

'And what would you do if I told you that this time you won't get anything at all?'

'I would re-examine the situation. I would search for the error in my calculations.'

'Well, an error there certainly is. Because this time you won't get what you want.'

'D'you mean that seriously?'

'Of course I do.'

'You mean you don't want to marry me?'

'Exactly.'

She noticed that he assumed a rather surly, threatening air; then he appeared to gain control of himself and rose to his feet, adjusting his tie as he did so. 'Dear Leonora,' he said, 'evidently there really *is* an error.' He put out his hand; she looked at his hand, hesitated, and then burst into brief laughter. 'No,' she said, 'I was joking. There is no error.'

Moroni, who, a moment earlier, had been sure that he was going to be rejected, was again astonished. 'There isn't?'

'Of course not,' said Leonora, turning red and biting her lips.

'That means that with you too I shall get what I want.'

'You've already got it.'

'So then, it's "yes"?'

'Yes, of course,' repeated Leonora, turning even redder.

But she realized that Moroni was now looking at her in a new way, covetously and stupidly, like a piece of personal property of which he could make whatever use he wished. As if to delay being used in this way, she rose suddenly and, coolly adopting the familiar 'tu', said: 'Wait for me here. I'm going to tell my family. I'll be back in a moment; wait for me and think about me.'

She passed close to him, and when Moroni awkwardly tried to put his arm round her waist, she stopped and gave him a quick, light kiss. Then she left the room and went straight to the dining-room. She was met by the usual clamour from her brothers and sister. She said, with mock solemnity: 'Give me your congratulations. This time we've done it.'

Her father, without commenting in any way on the event, shook out his pipe into the ash-tray, got up and said he was going to rest: and would they try not to make the usual din with the record-player until four o'clock? Her mother did not conceal her own satisfaction: two kisses, one on each cheek, showed Leonora that her present relief was equal to the anxiety she had hitherto been feeling. The comments of her brothers and sister were, naturally, different. She stood up to them in a fierce, childish manner, shouting at them, insulting them, fighting with them and even chasing her sister and showering blows upon her. 'And now you can all go to hell,' she concluded, panting for breath; 'I'm going back to my fiancé.'

Once she was in the passage, however, she hung about in distress in front of the closed door of the drawing-room. She was aware that these were the last days of her family life; and her heart sank. And, knowing that she had a faithful nature, she foresaw that she would be a good wife to Moroni, even if she did not love him; and thus, by force of circumstances, she would be led to become his associate. She would bear him children, she would share his ideas, she would defend his conduct. Her heart trembled as she thought of all these things, her hand resting on the doorhandle. Then she plucked up courage and went in.

In a Strange Land

It had rained for three days; and a woodland smell, evoked by the warm, abundant rain of autumn, rose up from the piles of dead leaves in the suburban avenue. This smell gave him a sudden desire for happiness, which for him, at that moment, would have meant being conscious of doing things that he liked. Instead of which, he thought as he made his way towards the last block of flats at the far end of the street, everything that he did, for the present, anyhow – studies at the University for which he did not feel himself adapted, friendships which he felt to be ephemeral and unworthy, reading which failed to nourish him, amusements which bored him – everything seemed to bear the mark of sterility and gratuitousness; and everything, as he was lucidly aware, might have been replaced without harm by something else, something quite different, something contrary, in fact. On the whole, he concluded bitterly, it was as if he had arrived in a strange land and knew himself to be condemned by his own inexperience and ignorance to see the people he ought not to see, to go to the places where he ought not to go and do the things he ought not to do.

With these thoughts running through his mind he reached the third floor of a building full of glass and rare woods and marble, of an excessive, almost painful modernity; and now he was ringing at the selfsame door that had seen him almost every day during the last months. The swarthy, hirsute maid, almost a hunchback and almost a dwarf, whose appearance gave immediate evidence of the contrast between the provincial, rustic character of the family and the modernity of the surroundings, opened the door to him and at once left him, saying that the Signorina was expecting him. Lucio went through into the living-room. This was a big room, greater in length than in width, with a continuous window along the street side, and, owing to its lack of furniture and the neat appearance of its wax-polished wooden floor, it made one think of a gymnasium. At the far end of the room, however, there was a big, ragged sofa, round which, on the floor, were to be seen a number of objects which normally are placed on pieces of furniture – a record-player, a tray with a teapot and cup, some records, a few illustrated magazines, the telephone and the telephone directory, an ashtray full of lipstick-stained cigarette-ends.

Baba was lying on the sofa, her feet up in the air and her head down; she got up as Lucio came in, not in order to greet him – which would have been contrary to the rules of her behaviour – but rather to change the record on the record-player. Baba had thick, brown, woolly hair, an exuberant figure and a pleasant, though compact and simple, face. If it had not been for her blue trousers and red sweater, thought Lucio as he glanced at her, she would have looked like a healthy country girl. But her large, unmoving black eyes, with pupils cut across halfway by heavy, sleepy looking lids, had in them a dazed, drugged, slightly imbecile expression that harmonized with her mode of dress and behaviour. Without looking at Lucio, she said: 'I warn you, it's a bad day today. I feel strange.'

Lucio sighed and, as he squatted down on the floor, answered: 'When *don't* you feel strange?'

Baba did not reply; she placed the disc on the record-player and then went and threw herself down again on the sofa. Lucio crawled over to her and made as though to take her hand; but he withdrew quickly with a subdued cry of pain: he had burned himself on a cigarette which Baba was holding between two fingers, with the lighted end hidden in the palm of her hand. He reflected angrily that it served him right: he was paying court to Baba without conviction, in the expectation, as with all the other things in his life, that something natural would spring all of a sudden from sterility and barrenness; instead of which, this was the result. In the meantime from the record, after the opening notes of a guitar, came a voice that appeared to be suffering from a grotesque kind of languor, as if the singer could not quite remember the words of the song. Lucio jumped to his feet and went and looked at the record-player. 'This is a seventy-eight record,' he cried, 'and you've put it on at thirty-three.'

'Oh yes, of course it is,' drawled Baba.

'But why?'

'Don't know.'

The song grated upon the ears with a false intonation which was expressive, though in an obscure way. Lucio stopped the record-player, and Baba cried: 'Why did you stop it?' She jumped up from the sofa brandishing, in a threatening manner, a hunting-knife which she carried in her belt; then she calmed down and went and flattened her nose against the window-pane. After a moment she cried out in a voice of terror: 'Look, look!' Lucio got up unwillingly and went to the window. The wide road below was sprinkled with dead leaves, and in the middle of it, in a depression in the asphalt, was a mirror-like pool in which sky and clouds were reflected. A large transport van, yellow and black, was standing on the far side of the road, with two enormous dappled white horses. The doors of the van were open and three men were unloading from it an ugly black chest, in the Quattrocento style; meanwhile one of the horses was scraping at the asphalt with its hoof and at the same time fulfilling, at regular intervals, the needs of nature. Baba went on insisting: 'Look! Look at that horse! Isn't it terrible?' But Lucio, concluding that Baba was once again trying to be original – completely lacking, as she was, in all interests and affections – did not even answer her. He recollected now the woodland smell of the rain, and wondered why in the world, instead of going for a walk, he found himself in Baba's flat. When he turned back into the room, he saw that she had gone and sat down on the sofa again and, bending over, with her head down, was trying to do a very difficult thing – to tear the telephone directory in half. Then she said to him: 'They say it needs exceptional strength to tear a telephone directory in two. Let's see who's stronger, let's have a trial of strength. I'll try and tear the book from the letter D onwards. Then you can try it in turn.'

'But a telephone directory is a useful thing,' remarked Lucio. 'What will you do without one?'

'I'll ask the operator the number. Or perhaps I'll stop telephoning.'

He watched her open the book and spell out: 'D'Amico, D'Amico, D'Amore.... Look, I'll tear it, beginning from D'Amore...' and then, with the book open, try vainly to tear it. The door at the far end of the living-room opened and Baba's father, a short, thick-set, brutal-looking man with a big head of black, woolly hair threaded with silver, came in angrily shouting something in a rough dialect which to Lucio was almost incomprehensible. Baba, without turning a hair, paid him back in his own coin, so it seemed, in the same dialect. Lucio gathered that the subject of the dispute was, in fact, the telephone directory, which her father, after a few more words of abuse, came and took, without troubling to respond to his greeting. When her father had left the room, Baba, with characteristic vagueness, devoted herself with great care to cleaning her black, broken nails with the point of her hunting-knife. It always happened like this, Lucio reflected; Baba started something, then a second thing, then a third, and then got tired in the middle of it, as though she realized the uselessness and absurdity of what she was doing. After a moment's silence, he said to her, by way of starting a conversation: 'By the way, I'm reading a very interesting book.'

'What's that?'

It was true: he had just been reading a popular scientific book on the subject of atomic energy which had much impressed him. And so, as if forgetting that Baba was almost illiterate, he began explaining, with great warmth, the properties of the atom. Baba listened, looking at him with her eyes half-hidden by their heavy lids, her beautiful, idiot eyes in which the sleepy expression seemed for once to be mingled with some sort of surprised curiosity. Finally she asked: 'Why d'you tell me these things?'

Disconcerted, Lucio replied: 'Because I thought they might interest you.'

'They don't interest me at all and I don't understand a thing of what you're saying.'

'Then tell me what does interest you.'

'I don't know.'

Lucio thought for a moment and then resumed, 'Would you like to go to the cinema?'

'No, I don't want to.'

'Would you like to go for a drive in the car?'

'No, not that, either.'

'Shall we go and eat ices?'

'No, for goodness' sake!'

'Shall we stay here?'

'No, I don't really want to stay here.'

'You must say what you *do* want.'

He saw her unsheath the knife again and thrust it violently into the arm of the sofa. 'This!'

These were Baba's usual oddities, and for some time now Lucio had lost all curiosity as to why she indulged in them. He felt that there was nothing left for him to do but flirt with her; but it was a feeling of desperation, for, although she attracted him, Baba had for some time past disgusted him with her meaningless eccentricities. He rose to his feet, went and sat down on the sofa and almost mechanically placed his arm round the girl's waist and made as if to kiss her. Immediately he received a violent shove, so vigorous that he nearly fell on to the floor. 'I've told you I feel strange,' said Baba, 'and you come and talk to me about love. Are you crazy?'

Lucio was suddenly conscious that he was losing patience; and it seemed to him that this was not so much because of Baba and the rejected kiss as because of his whole life, which for too long had resembled Baba herself and his relationship with her. He said furiously: 'It's you that's crazy.'

'All right, it's me that's crazy. But don't you try and kiss me again.'

'Tell me then yourself what you want us to do.'

'Let's play a game like this. I...' From her expression,

Lucio saw that Baba did not know what she was going to say, and he did not allow her to finish. He raised his hand and gave her a slap.

Baba at once replied with a slap that was equally violent. Then Lucio felt a fierce hatred blazing up in his heart. Perhaps, he thought as he seized Baba by the hair and threw her flat on the sofa, perhaps this, precisely, was the natural thing he had been waiting for all the time, the thing that would spring from the stupid, sterile situation in which he found himself. He was trying now to slap Baba again and Baba, on her side, with hatred no less violent, was trying to scratch his face and strike him in the stomach with her knee. They struggled in this way for some time, then rolled on the floor, still hitting each other savagely; finally Baba succeeded in freeing herself and ran away out of the room, shouting at him unexpectedly: 'Telephone me tomorrow morning.' Lucio, still out of breath, stood up, smoothing down his hair and clothes as best he could, and then went out into the hall. A door was ajar, and a woman's voice, possibly that of Baba's mother, could be heard shouting something incomprehensible in the same rough, vulgar dialect, in a tone of irritated reproof. Lucio went out on the landing and closed the door behind him.

In the wide suburban street, as he walked along beside the plane-trees, he noticed once again the woodland smell awakened by the autumnal rains and became aware that, by contrast, he was acutely and stupidly unhappy. Was it possible, he thought, that his life could never resemble that smell, so good and so alive; and that he was condemned, on the other hand, to do the things and to be with the people he did not like? He realized that he found no enjoyment in anything and did not understand anything; like a stranger in a strange land who is forced, before he can find his bearings, to make a number of mistakes. But this comparison, which before had appeared to him disheartening, now comforted him a little. After the mistakes, who knows? he went on to think, perhaps the right things would emerge.

The Honeymoon

After the train had left the station and had begun to gather speed, the bride said that the wedding ceremonies had tired her very much; it was a great relief to be alone at last. Giovanni answered jokingly: 'I think the main pleasure of a honeymoon consists in getting away from all the people who want to make much of the newly married couple.' No sooner had he uttered these words than he realized that they came strangely, to say the least, from the mouth of one who, like himself, had been married only a couple of hours previously; and he felt he should excuse himself, in an affectionate way, to his wife. But he did not have time, for she herself said, with a smile: 'Provided they really love each other, of course. But I believe a good many couples would prefer to prolong the celebrations as much as possible in order to put off the moment when they find themselves alone.' Giovanni said nothing; he stood up and started arranging the suitcases on the rack. Just at the moment when he was raising his arms to move the largest of them, his wife's remark, which had already slipped out of his mind, came bouncing back out of the silence as a ball bounces when thrown against a wall. He could not help pausing for a moment with his arms raised and his eyes fixed upon a travel poster showing the Lake of Como. 'Provided they really love each other.' Why had his wife made that remark? To whom had she wished to allude?

He finished arranging the suitcases and then sat down again opposite his wife, who now had her head turned towards the window and was apparently gazing at the bare, brown landscape glistening in the clear winter sunshine. Giovanni studied his wife's figure for a moment and then, with the sensation of making a genuine discovery after much confused enthusiasm, realized suddenly that there was no true relationship between them, or rather that there was the same relationship as might exist between a traveller without curiosity and some moderately attractive and interesting woman in the same compartment. He noticed that his wife had arranged her fair, fine hair in a new manner, combing it upwards; and this unaccustomed hair style confirmed the feeling he had of being face to face with a complete stranger. Furthermore, her white, cold face, with its thin, bizarre features, did not appear to him to be illuminated by any trace of affection; it seemed like a dead star from which it would be vain to hope for either light or heat. But he at once became aware that he was crediting his wife with his own lack of feeling; she was simply a mirror in which his own apathy was faithfully reflected.

It occurred to him that he ought to talk to her; through speech, perhaps, this feeling of incommunicability would vanish. But what was he to say? The only thing to say, he reflected almost with fright, was that he had nothing to say. He looked round the sleeping-car compartment, full of glossy wood and brass and velvet, seeking a pretext for conversation. Then he looked at the window with the sun flooding in. 'What a beautiful day, isn't it?' he said hurriedly.

Without turning round, his wife replied: 'Yes, very beautiful.'

Giovanni wondered what had made his remark so different from the identical remark made in other circumstances; and he realized that, perhaps for the first time since he and his wife had come to know each other, he had meant precisely what he had said, neither more nor less; which was, in effect, nothing. On other occasions, on the contrary, the remark about a beautiful day had had the value of a sentimental approach, had served, in short, as a means of communication. He wanted to be quite certain, and went on: 'D'you want to read the paper?'

'No, thank you, I'd rather look at the landscape.'

'We shall soon be passing through Civitavecchia station.'

'How far is that from Rome?'

'I think about thirty-five miles.'

'What is there at Civitavecchia? A port?'

'Yes, it's the port from which one leaves for Sardinia.'

'I've never been in Sardinia.'

'I have; I spent a summer there.'

'When?'

'Four years ago.'

She fell silent, her head turned towards the window; and Giovanni, in despair, wondered whether by any chance she had noticed that he was talking to her in a mechanical fashion, with meaningless words, like the columns of words in the pages of a dictionary. On reflection, he decided that something must have been discernible; for there was, in fact, a kind of determined obstinacy in the way in which she was looking at the landscape. Moreover – a sure sign of antagonism – she was frowning and biting her lower lip. Giovanni sighed, took an illustrated magazine at random and turned over its pages. His eye fell on a crossword puzzle – a thing he had not attempted for a long time – and it occurred to him that this was an occupation very much in harmony with his present state of mind. He fumbled in his pocket, looking for a pen, and, failing to find it, said to his wife: 'Can you please lend me your pen?'

At the same moment, his wife turned to him and said: 'I'm sorry, but can you lend me your pen-knife?'

The two sentences met and crossed in the air, and it occurred to Giovanni that at any other moment they would have both burst out laughing at this odd coincidence; but on this occasion neither he nor his wife laughed, as though they were conscious that there was nothing funny in it. In actual fact, Giovani reflected, they had been married a few hours before, in front of an altar, according to a centuries-old rite which intended that they should be united and in close communication for ever; instead of which they were already reduced to speaking to one another as if they were reciting language exercises from school textbooks: 'The wife has a pen, but the husband has a pen-knife.' He held out the object she had asked for, and inquired: 'Why d'you want a pen-knife?'

His wife, in turn, held out the pen and replied: 'To peel

an orange. I'm thirsty.'

Silence then followed. The train was now moving at a great speed beside a sea of a harsh, sparkling blue; Giovanni was trying in vain to discover what a scientific discovery capable of great developments, in four letters, could be; his wife was peeling her orange with head bent, in the attitude of a reserved female traveller who neither gives nor asks for confidences. Giovanni at last found the word he wanted – 'atom'; and the thought occurred to him that this word had far more meaning for him than the word 'love' which, theoretically, should have designated the present relations between himself and his wife. He tried to say to himself mentally : 'I love my wife,' and realized that the phrase sounded to him as empty and arbitrary as an affirmation that is not susceptible of proof. Then he thought : 'The orange is in the hand of my wife' and immediately felt that he had formulated a much more solid and truthful idea. He raised his eyes : the orange was, in fact, in the hand of his wife, and she was gazing fixedly at him, with an air of consternation. Embarrassed, he said : 'We get to Paris at nine o'clock tomorrow morning.'

'Oh yes,' replied his wife in a barely audible voice; then she rose and, without any kind of explanation, hurried out of the compartment.

As soon as he was alone, Giovanni became aware, to his surprise, that he felt a sort of relief. Yes, there was no doubt, the fact that his wife had gone out almost gave him the illusion that she did not exist; and this illusion aroused in him a feeling that was not very far removed from happiness. It was a negative happiness, like that of a person who is suddenly conscious of the cessation of a headache or some other physical pain; and yet, undeniably, it was the only happiness he had felt since he had entered that compartment. Consequently, he went on to think, to his terror, as soon as his wife came back he would feel unhappy again. And so it would be as long as they lived, since they were married and there was nothing to be done.

Suddenly his wife's hasty withdrawal a few moments

earlier appeared to him significant. Obviously she had been aware of his preoccupied, mechanical coldness and had gone out because she could not bear it any longer. What was there strange about that? Even a blind man would have noticed it; all the more so, a sensitive, intelligent woman, on the very day of her wedding, at the beginning of her honeymoon.

The train gave a prolonged whistle and started to slow down, while the blue, dazzling sea disappeared behind a row of yellowish tenement buildings. The train stopped beneath the arched roof of a station; a sonorous voice cried 'Civitavecchia'; doors began banging as they were opened and shut. Giovanni rose and opened the window, desiring to clear his head in the cold air. And then, beyond the crowd of travellers getting into or out of the train, beyond a handcart all set out with magazines and books, he saw his wife, easily recognizable by her fair hair and her greyish-blue two-piece dress, making her way hurriedly towards the exit. He thought immediately that she was running away: certainly she was going towards the station square where she could jump into a taxi and be driven back to Rome. Thus her silence was explained, and her flight from the compartment shortly before. At this thought, Giovanni suddenly felt himself assailed by a desperate anxiety; he rushed out into the corridor, reached the door and jumped down.

But as he looked up, he saw his wife coming to meet him, smiling happily. They took each other by the arm and Giovanni could not refrain from pressing her arm with his. They got into the train again as the whistle was blowing and the train already beginning to move. Once they were back in their compartment, quite unexpectedly she threw her arms round his neck and kissed him passionately. Then Giovanni heard her stammering: 'If you knew how frightened I was! I was looking out of the window at the end of the corridor, and I thought I saw you get out of the train and go off towards the exit, as if you were running away from me. So I ran after you and took you by the arm. But it wasn't you, it was someone who looked like you and who was dumbfounded when I spoke to him and called him by your name.'

'But why were you afraid I should run away?'

'Because a little time ago I had a horrible feeling. It seemed to me I no longer felt anything for you, that I couldn't even speak to you, and I was convinced you had noticed it, and so you had preferred to run away rather than stay with me.'

Censure

One evening Tarcisio, coming home earlier than usual, found his wife with his friend Silvio in a posture which left no doubts as to the nature of their relationship: sitting on the sofa, in front of the table laid for three, their backs to the door by which he entered, they were in one another's arms. Tarcisio had never thought that his wife could be unfaithful to him and therefore could not get over his surprise and did not begin to suffer until after his friend had already run away and his wife had re-settled herself into a conventional position, her legs crossed and a cigarette between her lips. Immediately afterwards she suggested to him, in a hurried manner, that they should part; but she spoke without any bitterness, as though she wished above all to avoid any sort of explanation; and Tarcisio was obscurely grateful to her for this haste: he also, he felt, did not desire to discuss, to analyse, to investigate, to understand – all of them useless things in such cases. But he wished to gain time and therefore answered that he would think about it; in the meantime he was not hungry and did not want anything to eat; he would sleep that night on the sofa in the sitting-room. His wife made no objection; she rose, went into the adjoining bedroom and came back with a couple of blankets and a pillow which she placed on the sofa. Tarcisio noticed that she did these things without showing any trace of feeling, as though in tacit agreement with him, and again he was grateful to her. Then she went away; Tarcisio turned on the radio and listened for a couple of hours to a programme of popular songs and light music. Meanwhile he smoked one cigarette after another and did not think about anything. Having passed two hours in this way, he turned off the radio, took a crust of bread from the table and ate it slowly; then he took off his shoes, lay down on the sofa and put out the light.

He slept long, for perhaps ten hours, and when he awoke

and looked round him he had the feeling that he had slept
not merely through that night but also through the two
years of his marriage and that he had in fact dreamed
that he was married and had lived happily with the wife
whom he loved. He wondered what was the cause of this
sensation of a dream and concluded that it derived from the
consciousness of suffering and at the same time of not feeling any pain. A painless pain, in short, he finally decided.
He had now had a bath, had shaved and dressed and, sitting on the sofa, was finishing drinking the tea which the
maid had placed on the table in front of him. On the far
side of the door he heard the voice of his wife speaking on
the telephone, in the bedroom. Then the door opened and
she appeared on the threshold.

She was in her nightdress; her beautiful, rather massive,
body was outlined in vague, languorous contours through
the varying transparency of the fine, crumpled material.
'Signora Stazi is on the telephone,' she said, 'and she wants
to know what we have decided about the flat.'

Tarcisio noticed that his wife's tone of voice was neutral,
that is, neither hostile nor ashamed, nor yet normal; neutral, or in other words very like the voices of people who
talk to us in dreams; and once again he was conscious of
being grateful to her. 'What flat?' he asked.

'The flat we were to go and see this morning.'

At last Tarcisio remembered: they had decided to
acquire a new flat; the one they were living in was too small.
'Very well,' he said; 'tell her I'll come as arranged.'

His wife went out; and Tarcisio, taking out his pocket-
book, began reading over his engagements for the day.
Everything was, in fact, noted down in good order: the
appointment with Signora Stazi, a second appointment with
his stockbroker, and then, immediately before lunch, an
appointment with a mysterious 'S.T.', followed by a question-mark. In the afternoon there were a couple of recep-
tions and in the evening an invitation to dinner. But the
appointment with S.T. focused Tarcisio's attention. Actually
he did not remember at all who this S.T. could be. In his

mind he went over the preceding day, in the hope of track-
ing down the telephone call or the meeting that had caused
him to make a note of these initials, but he found nothing.
The appointment with S.T. must have been noted several
days earlier, as sometimes happened. In any case, he
thought, it must have been someone whom he considered
either very intimate or very disagreeable : intimate because
he had thought it sufficient to indicate the person by initials
only; disagreeable because it was in this manner that he
was accustomed to jot down the names also of people
whom, for some reason, he did not wish either to know or
to associate with. The question-mark, moreover, seemed to
confirm this latter hypothesis, since it indicated a doubt as
to the expediency of receiving the mysterious visitor.

In the midst of these thoughts he heard the front-door
bell ring; then the door of the sitting-room opened and Signora Stazi came in. Signora Stazi was well-known to Tarcisio : well advanced in years, thin and worn and probably
unhappy, she took pleasure, in her own verbose manner, in
other people's happiness; and of this almost vindictive
pleasure she made use in her occupation as a house-agent.
In a harsh, despairing voice she would expatiate upon the
happiness her clients would enjoy as soon as they moved
into the flats she recommended; listening to her, you could
not help supposing that she herself, on the other hand, lived
in a sordid hut with no conveniences. As she came in, Signora Stazi said to Tarcisio : 'I ought to have come at three
o'clock, but at three I had another engagement and so I
arranged with your wife to come now. I hope I'm not disturbing you'; and Tarcisio wondered whether by any
chance the initials S.T. stood for the first two letters of the
name 'Stazi'. But, apart from the unlikelihood of his having
noted down a name by its first two letters, the times did not
agree : the appointment had been changed that same morning and he had certainly written down the initials at least
two days before. Meanwhile his wife had come into the
room, fully dressed; and they all three left the house.

The road along the Tiber embankment was black and

wet, the sky was black, and as Tarcisio drove along beside
the row of pale buildings he started thinking again of his
wife, who was sitting beside him, still and silent. The painless pain, as he realized, persisted; and above all he feared
lest it might become truly painful and consequently unbearable. This, he said to himself, would certainly happen if he
demanded an explanation: first of all he would learn the
real extent of her unfaithfulness which, for the moment, as
far as he knew, was limited to a kiss; then his wife, in order
to defend or justify herself, would bring up goodness knows
what grievances against him; he would have to counter-
attack by accusing her in return; and so a whole quantity of
things would come out which in reality did not exist because they had never mentioned them. But could he avoid
speaking? Tarcisio looked at his wife's face, slightly plump,
delicate, with fine, whimsical features framed in soft fair
hair; and he realized all of a sudden that the two of them
had never really spoken; and that, of all the many things
about which they had kept silent, perhaps adultery was not
the most important. Why therefore begin speaking just at
this moment, on so inopportune an occasion?

Meanwhile he was driving in a more or less automatic
way, and he started at the sound of Signora Stazi's voice
saying: 'Now, turn to the right here. You see what a quiet,
intimate, cosy little street. I've taken steps to find out who
lives here, and I can guarantee that they're all a good class
of people.'

Tarcisio said nothing. He stopped and put on the handbrake, then followed his wife and Signora Stazi up the staircase of a small, three-storeyed building with a blue and
green façade. Signora Stazi's voice now reached him, harsh
and yet remote, as though through a pad of cotton-wool:
'Luxury flats.... On the first floor, an industrialist whom
you certainly know.... On the third, an American
couple.... Each flat has its garage for three cars.... Here's
the entrance-hall, very spacious, with a hanging-cup-
board.... This is the big drawing-room for receiving
friends in a serene, calm, elegant atmosphere.... And this

is a smaller sitting-room for the intimacy of family life, for radio, for television.... Here's the bedroom: don't you feel, Signora, that you've already lived in it, slept in it, dreamed in it? ... Here is a room for you, Doctor: you could make it your study, with your books and book-shelves, your writing-table, your sofa and armchairs.... And now do look at this kitchen and dining recess.... This is the way to the guest-room and the servants' rooms.... And do look at this bathroom: isn't it wonderful?'

The voice of Signora Stazi, deathly sad as it was, yet seemed to Tarcisio to have in it a certain measure of truth; yes, he thought, they could be happy in this flat if only they wanted to be, there was no reason why they should not. 'And now, this is the room I was keeping to the last – the room in which your children will sleep and live: spacious, light, cheerful, with this magnificent terrace, full of sun-shine, on which, in fine weather, the children can play and take the air.' Signora Stazi's voice had never been so sad as at this moment when she was speaking with enthusiasm of Tarcisio's future children.

By now they had finished looking at the flat: Tarcisio told Signora Stazi that he would give her an answer in two days' time at the latest, and he then suggested driving her home. She continued to extol the qualities of the flat all the way, it might be said, to her own front doorstep – a pane-gyric which was in any case superfluous, since Tarcisio had found the place to be suitable in every respect and was thinking of buying it. Having dropped Signora Stazi at her door, he realized it was late and that the meeting with his stockbroker was no longer possible. It was lunch-time, and usually they had lunch at home. But Tarcisio recalled the appointment with the unknown S.T. which was noted in his book, and all at once he felt a profound repugnance at the idea of being found at home by the mysterious visitor. His wife now appeared calm and satisfied; she too, it seemed, had liked the flat. He started the engine and then asked: 'How about having lunch at a restaurant?'

'Yes, let's do that.'

'Where d'you want to go?'

'Wherever you like.'

Once they were inside the restaurant, sitting side by side on a low divan, underneath a large mirror, in front of a table already laid, Tarcisio noticed that his wife had laid her hand on the seat-cushion and felt a desire to squeeze it, in sign of reconciliation. But was it not too soon? After he had ordered the food and the wine, he said at once: 'I wrote down in my pocket-book the initials of someone whom I ought to be seeing at this very moment, just before lunch. Only I'm quite unable to remember who it can be.'

'What were the initials?'

'S.T. I put a question-mark beside them, which means it's not a person I particularly want to see. Who can it possibly be?'

His wife mentioned various names: Severino Tocchi, a carpenter; Stefano Terenzi, a decorator; Santina Tipaldi, a masseuse; and then, as if continuing the list, and still in the same neutral voice, she mentioned the name of the friend with whom Tarcisio had surprised her the evening before – Silvio Tommasi. Tarcisio replied at once with perfect naturalness: 'It couldn't possibly be Silvio. I would have written his name in full. Besides, I shouldn't have put a question-mark. Why a question-mark?'

'Are you quite sure you didn't write it yesterday evening, after we saw each other?'

'But I didn't speak to Silvio.'

'You may have made an appointment with him some days ago, possibly an invitation to lunch. Then, yesterday evening, you may perhaps have added a question-mark.'

'But I don't remember having had my pocket-book in my hand yesterday evening.'

'It may be that you did it without being conscious of it.'

They went on discussing the matter in this way in a tone which became more and more detached, serene, impersonal, almost scientific. Finally Tarcisio said: 'Oh well, I ought anyhow to telephone home now to find out whether this S.T. arrived or not.' With these words he rose and went over to the telephone-box.

The maid answered at once that someone had indeed arrived and was waiting in the sitting-room; it was not a gentleman, however, but a lady. Tarcisio wanted to say: 'Ask her who she is and what she's called', but he stopped himself in time. Why in the world should he have to know anything about this mysterious female visitor, seeing that he had not wished to know anything about his own wife? Finally he said: 'Tell her that I'm not in Rome, that I'm abroad and it isn't known when I shall be back.' The maid replied that she would do so; and Tarcisio went back to his table.

It seemed to him now that he could make the gesture he had been tempted to make shortly before. He put out his hand and grasped his wife's hand as it lay on the seat of the divan. She returned his pressure.

You Went to Sleep

The iron gate was ajar; and before they went in, Girolamo's mother drew his father's attention to the notice which said that claims could be made only in the morning, between ten and twelve. 'Absurd,' she remarked; 'and if, like me, you have the habit of getting up late in the morning, what's to be done?'

Girolamo did not wait to hear his father's reply; releasing himself from his hand, he was the first to enter the enclosure containing the kennels. There was an open space floored with dull white cement; then the office building, low, yellowish, straight opposite the gate; then on the left, the cages where privately owned dogs were being kept under observation, and on the right the rows of kennels for stray dogs. Girolamo said anxiously to his mother: 'Mummy, the black griffon was in kennel number sixty.'

His mother did not answer; but she said to his father: 'You must find the attendant. A fair-haired young man. In the meantime we'll look at the dogs.' His father lit a cigarette and then went off towards the office building. She took Girolamo's hand and walked away with him towards the kennels.

The enclosure was plunged in complete silence, a silence at once heavy and full of suspense, which the faint wild-beast smell that hung in the air seemed to endow with a significance of anguished expectancy. But as soon as Girolamo and his mother appeared in front of the first kennel, first one dog, then two, then three, then the whole lot began to howl. Girolamo noticed that these howls varied greatly, from shrill yelping to deep barking, just as the dogs that gave voice to them were also of various kinds; and yet it seemed to him that one single note united these discordant sounds – that of a heartrending and perfectly conscious entreaty. He felt that all this barking was addressed to him, and he longed to take the dog he had chosen and go away as quickly as possible. Pulling at his mother's hand, he repeated again: 'Mummy, the black griffon is in kennel number sixty.'

'Here is kennel number sixty,' said his mother.

Girolamo went over and looked. Five days before, when they had come in the afternoon, the kennel had been occupied by a small, shaggy black dog with coal-black eyes and shining white teeth, a dog of frenzied, pathetic liveliness which, the moment Girolamo appeared, had rushed towards him barking and holding out its paw to him between the bars. They had decided to take this dog; but had been told to come back in the morning which was the time when claims could be made. Now, however, the kennel appeared to be empty; or rather, Girolamo could see, curled up right at the back, a little brown, fox-like creature looking at him with sad, dim eyes and quivering all over from time to time as if with a recurring shudder of disgust. In a voice already filled with despair, Girolamo said: 'Mummy, the griffon isn't there.'

'They must have put it in another kennel,' said his mother in an evasive tone, 'unless perhaps its master came and took it back. We'll ask the attendant.'

At that moment Girolamo's father came back from the office building. 'The attendant will be here in a minute or two,' he said.

'Let's go and see the dogs in the meantime.'

Heedless of Girolamo who wanted to wait for the attendant at kennel number sixty, his parents walked away and started examining the dogs one by one. Girolamo, through a mist of bitter uncertainty, heard his mother say to his father: 'The other day there were a couple of pure-bred dogs. A boxer and a setter. Strange, isn't it, that dogs like that should turn up here?'

'People lose them,' answered his father. 'Or they abandon them deliberately. Many people dream of abandoning in the same way someone who is a burden on them, and they take it out on their dogs.'

The dogs continued to bark despairingly; and Girolamo

wondered whether the barking of his griffon was contrib-
uting to the uproar. His father remarked quietly: 'You
know, I have the impression that mongrels howl more dis-
mally than pure-bred dogs.'

'Why should that be?'

'Because they realize they're not pure-bred and that
there's less likelihood of their being rescued.'

His wife shrugged her shoulders. 'But they don't know
what it means to be pure-bred or mongrels. It's human
beings who make these distinctions.'

'No, they know because they see they're treated worse,
and anyone who sees himself treated worse thinks at first
that it's the fault of other people, then, what with one thing
and what with another, he ends by thinking it's his own
fault. Of course being a mongrel is not a fault in itself; but
it becomes one because of the different treatment.'

'There you are again, with your usual subtleties.'

They stopped at random in front of a kennel. A dog
which was still a mere puppy, comic and ugly in appearance, dappled yellow and white, with enormous paws and
head and a tiny body, rushed at the bars and, standing on
its hind legs, began yelping in a highly expressive fashion,
trying at the same time to lick Girolamo's hand and to put
its paw into his palm. Girolamo's mother read aloud from
the identification card: 'Cross-breed. Found in Via delle
Sette Chiese.' And then, turning towards his father, she
added: 'There's one of them that's really ugly, poor little
thing. But where is Via delle Sette Chiese?'

'In the neighbourhood of Via Cristoforo Colombo.'

The mongrel yelped and writhed excitedly, seeking to
place its paw in Girolamo's hand, as though it wished to
form a pact of friendship with him. Girolamo finally took
hold of it; and the dog appeared to be slightly reassured.
Girolamo's mother asked: 'They say that mongrels are
more intelligent than pure-bred dogs; d'you think that's
true?'

'I don't think so. It's a report put about by the pure-bred
dogs,' said her husband jokingly.

'And why?'

'In order to depreciate intelligence in comparison with other qualities such as beauty, sense of smell, courage and so forth.'

They stopped in front of another kennel which contained – big as the kennel itself and with a look of being on the defensive – a worn and wasted Alsatian, old, probably, with a yellowed, mangy coat and unhappy, red, vicious eyes. As Girolamo was about to approach, the dog rushed forward with a growl, showing its sharp white teeth, its appearance suddenly improved and rejuvenated, as it were, by its outburst of rage. Girolamo jumped back in fear; but at the same time, when he compared the intelligent, heart-rending yelping of the little mongrel found in Via delle Sette Chiese with the Alsatian's stupid growling, he felt that the latter, which had not even the comfort of understanding what was happening to it, inspired more pity than the former. 'This one,' said his mother, 'yes, this one is vicious. But perhaps he has rabies?'

'No, if he had, he wouldn't be here. He's protesting because he's been shut up, that's all.'

Girolamo gazed intently at the Alsatian; and it seemed to him that, by taking an interest in it, he found some relief from a serious trouble that weighed upon his heart. Then he understood: it was the thought of the griffon which had not yet been found. He asked suddenly: 'Mummy, how about the griffon?'

'We shall know as soon as the attendant comes.'

They were now standing in front of a kennel in which there was a small mongrel gun-dog, which was lying on its side breathing with difficulty and trembling. Girolamo felt his heart sink. 'What's the matter with him?' he asked. 'Is he ill?'

His mother thought for a moment and then said: 'No, he's not ill; it's just that he's distressed.'

'Why?'

'Wouldn't *you* be distressed if you'd got lost and been taken to a strange place far away from your family?'

'But his master will come and look for him, won't he?'

'Yes, of course he'll come.'

'Ah, here's the attendant,' said his father.

The attendant was a young man with fair, close-cropped hair, a pointed nose and intensely blue eyes. He came over to them with a swaying walk and greeted them from a few paces' distance. Girolamo's mother said: 'We've come about that little black griffon. D'you remember?'

'Which griffon?'

'The one in kennel number sixty,' said Girolamo, stepping forward.

'Did you see it in kennel number sixty?' said the young man, in a drawling country accent. 'But that one isn't here now.'

'There, Mummy, you see...' cried Girolamo.

She made a sign to the boy; then, turning back to the attendant: 'Did they come and fetch it away?'

'No, but since the three regulation days had passed, plus two other days, we...' – the young man seemed to be searching for a euphemistic term, but finally resigned himself to telling the truth – 'we sent it to the gas chamber.'

'But we said we would come and take it away.'

'Signora, you said so, but then you didn't turn up. That's the rule.'

'How many do you put away each week?' inquired Girolamo's father at this point, going over to the young man and holding out a packet of cigarettes. The young man thanked him, took a cigarette which he placed behind his ear, and replied: 'Well, ten or fifteen a week.'

Girolamo was still puzzled. Finally he asked his mother, with profound anxiety: 'But what is the gas chamber?'

His mother hesitated and then said curtly, in an instructive tone of voice: 'Stray dogs are killed because they might spread rabies, which is a terrible disease. So they're put into the gas chamber where they die without suffering.'

'So the griffon is dead?'

Girolamo's father placed his hand on the boy's shoulder and said: 'I'm afraid so.'

They walked away towards the gate. Girolamo's mother said to him: 'Today there was no dog I should have liked to have. But one of these days we'll come back again and get one. Is that all right?'

Girolamo said nothing. He now recalled the mongrel which had put its paw in his hand; but it seemed to him that henceforward it would never be possible to save either that or any other dog. Everything, he felt, was tangled up in inexplicable confusion and indifference. They crossed the road and went to the car. His father said, as he opened the door: 'You've made me lose a whole morning with this business of the dog. Now I must run off to the office.'

They got in and sat down, all three of them, on the front seat. Suddenly Girolamo said: 'Mummy, I knew we ought to have gone the day before yesterday. And I told you, Mummy. I came to your room yesterday and the day before, and I told you.'

The boy's tone appeared to surprise his mother, who answered rather stiffly: 'Yes, you came, but I couldn't go out because I was tired and I needed to rest.'

'But why, Mummy, why didn't you come, why?'

'I've told you. Because I went to sleep.'

'Yes, you went to sleep, Mummy, you went to sleep.' Girolamo, all of a sudden, started sobbing so violently that his father, who was on the point of moving off, stopped the car again and said: 'Come now, don't cry. Next week Mummy will find you another one.'

Girolamo went on repeating, in a loud voice that surprised even himself: 'You went to sleep, Mummy, you went to sleep, you went to sleep.'

His father, re-starting the engine, said again: 'Come now, don't cry. Men don't cry.' His mother remarked: 'This boy hasn't been very well for some time. He's too excitable.' The car moved off.

The Man Who Watched

After lunch they rose from the table and went and sat near the fireplace. But no sooner had Valerio sat down than he realized that he could no longer endure to stay with Lavinia and the lawyer Rossi. Lavinia's mysterious, disconcerting impartiality in face of the rivalry which had revealed itself from the very beginning between himself and the lawyer had at first astonished, then grieved him, and finally made him indignant: the lawyer had known her for a few days, he himself for two years, and they were going to be married. So he jumped up and said he must go. It seemed to him that the lawyer welcomed his departure with relief and perhaps with gratitude. Lavinia also rose to accompany him to the door.

In the entrance hall she said to him gently: 'It's best for you to go away.'

'Oh, and why, may I ask?'

'Because, when people are jealous like you, it's better for them to be alone.'

Valerio would have liked to reply that it was not his fault if he was jealous; but he hadn't the time, for Lavinia added: 'Anyhow, come back in half an hour. Then we'll go out for a little. I want to take the dog for a walk.'

Once he was alone on the landing, Valerio hesitated for a moment and then, taking from his pocket a key which Lavinia had given him some time before, went back into the flat. He had some sort of an excuse ready in case he ran into Lavinia; but the entrance-hall was empty. He opened the door of Lavinia's bedroom, skirted round the low, wide bed and went out through the open french window. The flat was on the top floor, tiny in itself but in the middle of an immense roof-terrace. Valerio followed along the wall and, having reached the window of the sitting-room, went forward at first cautiously, then more boldly, and looked in. Lavinia was sitting with her back to the window and the lawyer was sitting close to her, in profile. Valerio realized that neither Lavinia nor the lawyer could see him; and so, keeping a little to one side so that he could jump back at the slightest warning, he set himself to watch.

He noticed at once that the very nature of the feeling of jealousy that urged him to play the spy prevented him from observing anything at all which was not Lavinia. The furniture in the room, the floor, the walls, the lawyer himself seemed all to be enveloped in an atmosphere of obscurity and imprecision; only Lavinia was clearly visible to his eyes as also to his consciousness. She was sitting on a little chair which was too narrow for her, so that her hips – the hips of a young, big woman – projected slightly, giving a lively sense of roundness and softness. From her golden head, with its fine, thick hair pulled back into a high, oval coiffure, a warm, rosy light seemed to fall upon the whole of her palely-clad figure. She was wearing a grey skirt and a white blouse whose transparency allowed the colour of her skin to shine through it. She had a very slender waist, broad shoulders and a long neck, with a few curls at the back of it. Valerio could see from the movement made by her shapely bust as she stooped forward towards the little table, that she was pouring out the coffee. Then Lavinia turned as she handed the cup to the lawyer; and began, so it appeared, to speak. But Valerio could not hear the words; and so, after the gesture with the coffee-cup, the scene became, for him, mysterious and incomprehensible though still enveloped in an air of guilty suspicion.

What could those two be saying to one another? Lavinia had turned slightly towards the lawyer, and the latter was speaking with great, possibly excessive, warmth, breaking off to listen to a remark from Lavinia and then resuming. Every now and then Lavinia made one of those useless, languid gestures that women make: she would pass her large white hand over the back of her neck, pressing slightly against her hair; or she would place that same hand on her knee as though to look at it – or perhaps, indeed, to let the lawyer look at it. Her knees were visible because she had twisted round a little; and the calf of her long, elegant leg was also visible. Valerio, all of a sudden, realized that he almost wanted Lavinia's knees to touch those of the lawyer, which in any case were not so very far away. He really suspected that there was something between Lavinia and the lawyer and felt the need of a proof, not so much of her innocence as of her guilt.

But the proof did not come. The two went on talking, more and more mysteriously, they moved on their chairs, they almost, but not quite, touched one another, they did not embrace, they did not kiss. After nearly twenty minutes of contemplating this mute and meaningless scene, Valerio began to feel bored and at the same time ashamed. He had wished to spy out guilt inside the room; but now he began to be aware that the guilt was outside, on the terrace. It was he himself, so furtive, so underhand, so burdened with unhealthy curiosity, who was the guilty one; not those other two who were calmly conversing. And, together with the shame at what he had done and was still doing, there came to him a violent, passionate feeling of remorse towards Lavinia, who was not betraying him nor had any intention of doing so. He was already preparing to go away when, by chance, he raised his eyes and caught sight of himself in the looking-glass above the fire-place, at the far end of the room.

The glass reflected only his head, with an effect that was almost macabre, as though it were the head of a man who had been decapitated. Furthermore, the head bore the distorted expression of such a man, the anguished eyes, the pallor, the look of horror. Standing, so to speak, on the marble mantelpiece, it was impossible for the head not to have been seen by Lavinia, who was sitting straight in front of it. Here was the explanation, Valerio immediately thought, of the apparent innocence of the scene between her and the lawyer. Lavinia had seen it, had perhaps warned the lawyer, had anyhow taken good care not to make any sort of imprudent gesture. Valerio, at this thought, felt his feeling of shame vanish to be replaced, once more, by jealousy.

By this time, however, the half-hour had passed. And now Lavinia rose to her feet; and the lawyer rose at the same time. Valerio had only just time to run round the terrace, cross the bedroom, slip out through the entrance-hall and run down a couple of flights of stairs. After a moment he heard the sound of voices and the hum of the lift going up, then a banging of doors and the hum of the lift going down. He went up the two flights of stairs again and rang the bell.

Lavinia herself came to open the door, ready to go out, with the dog on the lead, an excitable little black griffon which yelped and danced, mad with joy. 'You're punctual,' she remarked in an ambiguous tone, half reproving, half ironical, 'but, as you see, so am I. I sent off the lawyer somewhat abruptly. Let's go, then.'

A few minutes later they were out in the country. Valerio was driving and did not speak; beside him, Lavinia kept her hand on the collar of the dog which was straining forward frantically at the window. Finally she asked: 'What did you think of the lawyer Rossi?'

'Loathsome,' replied Valerio without turning.

After this question and answer, they were silent again for some time. They drove for a good distance along a main road flanked with spring-like plane-trees, whose pale, almost livid buds struck a discordant note against the black, stormy sky; then Valerio turned off along a side road, between two rows of hills covered with cornfields, green and treeless. From this country road, paths led off every now and then, winding upward towards the hills. Valerio stopped the car at a fork in the road and said they might perhaps walk a little. Lavinia opened the door and the dog hurled itself out, barking, and very soon vanished amongst the high corn. They went off up the path.

They walked a little distance. Lavinia, holding the dog's lead, was in front of Valerio; he himself held back a little, so as to see her better. He always did so when they went for a walk because he loved her passionately and could never have enough of gazing at her. Lavinia knew this and was pleased; and so she always walked with a kind of aesthetic consciousness, rather like a mannequin between two rows of spectators. When it seemed to Valerio that he had looked at her long enough, he said brusquely: 'Let's go this way,' pointing to a little sloping meadow a short distance away, sheltered by a hedge. Obedient and docile, Lavinia turned off the path and walked towards the meadow.

The grass was very tall, thick and tangled, reaching almost to their hips and impeding their steps. 'Let's lie down now,' suggested Valerio as they came near the hedge. Standing amid the grass, Lavinia hesitated. 'I don't know why,' she said disgustedly, 'but this place frightens me. There might be snakes here.' Valerio shook his head: 'Snakes indeed! Come on, lie down'; and he took her by the arm, almost forcing her. Once more she obeyed and lay down rather awkwardly, as indeed might be expected of a tall, beautiful woman who is anxious to move gracefully. Finally they lay facing each other, both leaning on an elbow, Lavinia opposite to Valerio, who had his back to the hedge.

For some little time they did not speak. Lavinia had picked a blade of grass and was chewing it. Then she looked up and smiled at him, at the same time enfolding him in a blue glance of singular intensity, which Valerio felt immediately on his skin with a suddenly soothing and beneficent effect, as one is conscious of the warmth of a ray of sunshine or the caress of a light breeze. Then she asked him: 'Why are you so jealous?'

'Who wouldn't be?' he replied. 'Anyone would have thought that, for you, that lawyer and I were of equal importance.'

'He was a guest; I had to pay special attention to him.'

'At one moment he touched your hand lightly with his.'

'I didn't notice it.'

'I was almost sure that he was pressing your foot under the table.'

'You're being absurd. D'you know why I invited the lawyer Rossi?'

'Why?'

'About the annulment. I want to put the case in his hands; I've lost confidence in my present lawyer. So you see, in reality I invited him for your sake, if it's true that we're going to get married after the annulment comes through.'

The dog, meanwhile, was rushing about amongst the corn, barking. It was a lively but exceedingly timid animal. From the overcast sky above the hills came a single sharp, hollow clap of thunder. The dog, frightened, at once ran over to them and went and lay down close behind Lavinia.

Valerio now felt reassured again. Lavinia had an extraordinary quality of which he was distrustful but from which he could not escape – an intense, profound sweetness which filled him with a desire to lose himself in it, to drown in it as though in an abyss of maternal love. 'Forgive me,' he said at last. 'I promise you I'll never be jealous again.'

He saw her smile, but she did not speak. The dog was now standing behind her with its nose in the air and its ears erect, its nostrils quivering; it was looking at some unidentified object behind Valerio's back. Lavinia, too, seemed for a moment to be looking at the hedge behind Valerio. Then he saw her frown and lower her eyes to the ground. He put out his hand and began gently stroking her cheek in a caress which, in its intention, should have ended in a kiss. To his surprise, she turned her face aside, then took his hand and moved it downwards, away from her. Puzzled, he then leaned forward and tried to kiss her. But he succeeded only in lightly touching her chin. Lavinia pulled her head back and said: 'No, sit still.'

'But why, can't I even kiss you now?'

'I don't want you to.'

He saw her move uneasily on the grass; the dog, behind her, was still standing stiffly, its ears erect and its nostrils quivering. Lavinia, all of a sudden, rose with an effort from her bed of grass and said: 'I'm afraid it's going to rain.

Let's go home.'

Valerio followed her, disconcerted, and joined her on the path. 'Didn't you notice,' she said then, in a low voice, 'that there was somebody watching us from behind that hedge?'

'No, no, there wasn't anyone.'

'I tell you, there *was* someone. I saw him.'

Valerio turned and, to his surprise, perceived a small farmhouse at no great distance from the meadow where they had been lying. How in the world had he failed to notice it? At the same time a human figure detached itself from the hedge, was visible to him for a moment, then disappeared – a country youth with a brown face and a peaked cap pulled down over his bright eyes.

'I saw him from the beginning,' said Lavinia. 'Now you understand why I didn't want to kiss you.'

And so, Valerio could not help thinking at once, Lavinia had seen, from the beginning, the youth behind the hedge, just as shortly before she had seen, from the beginning, himself on the terrace. Again he felt jealous; and at the same time ashamed, too, at resembling the boy hidden behind the bushes. So there was no end to jealousy; and there would always be a looking-glass to warn Lavinia of his presence and to make her behave prudently.

Repetition

In the lift, Giorgia retreated into a corner, her eyes downcast; and Sergio said: 'Don't look like that. After all, what I'm asking of you is a thing of no importance. Afterwards we'll part company and never see each other again.'

'It's not a thing of no importance,' answered Giorgia. '*I'm* sorry, too, that everything's over between us. And to pretend to begin all over again seems to me cruel. It's only you who could have thought of such an idea.'

The lift stopped and they came out on to the landing. Sergio looked at the watch on his wrist. 'It's eleven o'clock,' he said. 'You arrived at five minutes past eleven, on this same day and in this same month of May. Only the year is different: three years ago.'

'Well, what am I to do, then?'

'Wait here on the landing and at five minutes past eleven ring the bell.'

Sergio took the key from his pocket, opened the door and went into the flat. A pent-house flat on the top floor, it was not large and the whole place was crowded with books. Sergio went along the narrow passage between two book-laden shelves, into the study. Everything was as it had been three years before, except that the shutters were drawn over the window, whereas, on that day three years before, the shutters were open, and he recalled seeing the wind shaking the bright, glossy foliage of the wistaria on the roof-terrace. He pulled back the shutters; the wind was blowing, as on the other day, and there was the wistaria. Then he went and sat down at the desk and took up the book he had been reading that morning, a monograph on the painter of the picture on which he had to give an expert opinion.

The bell rang, as on that other morning, and Sergio felt his heart flutter. He rose and went quickly into the hall and opened the door. She was standing on the threshold, absolutely the same, with the same dress, the same shoes, the same handbag. And perhaps, he thought, perhaps with the same intense look in her green eyes, and the same pointed lock of black hair on her white forehead. 'Who do you want?' he asked, starting to repeat the scene of three years before.

Giorgia, in turn, recited with an effort: 'Signor Lanari apologizes for not being able to come. I am his secretary.'

'Please come in.'

Sergio preceded her into the passage and thence into the study. Here he did exactly the same things as he had done that morning. First he went in behind his desk as though to sit down in his armchair; then he changed his mind and went over to the leather sofa in front of the window, saying: 'Look, let's sit here, we shall be more comfortable.'

Giorgia sat down, looked at him for a moment and then said angrily: 'No, I can't do it.'

'But what's the matter with you?'

'You attracted me at once, that morning, and I sat down in a certain way, so that I could touch your knees with mine at the first opportunity. But how can one do such things again, in cold blood?'

'Why not?'

'The feeling that made us do them no longer exists, and it all seems ridiculous or even disgusting. Well, I'll do it, but I'm ashamed of doing it, whereas that morning it gave me a wonderful feeling.' She slid a little way along the sofa, almost violently, towards him, and crossed her beautiful, long, straight legs; then, in a slow, laboured voice, as if she were climbing a difficult slope, she went on reciting: 'As I said, Signor Lanari has had to stay in the hotel because he was expecting a telephone call from Milan. In the meantime he sends you the photographs of the picture. He asks you to look at them and then tomorrow morning he will telephone and make an appointment.'

She breathed a sigh of relief and looked at the window. Sergio said harshly: 'Not like that. After you said those words you looked into my eyes.'

'In what way?'

'It was the loveliest look I have ever seen,' said Sergio, suddenly moved. 'A look – how shall I say? – of entreaty and at the same time of command.'

'You bet it was!' said Giorgia thoughtfully. 'I was so afraid you'd send me away; you seemed so serious, so angry, in fact. And so I looked at you to make you understand that you must find some pretext for keeping me.'

'Well, come on then, try!'

'All right, now I'll look at you as I did that morning.'

They looked at one another and Sergio felt a pang of distress. Yes, it was the same look and yet at the same time it was not. He said in a low voice: 'Will you show me the photographs?'

'Here they are.'

Sergio took the yellow envelope from Giorgia's white, thin hands and, as on that far-off day, drew out the photographs and began looking at them. He recalled that his eyes, that morning, had grown misty and his hands had trembled as he quickly examined the photographs and realized, confusedly and as though in a dream, that the picture owned by Signor Lanari, a rich industrialist from the North, was worth nothing, being merely a copy from a quite well-known original in a foreign gallery. Finally, as on that other morning, he said: 'Signorina, there's no need for Signor Lanari to telephone me tomorrow morning. The expert examination is already finished. D'you know how much this picture might be worth?'

'How much?'

'As it is merely a copy, the only value lies in the blank canvas and the frame. Between ten and fifteen thousand lire.'

'But Signor Lanari told me it was worth about two hundred million.'

'Signorina, it's a copy, and of a well-known picture into the bargain. You know what a copy is? A painter of a certain technical ability makes a very careful study of an Old Master and then paints a picture which is, so to speak, perfect, to the order of some unscrupulous dealer who passes it off on someone like Signor Lanari. I said perfect, but not genuine. A copy is therefore something which is perfect but at the same time sham.'

'What am I to say to Signor Lanari, then?'

'That his picture is a sham.'

'At that point,' exclaimed Giorgia, 'I felt desperate. I thought you had not noticed the look I gave you, and I decided to make myself more clearly understood. So I pushed my knees towards yours, like this.'

Sergio was troubled. Interrupting the game of make-believe, he asked: 'Did you like me so much, then?'

Giorgia answered with sincerity: 'Yes, terribly. If at that moment you had sent me away, I think I should have fainted before I reached the door.'

'I understood that, and in order to gain time I started asking you about your work, about Signor Lanari and so on. Shall we try to re-enact this part of the scene?'

'Very well, let's try.'

Sergio said hastily, as on that other morning: 'So you're Signor Lanari's secretary?'

'Yes.'

'What do you do with Signor Lanari?'

'I'm his secretary.'

'I'm sorry; what I meant was, what does your work consist of?'

'Oh, typing out contracts and business letters, taking down conversations in shorthand, making appointments.'

'But you're very young.'

'Not so very. I'm twenty-four.'

'And is Signor Lanari young?'

'Oh no, he's an old gentleman, very respectable, with white hair and several grandchildren.'

'And does he like pictures, Signor Lanari?'

'I don't think so. This picture was given to him in payment of a debt.'

Sergio was suddenly conscious that the words were more or less the same but the feeling was different. Three years before, at each of these very ordinary remarks he had felt, with her knees pressing hard against his, that he was taking an upward leap, further and further upward, into the heaven of intimacy. Now, on the other hand, he felt he was plunging downward, further and further down, into the abyss of regret and impotence. Abruptly he suggested: 'Let's cut it short. I couldn't invent anything more to say and I became confused and finally I said to you: "D'you know you have very beautiful eyes?"'

'I don't remember at all now what I answered. What did I answer?' inquired Giorgia.

Sergio replied bitterly: 'You didn't answer. You looked at me in silence. And I raised my hand and stroked your cheek, like this.'

He raised his hand and stroked Giorgia's face and she allowed him to do it, gazing fixedly at him with her eyes wide open. 'Not like that,' said Sergio. 'You lowered your eyes. Lower your eyes. With an expression of the greatest sweetness. That's better.'

He saw her lower her eyes; and then, as though in a kind of deliberate, desperate ecstasy, he seemed to see himself and Giorgia again at that far-off moment three years before, and he hoped, he hoped intensely that the present moment was identical with the past moment, in every sense, in fact that it was actually the same moment recovered from the stream of time, brought to life again and located, just as it was, in the present. He said softly: 'You lowered your eyes and then you raised your hand like that – that's right; you took my hand, you pressed it for an instant against your face – yes, that's right – and then you turned it half round and kissed the palm. And all the time with your eyes closed.'

He recalled that at that point he had bent forward and embraced her, and so their love affair had begun; and again he hoped that, thanks to that moment which had been so perfectly reconstructed, everything would be repeated, just as if the time had indeed never passed. But Giorgia thrust his hand away and rose to her feet: 'I can't go on any longer; enough, enough, enough!' Sergio, too, was upset; he, also, rose from the sofa.

'Then, it was beautiful, now it's merely disgusting,' said

Giorgia. 'Really I don't know why you force me to do this play-acting. Perhaps because you're hoping to start all over again. In that case you're mistaken. I haven't any intention of it.'

'No,' said Sergio, 'I don't want to start over again. It would be a different thing, whereas I want precisely that particular thing and nothing else. I made you do this play-acting, as you call it, because I wanted to re-live that moment which was perhaps the most wonderful moment of my life.'

'That moment is past for ever and will never come back again,' she said, less harshly now, almost as if she too regretted it. She went over to the window and looked out.

'But I cannot admit that it's past. I have it here, in my memory, so living, so true. That moment ought to repeat itself.'

She turned slowly and looked at him with compassion. 'It's suitable that you, of all people, should speak to me like this, since you explained to me so well, that day, what a sham was. That moment, then, was worth millions, milliards; all the riches in the world wouldn't have been enough to pay for it. But what we've done this morning is a sham, worth only a few lire. Isn't that so?'

She left the window and went towards the door, beating the long black gloves that she held in her hand against her leg. 'I'm no longer the person I was that morning and you're no longer the person you were. We're two different people. Nor, on the other hand, are we actors, a pair of good actors who can re-enact a scene to perfection. Besides, even if we were, who should we be acting for? For ourselves? Actors don't act for themselves but for a public. Good-bye.'

Sergio did not reply but went across to the window. The May wind, gay and impetuous, shook the foliage of the wistaria, just as it had on that other morning. And everything might have been as it had been that morning. Behind him, the door closed.

Lorenzo stopped the car and turned towards the youth. 'Well then, are you coming up or d'you want to stay here?'

He saw him shrug his shoulders, with an expression of arrogant laziness. 'Who's going up? I'm not – not even dead.'

Lorenzo looked at him for a moment without speaking. The handsome, depraved face, very dark, with its black, moist eyes of feminine size and shape, its short, sensual nose, its fleshy, glossy, full lips, was repugnant to him and, even more, surprised him: how had the boy's parents failed to notice anything? It was a face that spoke for itself. Lorenzo, annoyed, said: 'Lionello, if you're going to take it like this, it would have been better not to come to me.'

'But, *avvocato*, how ought I to take it?'

'D'you realize you may end up in prison?'

The boy looked at him, settled himself back on the cushions of the car, half lying down, his head thrown back and his neck rising round and strong above his summer jersey; but he said nothing. It was his way of answering embarrassing questions. Lorenzo persisted. 'May one at least know why you did it?'

Again silence. The look in the boy's eyes, filtering downwards through his long lashes, irritated Lorenzo. 'Why did you come to me, then?' he asked.

This time Lionello decided to speak, slowly and disdainfully. 'I came to you because I thought you were more understanding. But if you ask me these questions, then it means that I made a mistake and did wrong.'

'Did wrong in doing what?'

'In coming to you.'

Lorenzo jumped out of the car and slammed the door hard. 'All right then, stay here, I'll go up.' But, just as he was walking past the car, he saw the boy raise his hand in a languid gesture of appeal, without, however, modifying his listless, lounging attitude. He stopped and inquired irritably: 'Now what d'you want?'

'Cigarettes.'

'Here you are.' Lorenzo threw the packet straight at the boy and then went on into the entrance hall. As he stood in front of the lift he noticed, out of the tail of his eye, a female figure, outside in the street, approach the car and speak to Lionello. He recognized her at once; it was the boy's sister, Gigliola. While Lionello had the face and the manners – whether cultivated or spontaneous, it was impossible to be sure – of a young hooligan from the suburbs, Gigliola, for her part, with her supple body that swayed too much from the hips, her flat, foreheadless face, her eyes that were too large and her mouth that was too wide, had much of the corresponding female type. Lorenzo lingered purposely beside the lift so as to allow her to come up with him. Finally, in fact, he saw her approaching, walking across the shining marble of the spacious hall, half naked in her little dress which looked as though cut out of a handkerchief and which left her shoulders uncovered, as well as her arms, the upper part of her bosom and her legs up to above her knees. Lorenzo noticed that her fashionable hair-style, in the form of a tall, oval crest, confirmed and emphasized the extraordinary lowness of her forehead, not more than two finger-breadths high, and the breadth and animal-like robustness of the lower part of her face. Gigliola entered the lift and, without greeting him, asked Lorenzo: 'What's wrong with Lionello? Why won't he come upstairs? And why is he hiding in your car?'

Lorenzo, in turn, entered the lift and said, as he closed the door: 'Lionello is in trouble.'

'He's got himself into a mess, has he?'

'A very bad mess.'

'But what has he done?'

'My good girl, if I told you, the whole of Rome would get to know in a moment.'

'I think I can make a pretty good guess, all the same. Lionello and the other boys were always saying they wanted to do something to break the monotony of life.' She uttered these words as though quoting them from memory, with an ingenuous, blunt seriousness which made Lorenzo smile almost against his will. 'Ah, they said that, did they?'

'Yes, and they also said they would do something to make all the newspapers talk about them. I wanted to go in with them but they wouldn't have me. They said such things were not for women.'

The lift came to a stop and they got out on to a landing which, no less than the hall, was glossy with marble. Lorenzo turned towards the girl and took her by the arm. 'Now mind what I say: if you are fond of your brother, the things you've just told me, you mustn't mention to anybody.'

'I won't say anything, if you tell me what Lionello has done. Otherwise...'

She did not finish, for Lorenzo seized hold of her by both arms, exclaiming: 'Don't play the fool. You mustn't say anything, and that's that.'

He gripped her tightly and noticed that she looked at him with an expression that was far from offended. Then she said, in an almost flattered tone of voice: 'What a way to behave!'; and at the same time made a slight forward movement, a provoking movement, with her belly. At that, he let go of her immediately and said hurriedly: 'On the whole, Lionello is less heavily compromised than the others. If you don't talk, he may even get away with it. And stop playing the fool.'

'What a way to talk! The family lawyer!' mocked the girl. The door opened and a manservant in a white jacket ushered them into the anteroom.

'Good-bye, *avvocato*,' said Gigliola, and went off, humming and dancing along, into the darkness of a corridor. The manservant showed Lorenzo into the drawing-room.

Lionello's mother, Giulia, was wandering round the room with a little bald man who held a measure in his hand. She shook Lorenzo's hand as she passed, saying: 'Forgive me, I have to discuss the question of summer chair-covers for a moment with the upholsterer. I'll be with you in a minute.' Lorenzo wondered whether it was advisable for him to speak to Giulià before seeing her husband; in the end he decided that it might be useful : in that house everything depended, fundamentally, on her. Meanwhile he had sat down in an armchair and was watching her as she discussed matters with the tradesman. She was tall, thin, narrow, dressed in grey and black, with the lifeless elegance characteristic of many women who are very rich and very domesticated. In her carefully arranged brown hair there were already a few white threads; her blue eyes, small and deep-set, had in them a disquieting sparkle; her face, of a perfect oval shape, had a slightly swollen look, on account perhaps of the smallness of her nose.

Giulia finally dismissed the upholsterer, came and sat down beside Lorenzo and began talking to him, as usual, about her family, to whom she devoted herself tirelessly and who gave her, in her own words, worry enough to kill her. She spoke in great haste, linking up one sentence precipitately with another, even when the sense did not require it, rather like a frenzied smoker lighting a fresh cigarette from the butt of the preceding one. Anyone would have thought she was afraid that Lorenzo might interrupt her, and that she knew in advance that he had something disagreeable to tell her. Several times Lorenzo attempted to insinuate the phrase which lay on the tip of his tongue : 'Listen, Giulia; on the subject of your children, I must speak to you about Lionello ...'; but each time he came up against a wall of words that was at the same time both mobile and impassable. Strangely, thought Lorenzo, whereas in her conversation there was apparent the complacency of one whose conscience is at rest and who has nothing to reproach herself with, the haste, the frenzy almost, with which she talked seemed to indicate a profound, though perhaps unconscious, anguish. She had started by talking about the summer covers for the furniture; from the covers she had gone on to holidays at the seaside and in the mountains; from holidays she had enlarged upon the fashion for yachts, or, as she called them, boats; from boats she had slipped to the subject of her two children, who for her were 'my babies', and who had actually both been invited on to one of these boats; and now, without any connexion or any interruption, she had begun describing, in all its minutest details, a small party which Gigliola and Lionello had given, some evenings before, for their friends, on the roof terrace of the house. 'They even did variety turns. But they turned us out, Federico and me, saying: "Not suitable for adults. Only for minors of eighteen years old." Witty, wasn't it?'

The door opened and Federico, the husband, came in slowly, with the exhausted step of one who is emerging from a long, forced immobility. He was tall, athletic, but with slightly bent shoulders; his face with its handsome, symmetrical features, was closely marked, all round the blue eyes and the still youthful mouth, with fine wrinkles; his brow, at first sight, appeared ample and luminous, but if you looked more carefully you became aware that it was simply bald. Unlike Giulia who was unable to restrain her chatter, Federico, as Lorenzo knew, restrained himself all too much, reducing conversation to a series of half-sentences and head-shakings that seemed to betray an anguish which, fundamentally, was not very different from that of his wife. Federico went up to Lorenzo and, as though making a show of ignoring his wife, greeted him with cordiality that appeared to cost him a painful effort. Lorenzo looked at him and realized that his friend must have passed, as usual, a bad night: he suffered from insomnia and, as he himself expressed it, his nervous system was all to bits. Federico said briefly, in a subdued voice: 'Let's go on the terrace, shall we?'

They went out on to the spacious terrace, which was indeed a veritable 'hanging garden' suspended in front of a panorama of the city. It was hot, and the summer sunshine fell scorchingly upon the brick paving between the brief shadows of shrubs in boxes. Federico went towards a corner of the parapet from which there was a view over the

Tiber and over Monte Mario. He walked with long steps and moved his head this way and that, jerkily, like a man who feels himself choking and seeks in vain for air. As soon as they were far enough away from the drawing-room, Lorenzo said: 'Listen, I must speak to you.'

Federico was now looking down; he seemed to be staring straight at Lorenzo's car standing beside the pavement, small and solitary in the middle of a big, grey space of asphalt. Turning, he said: 'Speak to me? I'm sorry, but this morning it's not possible.'

Lorenzo opened his eyes wide in surprise: 'It's not possible? Why?'

He saw Federico's whole face contract, as if with cramp or some other sudden pain. Then Federico answered: 'It's impossible. My mind is not calm enough. I haven't closed an eye all night, in spite of sleeping-draughts, and, in short, I don't feel well.' He said yet other things of the same kind; and both the drawn, shrunken face and the spasmodic, jerky tone of voice were those of a man who is really suffering. This suffering made Lorenzo think that, perhaps, it would not be prudent to speak to him of his son. He persisted, nevertheless: 'Mind you, this is something that cannot be put off.'

Federico again cast a glance at the car, down in the street, in which Lionello was waiting; and he replied: 'There are no things that cannot be postponed. They seem always so urgent, and then ... I beg you, come back to-morrow, come tomorrow morning, even; I shall have slept, we shall be able to talk calmly.'

'But it's a thing that is really important.'

'Just because it's important, I don't wish to know it. I couldn't occupy myself now with an important thing.'

'Then you really don't want to?'

'Please don't insist.'

He had placed his hand on Lorenzo's shoulder and, imperceptibly, was pushing him across the terrace towards the drawing-room. Lorenzo had noticed that, each time he spoke, Federico's face was contracted by a sort of spasm, and in the end he privately decided not to tell him anything. He would do what he could for Lionello: Giulia and Federico who, each in their own way, did not wish to know anything, would learn of their son's misdeeds from the newspapers, or would not learn of them at all. He declined a bland invitation to lunch from Federico, said good-bye to him, then went and shook Giulia's hand and passed on into the anteroom.

As though she had been waiting for him, there, at once, was Gigliola, emerging from the shadows. 'Well,' she said, 'did you speak to Papa and Mamma?'

'No; and, in fact, please don't say anything to them.'

'But who's saying anything? However, you ought to be convinced.'

'Of what?'

'That the only person to whom one can say anything, in this house, is myself.'

'Perhaps you're right.' Lorenzo closed the doors of the lift. The cage started on its way down.

The Misanthrope

The idea of the expedition appealed to Guido, although he had only a slight acquaintance with Cesare, the young industrialist who had invited him, and none at all with the two girls, both of them employees of an airline company, who had come with Cesare. But no sooner had the car started off in the direction of the Lago di Vico, the goal of the expedition, than he regretted having accepted. He did not find his neighbour, on the back seat of the car, at all attractive. She was evidently very young; she had a soft, milk-white complexion, black eyes and very fair hair of a shameless peroxide tinge. Dressed in a knitted pullover of a brilliant, disagreeable whiteness, and a very tight, sky-blue skirt which displayed clearly the soft contours of her body, she seemed to Guido to be vulgar in an irreparable, innate manner, as though vulgarity, in her, were a congenital fact and not a moral characteristic. Very different, on the other hand, was the appearance of the other girl, whom Cesare had placed beside himself, on the front seat: she was lean, dark-haired, pale, elegant, with a long neck, a delicate face, a large, thin-lipped mouth and two enormous green eyes. Guido felt that Cesare had chosen the better of the two and had palmed off the worse on him. As they drove along, the fair girl sat brooding over him with her pitch-black eyes that looked like glass beads framed in velvet; finally she inquired: 'I say, are you a student?'

'Yes,' replied Guido, 'I'm studying law.'

'The law of the strongest,' said the girl, as pleased with this commonplace as if it had been a profoundly original remark.

'No, law in general.'

'My name's Iole. What's yours?'

'Guido.'

The girl said nothing, yet at the same time it seemed to Guido that she was talking because she was moving her

mouth. Then he looked more carefully and understood:
Iole was moving her mouth because she was chewing gum.
Guido reflected that this was a further objectionable feature
in the girl's character, and once more he was filled with
envy of Cesare who was now chatting, as he drove, with his
pretty neighbour. Indicating the back of the latter's slender
neck, shadowed with light curls, he said to Iole: 'Have you
known her long?'

'*Her?*' Iole's mouth, painted too bright a red, twisted into
a grimace. 'Why should I know her?'

'But don't you work in the same office?'

'There are so many of us, I can't know them all.'

'What's she called?'

'I believe she's called Valeria.' And then, lowering her
voice and leaning towards him: 'She's a Contessa, and she
thinks the world of herself.' She laughed and pulled the
chewing-gum out of her mouth in a long string which
became thinner and thinner until it broke and fell back in
an untidy flourish on her chin. Guido, disconcerted and also
rather disgusted, suddenly felt it was absolutely necessary
for them to change places so that he could have Valeria
beside him. They drove on for a mile or two and then he
exclaimed, as if by chance: 'I say, Cesare, would you mind
stopping at the next bar we come to? I'm dying for a cup of
coffee.'

'All right.'

When they reached the neighbourhood of La Storta, they
stopped at the rustic farmhouse with the little portico beneath which could be seen the glint of an *espresso* coffee-
machine at the far end of a big, dark room. Guido went to
the desk to pay, and beckoning to Cesare, whispered to
him: 'Could you do me a favour? Let's exchange girls; you
take Iole and I'll take Valeria. D'you mind?'

Cesare, with some surprise but without a shadow of jealousy, replied: 'Why, I thought I'd done the right thing, you
told me you liked blondes!'

'But this one's a peroxide brunette,' said Guido half-
jokingly.

'Very well,' said Cesare, 'I'll take Iole.' He spoke these words with the air of someone who finds a suggestion strange but has no personal objection to make to it. And in fact, when they had drunk their coffee and were going off towards the car, he said, without turning round, in a languidly indifferent way: 'Now girls, take turns. Iole comes in front with me and Valeria goes behind with Guido.'

Iole, curiosity aroused, inquired: 'And why?'

'Because two and two don't make three.'

They got in and the car started off again. Guido looked at Valeria and had a real sense of relief as he noted the girl's reserved, almost disdainful air as she sat beside him, keeping as far away from him as possible; exactly the opposite of Iole, who, on the contrary, had pressed heavily against him all the time with her wide, soft hips. They went on for some miles; Cesare was chatting and making jokes with Iole; but Valeria showed no sign, not merely of speaking to him, but even of looking at him. Finally Guido asked: 'What is your name?'

Without turning, the girl answered: 'Valeria.'

'You work at the airline company too, don't you?'

'Yes.'

'A lovely day, isn't it?'

'Yes.'

'Have you known Cesare long?'

'No.'

'I see you've been to the seaside already; you've got a good sunburn. Where were you? At Fregene?'

'No, at Portofino.'

'Ah yes, a lovely place. What's it like this year? Amusing?'

'That depends on the people you associate with.'

This last remark was, to Guido, like a flash of lightning on a dark night. He looked down at Valeria's long, thin hand and saw that she wore, on her index finger, a big ring with a stone upon which was engraved a coat of arms; then he looked at her eyes from which there shone out a look almost of terror, and at last he understood: the girl was a snob; and Cesare had made a bad mistake in inviting her together with the vulgar Iole; and she had accepted the invitation probably because she had nothing better to do; but was resolved to keep her companions at a distance and not to be too familiar with them. Putting his conjecture to the proof, Guido asked her a few more questions about the people with whom she associated at Portofino, and saw that he was not wrong: in the way in which Valeria pronounced certain names; in the stiffness and brevity with which she condescended to answer him; in certain commonplaces and clichés characteristic of smart society which she uttered as it were in inverted commas, as though to make it quite clear to him whom he had to deal with – in all these lay the confirmation of a pathological snobbishness which was anyhow too hidebound to be broken down during the brief period of a day's expedition. In the end Guido, discouraged, fell silent, almost regretting the vulgarity of Iole – though on second thoughts he felt that that, too, was unendurable.

He now had no further wish to speak to Valeria, who no longer seemed to him even to be attractive. He wondered whether it would give him any pleasure to kiss her and privately concluded that it would give him no pleasure at all: snobbishness disgusted him more than a physical defect. Suddenly the car stopped in front of a reinforced concrete shelter beneath which was a row of four yellow and red petrol pumps. 'We'll fill up here,' said Cesare, opening the door and getting out to unscrew the cap of the petrol tank.

Quickly Guido jumped out of the car, went over to Cesare and said to him in a low voice: 'I'm sorry, but would you mind letting me sit in front beside you, in place of Iole?'

'Why!' exclaimed Cesare, amused, 'don't you like Valeria either?'

'No, it's not that; it's the springiness of the car that makes me feel a little sick.'

Cesare paid the petrol pump attendant and then cried airily: 'Iole, you're requested to go and sit behind with

Valeria. Guido wants to sit in front because the car upsets his stomach.'

'What a delicate stomach!' said Iole; but she went willingly and sat beside Valeria, who now shrank back more than ever into her corner, a prey to her social terrors. The car moved off again.

Guido knew Cesare only slightly, but felt a liking for him. He liked Cesare's fine head, with its large, serious eyes, its straight nose and well-formed mouth, a head which would not have been out of place in a Renaissance picture or on a Roman coin. So he started chatting to Cesare who answered him, as he noticed, with intelligence and readiness and a curious quality of irony that was not in the least vulgar. In this way they touched on many subjects, all of them, however, of a private kind, so to speak – that is, relating to habits, tastes and individual life. Encouraged, Guido then introduced a question – of an entirely public kind, this time – on a matter which concerned him deeply: a sensational trial being held at that moment in which the accused were members of a criminal association in the South. The sensational quality of the trial derived not so much from the seriousness of the crimes, which indeed were terrible, as from the social and political implications. Guido took a passionate interest in this affair, partly because his family belonged to the neighbourhood in which the crimes had been committed; and it never even occurred to him that Cesare could see these things in a way different from his own, which was, in his opinion, the only possible way. And so he was much disconcerted when he observed that his companion had now fallen silent, with a distant, embarrassed expression on his face which seemed stubbornly to deny him the signs of understanding and approval he had expected. Finally Cesare said in a curt tone of voice: 'For me, all this is something that doesn't exist. I think of my work and my work doesn't permit me to concern myself with anything else.'

At these words Guido, in turn, became silent; he looked at Cesare with different eyes and was surprised at having thought he could share his ideas. It had been his face that had misled him, he went on to think, that face which was so handsome and so noble but which, to a shrewd eye, looked like a mask with imposing but empty features behind which was concealed the real face, very different and devoid of any sort of nobility. Suddenly he realized that he felt, for Cesare, a repugnance even stronger than for Iole and Valeria; just as, in fact, scepticism was more repellent than vulgarity or snobbishness. But what was he to do now? He had already changed places twice, and there was no escape.

At last they reached the Lago di Vico, a stretch of pale blue water amongst delicate green reed-beds, with the shadowy hills reflected indeterminately in its mirror-like surface. They stopped and got out of the car and made their way towards the little restaurant which stood on the lake shore in the shade of some leafy trees. Guido fell behind, and while the other three went and sat down at a table he walked over to a little landing-stage consisting of a couple of planks jutting out into the lake.

He felt profoundly disgusted and wondered whether it might not be possible for him to run away, reach the main road and there take the bus back to Rome. Valeria's snobbishness, Iole's vulgarity and Cesare's scepticism all seemed to him unbearable; but even more unbearable seemed the feeling of aversion which his three companions aroused in him. Then he looked down from the landing-stage at his own image reflected in the water of the lake and remembered, all of a sudden, how that very morning, looking at himself in the glass, he had been moved to anger and had exclaimed to himself: 'How unpleasant I am! How very unpleasant!' He had picked up a long, dry branch from the ground. He threw it on to his own image, which was at once shattered into numberless liquid, shifting reflections. Then he walked away towards the restaurant where the other three were already giving their order for luncheon to the waiter.

About three in the morning Giovanni had the following dream. It seemed to him that he was high up on a balcony without any balustrade, at the top of an extremely tall building closely encompassed by other buildings of equal height. These were the houses, or rather the towers, of a fantastic city which had grown entirely upwards; laden with pinnacles and spires, they were so lofty and so slender that they seemed to remain upright only by a miracle. Then the roar of an earthquake travelled across below the city, and suddenly Giovanni saw the houses as though in a concave mirror, leaning forward. The buildings leaned more and more, like reeds bent by the wind, and then, when tilted to the farthest possible angle, started collapsing, unhurriedly, in fact slowly and tidily, beginning with their copings and so on right down to the ground, in a steadily increasing uproar. And now the house at the top of which he himself was standing started tilting, farther and farther forward, until, in the end, he was forced to hurl himself into the void, into the great cloud of dust from the buildings already collapsed. He did in fact plunge forward, arms outstretched, with a cry, and as he cried out he awoke.

He opened his eyes and found that he was in darkness and that the roar of the earthquake and the collapsing houses was simply the noise of thunder from a storm which now flashed lightning at the window, illuminating the room, from time to time, with an uncertain light. The thunder at first rumbled distantly, then, after a pause, nearer and more loudly, and finally burst with a violent explosion that made the windows rattle. Immediately afterwards there was silence, and then he heard the vast, impetuous murmur of the rain falling in torrents outside the window.

Giovanni put out his hand under the bedclothes and had a moment of panic when he discovered that his wife's place beside him in the bed was empty. Then, as he stretched his

hand out further, he felt under his fingers the light folds of
the chemise on the warm body and realized that his wife
was indeed there; it was merely that she had moved over
towards the edge of the bed. Somewhat reassured, he
started thinking about his dream; and then, all at once, he
was seized with depression. It was true that it had been the
thunder which had, so to speak, suggested the dream of the
earthquake and the collapsing buildings; nevertheless it
was significant that, among so many possible images, the
thunder should have suggested precisely that one, the image
of the collapse of a city. Giovanni was conscious of a feeling of deep distress, as if, together with the fantastic houses
of his dream, his reasons for living had also fallen in ruins.
How many years had passed since, as a child, during a
similar thunderstorm, he had jumped in great haste out of
his bed and had run to his mother who was sleeping in the
next room and had sought her in the darkness, his fingers
on the thin stuff of her chemise, just as he had sought his
wife a moment ago? Thirty years, more or less. So thirty
years had gone by, he thought, more than half a lifetime.
Almost aloud, he said: 'How awful life is!'

Immediately, from the darkness, the calm, clear voice of
his wife inquired: 'Why do you say that?'

Giovanni was disconcerted. He had thought his wife was
asleep, instead of which she was awake and had heard him.
He in turn asked: 'What did I say?'

'How awful life is!'

'I don't know why I said it.'

There was silence. It had started to rain again, and then
there was an intense flash of lightning and the room, with
its objects and its colours, became visible, albeit entirely
unreal. The lightning ceased, and immediately afterwards
there was a sharp, violent clap of thunder. Giovanni said:
'For some time now there's been a thunderstorm every
night.'

His wife agreed. 'I've been awake for an hour already,'
she said. 'I woke up at the first clap of thunder.'

'And what did you do?'

'Nothing: I opened my eyes wide and watched the window which was lit up every five seconds.'

Giovanni was now vaguely irritated at the calm which was apparent in her voice. 'Nothing else?' he insisted.

'Yes, I thought of you.'

'You thought of me?'

'Certainly; does that seem to you strange?'

'It doesn't seem to me in the least strange,' replied Giovanni sharply, raising his voice in the darkness of the room, 'only I should like to know, please, what you mean when you say you thought of me.'

'I mean what I say. I just mean I thought about you.'

'And what did you think?'

'Really I didn't think anything. I just thought of you.'

'That's idiotic.'

'What d'you mean, idiotic?'

'An idiotic remark,' answered Giovanni, paraphrasing Shakespeare's line, 'made by an idiot on a night full of sound and fury.'

'Thank you.'

There was a long silence. The rain was still falling in torrents; through its diffused rustling sound could be heard the greedy gurglings of the drain-pipe doing its best to gulp down all the water that rushed into it from the roof. Giovanni's wife said: 'You still haven't explained to me why you said life was awful.'

Irritated afresh, Giovanni replied: 'First of all you must explain what "I thought of you" means.'

'It means exactly what it says.'

'Well then, I don't understand it.'

'Get along with you, you understand perfectly well.'

Giovanni wondered why his wife's remark irritated him so much; and finally it seemed to him that he understood: if the words meant nothing, then his dream was correct, and everything had fallen in ruins. 'No,' he said, 'really I don't understand. But let's take things in order. Seeing that, when you thought of me, you didn't think anything, tell me at least what you *did*.'

'What I *did*?'

'Yes, what you did in order, as you say, to think of me.'

There was a brief silence. Then his wife's voice began again, slowly: 'I huddled myself together, as if there'd been a fire inside me and I was warming myself at this fire. I concentrated, in fact.'

'And what was the result of this concentration?'

'That I thought of you.'

'That is, that you didn't think anything.'

'If you like. But I caressed you with my thought.'

'Wait a moment. This thought of yours – what is it? A hand?'

'No, it's not a hand. When I say that, I only mean I thought of you.'

'In other words, you didn't think anything.'

'But what need is there always to be thinking something?' exclaimed his wife with a certain impatience. 'It's feeling that's important, in some cases anyhow, not thinking.'

'In reality,' said Giovanni with profound bitterness, 'I'm nothing to you, that is, I don't exist. It's natural therefore that, to you, thinking of me means not thinking anything.'

For the first time there was a note of alarm in his wife's voice. 'But why d'you say that?' she said. 'What's the matter? What's happened to you tonight?'

'Nothing's happened to me. I had a dream and I woke up. That's all.'

'What was the dream?'

'I dreamt that an earthquake made a whole city collapse.'

In a quiet, reasonable voice his wife said; 'I don't see what *I* have to do with this dream. Besides, why d'you say that for me you don't exist? I swear that, if you happened to die, I should throw myself out of the window at once, at once. Now are you content?'

Giovanni thought for a moment and realized that he was not content. 'Do you mean by that,' he said, 'that you love me?'

'Yes.'

He protested violently: 'But what's the use of your love to me if you don't know how to express it? You huddle yourself together, you concentrate, you caress me with your thought, you jump out of the window; all of them things that don't affect me, that concern only yourself.'

'What would affect you, then?'

'That you should tell me, in a clear and precise manner, what you mean when you say that you thought of me.'

His wife, all of a sudden, started to laugh in the darkness. 'How obstinate you are!' she said. 'But don't you know that there are things about which one *can't* speak?'

'I think one can speak about anything,' said Giovanni.

'I, on the other hand,' replied his wife, '*I* think that, when there are things one can't speak about, it's best to keep silent.'

The Dream

The telephone started ringing when Silvio had already been asleep for some time. He stretched out his hand from underneath the sheet, turned on the lamp at the head of the bed and looked at the clock on the bedside table: it was a quarter past three. The telephone went on ringing. Silvio took off the receiver and asked: 'Who is it?'

A woman's voice answered him. 'It's me, Alina; don't you recognize my voice?'

Silvio replied gaily: 'Why, of course I recognize it. When did you arrive?'

'Half an hour ago. It seemed a long stretch from Milan, by car. I couldn't go fast because the car's running in. On the other hand it's a most beautiful car, blue. You'll see.'

'Where are you staying?'

'With my usual friends, in the house where we met – the Federicos.'

'Are we going to see each other?'

'Of course; otherwise why should I have telephoned you?'

'I'm pleased that you're here.'

'And I'm pleased that you're pleased.'

'Are you stopping long?'

'Alas, no. I'm leaving again the day after tomorrow, or rather tomorrow, seeing that tomorrow' – he heard her laugh – 'has already become today. But then I'm coming back and staying longer.'

'Well then, when shall we see each other?'

'Let's have lunch together,' answered Alina. There then followed a long and very detailed discussion on the restaurants which Silvio suggested one after another, and which Alina, for this or that reason, rejected. Silvio, indeed, could not help wondering at this fastidiousness – right in the middle of a love conversation, into the bargain. Finally Alina said: 'No; d'you know what I'd really like? I'd like to have lunch at that little place where you always go, close to where you live. Then after lunch we'll go up and you can give me some coffee.'

Silvio wondered whether this very promising suggestion was premeditated, and was left in doubt; it all appeared natural and yet at the same time predetermined. He answered, however, with genuine delight, that if Alina was satisfied he asked nothing better. 'Well, I'll ring off now,' said Alina, 'I'm dead sleepy. But wait a minute; listen.'

Silvio listened, and a small sound came to him out of the receiver; then the voice asked: 'Did you understand?'

'Yes, it was a kiss.'

'Good! Well then, until tomorrow – that is, today.'

Silvio replaced the receiver, turned off the light and for a while lay thinking about Alina and her telephone call. He had seen this beautiful, rather odd, girl only once, a month previously, at a party. Alina, as usual, had had to leave for Milan the same evening; and yet there had been something very like love between them during the two hours between the end of the party and her departure. Alina had promised him to come back in three days' time and anyhow to write to him; but she had not come back and she had not written. Now, thinking of her, Silvio realized that he loved her. Turning over in his mind, deliciously mingled together, the memory of their first meeting and the hope which their second inspired in him, he finally fell asleep.

Next day, he left the house a quarter of an hour before the time fixed for their meeting, and made his way to the restaurant. He lived in the old quarter of the city, in a penthouse flat on the top of an ancient *palazzo*. The restaurant was in one of the narrow lanes near by, only a short distance from his front door. And then, as he walked and reflected on his good fortune, Silvio could not help telling himself that everything was too wonderful, too perfect in fact, to be true. His reasoning was as follows: 'Nothing that is human can be perfect – which means, in my case, in conformity with my desires; therefore, in this love affair of ours, there must necessarily be something that does not do, something I don't know about, something that will not take long to reveal itself.' At this point he asked himself why it was that perfection made him suspicious, and finally he understood: there was, in perfection, something excessive which was not human and which, therefore, unless it were superhuman, could not but be apparent. Alina's behaviour towards him was, in point of fact, favourable to an excessive degree; for that reason it was to be feared that it might be merely a smiling mask covering a very different reality. With these thoughts in his mind he had now reached the restaurant; he opened the door and went and sat down at his usual table, in the corner under the window. The restaurant was of the rustic, or rather the sham rustic, type, with garlands of sausages and clusters of wine-flasks dangling from the low ceiling and numbers of photographs of film actors and actresses on the walls. There was no one there and it was almost dark. A waiter turned on the light and came over to Silvio. 'Good morning, Doctor. Are you alone?'

'No, I'm expecting someone; we'll need another place.'

'Will you wait, Doctor?'

'Yes, I'll wait.'

Silvio ordered an aperitif and, in order to pass the time, started counting the photographs of film stars that hung on the walls. It was not a big place, but there were many photographs. After he had counted the photographs on two of the four walls, he suddenly grew tired of it, looked at his wrist-watch and discovered that almost twenty minutes had already gone by. All of a sudden he was sure that Alina would not come. He was so sure of it that he leapt to his feet and went to the telephone, at the far end of the restaurant. He dialled the number of the Federicos' flat, where Alina had said she was staying; a voice that he did not know, a woman's voice which nevertheless was not that of the maid, answered him that the Signorina was not at home: if he telephoned in an hour's time, however, she was due to return for lunch. Silvio felt the blood leave his cheeks and asked in a very low voice: 'She's coming back for lunch, the Signorina?'

'Yes, certainly.'

'Did she not say anything about going out to lunch?'

'She said nothing to us.'

Silvio hung up the receiver, went back to his table and, calling the waiter, said that he would start eating. He was not hungry, in fact he had a very distressing feeling of nausea, but, since he was sure that Alina would not come, he was ashamed of waiting longer, in front of the waiter who knew him and would be able to guess his disappointment. After a short time the waiter brought him the dish he had ordered and Silvio started to eat slowly, embittered by the realization that, as always when one suffers very severe pain, appetite, instead of deserting him, was steadily increasing. Meanwhile he was wondering what could be the reasons for Alina's behaviour. He at once rejected the possibility of some uncontrollable circumstance, that is, of some outside event which could have prevented her not only from coming but also from letting him know that she would not be coming: the imperfection of that apparent perfection lay, in fact, in the thing itself, not outside it. Thus he came to the conclusion that, between a quarter past three that morning and twelve o'clock, something had occurred to make Alina change her mind. This something, he went on to think, seeking to superimpose the coolness of an objective examination upon the burning smart of his wounded pride, might be a moral, or rather a moralistic, scruple; it might be a change of heart due, at best, to the suspicion that she did not love him enough, or was not enough loved by him; it might be mere absent-mindedness or forgetfulness; or again, a piece of premeditated cruelty due either to a desire for revenge for something which he, without being aware of it, had done to her, or to gratuitous spite. As he continued, diligently but miserably, to eat his second course, Silvio examined, one by one, all these hypotheses, and in the end was forced to admit that all four of them were possible: Alina's character, in fact, was such that one might expect from her either moral scruples, or a recognition of error, or forgetfulness, or cruelty. Her manner was in fact so restless that one might suppose her to have a troublesome conscience or an irresolute temperament; on the other hand it was possible to imagine, from her character as a rich, spoilt society girl, that she might be scatter-brained or cruel. By this time he had completely finished his meal and a whole hour had gone by since the moment when Alina ought to have kept her appointment. Silvio paid his bill and went out.

He returned home by the same narrow streets through which he had passed on his way to the restaurant and which now, after his disappointment, seemed to him actually to have changed colour. He went up to his flat and, as soon as he was inside, without taking off his overcoat, rushed into his study in the half-darkness and gropingly dialled the telephone number of Alina's friends. The same female voice informed him that Alina had come in, had eaten her lunch in a great hurry and had then gone out again. Silvio turned on the light and began taking off his coat, looking at the desk as he did so. All of a sudden he paused, one arm still in its sleeve, the other out: on the pad on which the maid noted down telephone-calls, there was one from Signora Federico, Alina's friend, with a few lines informing Silvio that he was invited to a party there that same evening. He finished taking off his coat, went and lay down on the sofa and put out the light.

He now thought that he would go to the party and compel the girl to justify, somehow or other, her incomprehensible way of behaving. The methods he imagined himself adopting in order to confront her varied considerably: they ranged from a heartbroken request for an explanation, or a cold, pressing accusation, to a couple of slaps administered with methodical violence. Silvio spent the afternoon indulging in fantasies of this kind. Finally he dressed and went off to the party.

He found Alina, as he had foreseen, in the last of a series of small, crowded rooms, on the second floor of an old *palazzo*. A tall fur hat made her almost unrecognizable. Elegant, inattentive, frivolous, smiling and distant, Alina gave him her thin, ring-laden hand, asked him how he was and then turned her back on him and went on with an interrupted conversation. Silvio wandered round the rooms for a little and finally went home again.

As he went, he started thinking again about the events of that day and all at once it occurred to him that his association with Alina consisted of two parts which did not fit together and which, while they were plausible if taken separately, became absurd when linked to one another. The first part comprised their meeting of the previous month, followed by silence and absence and concluded by their second meeting that afternoon. The second part was the telephone call of the night before, during which Alina had shown herself so amorous. If one ignored the telephone call, he reflected, everything fell into place: Alina had had a moment of passion for him, a month earlier, then had regretted it, had decided to do nothing more about it and had tried to make him understand this at the party, by her kind but distant reception of him. All this, however, was rendered absurd by the telephone call. But how could one contrive to ignore the telephone call, since it had really happened?

He thought about it for some time and, in the end, said to himself that there was only one way of ignoring it, which was by admitting that he had dreamt it. By attributing it to a dream, everything explained itself. Furthermore, the telephone call had at least three characteristic qualities of a dream: it had occurred between two sleeps, at dead of night; it was very precise in its details (the car 'running in', the colour of the car, the time, the address, the discussion about restaurants, the kiss) as often happens in dreams; finally, notwithstanding this richness and precision of detail, it had no roots in reality; in other words, it was absurd.

But the fact remained that Alina had really come to Rome and that he had really seen her at the Federicos': here dream and reality became merged. Silvio reflected further and concluded that he could provide an answer to this objection too: however the thing might have been, whether he had dreamt it or whether it had really happened, it was nevertheless a dream because it was not to be explained in a rational manner. Nor, on the other hand, was he anxious to explain it, precisely because, since it had all the characteristics of a dream, he accepted it as such; as indeed one accepts dreams and, in general, all occurrences that are not worth explaining.

As they drove along a road glassy with rain, under a grey, wet sky, Tommaso observed his companion. She might have been a little over thirty; her smooth, flowing black hair hung down on either side of a pale, lean face, with an aquiline nose and brilliant black eyes. Lipstick of a very bright red gave her large, curving mouth the appearance of a wound. He looked down and noticed that, below her green skirt, she was wearing glossy black Wellington boots that came half-way up her legs. Finally he asked: 'Is it much further?'

'No, it's not far now.'

'Whatever made you think of building a villa in such a solitary place? I could understand if it was near the sea. But it isn't.'

'We built it there because the land was ours.'

'And when was it built?'

'About 1930, over thirty years ago.'

'In all those years, have you lived there all the time?'

'No, we used to go there until 1933, I think. Then we built the villa at Ansedonia and didn't go there any more.'

'Abandoned for twenty-seven years! But why?'

'Oh, I don't know. I suppose we didn't like it.'

'And what is the price? The agent told me, but I've seen so many villas recently that I've forgotten it.'

'Fifteen million lire.'

'Ah, yes. From what I understand, it's a very big villa.'

'Yes, it's big, but there aren't many rooms. A living-room and four other rooms.'

'According to the agent, it would be a good bargain.'

'Yes, I think it is.'

'Does the villa belong to you?'

'No, it belongs to my brother, my sister and myself.'

'But have you no parents?'

'No, they're dead.'

'Are your brother and sister married?'

'Yes.'

'Do they live with you in Rome?'

'No, they live abroad.'

'And you, are you married?'

'No.'

'You live alone?'

'No. But, Signor Lantieri . . .'

'Yes?'

'Excuse me. I have to show you the villa, but I don't consider that I have to talk to you about my private life.'

'You're perfectly right. Forgive me.'

Silence followed. But, strange to say, Tommaso realized that the girl's brusque reply had neither mortified nor surprised him. He wondered what the reason could be for this serenity on his part, and finally understood: both the price of the villa, which was very low considering the size of the building, and, in general, the girl's curiously disinterested and distant attitude, had about them something mysterious which excused, if not actually justified, his indiscretion. He looked at her mouth and was struck by the brightness of her lipstick, which looked like blood. From her face, white as paper, his eyes travelled to the road, which ran, grey and shining, towards the grey, steaming landscape, and then he noticed that, like the red of her lips, other colours too stood out in an unusual, brilliant way from the greyness of the autumn day – the golden yellow of the leaves of a climbing plant on the front of a cottage, the wet blackness of the trunks of certain trees, the almost blue green of cabbages in vegetable gardens, the red of the clusters of berries in the hedges. It was a cloudy, rainy day, he thought, but it was also an extremely beautiful day in which colours stood out and were resonant as voices in a great silence. He inquired of the girl: 'Is there any land round the villa?'

'The price includes two thousand square metres of garden. But the land all round belongs to us, and if you like you can buy more.'

'At what price?'

'A thousand lire a square metre, I think.'

Tommaso noticed again that the price was lower than the rate usually quoted in that district; but this time he said nothing. The girl changed gear and, leaving the Via Aurelia, turned the car into a country road, between two antique pillars. 'This is where our property begins,' she said.

'Then is this the approach to the villa?'

'Yes, there's no other road.'

The road wound along the bottom of a valley, between round, green, treeless hills on the top of which could be seen white farmhouses with green windows and red roofs, one on each hill. 'Are all these farms yours?' asked Tommaso.

'Yes, they're ours.'

Between one hill and another there were deep, narrow valleys, some of them cultivated, some left to scrub or woodland. Tommaso counted, on the left of the road, four hills and as many valleys; then the car turned sharply and proceeded along a small side road towards one of these valleys, at the far end of which could be distinguished, among the trees, the vague, grey outline of a building. 'The villa's not on the sea,' said the girl, with an absent-minded, careless air, 'but it's very near the sea. Five minutes in a car and you're at the beach, on the other side of the Via Aurelia.'

They crossed a little bridge over a deep ditch and then the lane plunged into the scrub, which seemed to become steadily higher and thicker as they went on. All of a sudden the girl stopped the car in front of a wooden gate with a chain and a big padlock on it, both of them rusty. Beyond the gate, only part of the façade of the villa could be seen because of the trees. Tommaso noted with surprise that this façade had nothing attractive and rustic about it, as might have been expected in such a place; on the contrary, it was a gloomy, square structure, grey-cement-coloured, rather like a neo-classical temple, but of the type of neo-classicism which, round about 1930, had been known as the 'twentieth-

century style': a plain pediment, a peristyle with square
pillars, brutal and squat and having neither capital nor
base, a square stone door like that of an Egyptian tomb.
The girl, in the meantime, had got out of the car and was
fumbling with the padlock on the gate which, in the end,
opened. 'Why, is it the first time you've been here?' Tommaso asked.

'Almost. I haven't been here for years.'

The eucalyptus-trees lining the short approach to the
house opened out in front of a paved forecourt, on the far
side of which, fully visible now, stood the enormous,
gloomy cube of the villa. Behind and all round the villa
there were many trees, and behind the trees rose the slopes
of the hills. Tommaso noticed an odd fact: in spite of its
having been deserted for twenty-seven years, nature had
kept at a distance from the villa: the walls were bare, with
patches and seepages of damp but no creepers; no green
moss had invaded the cracked and crumbling steps that led
up to the door; no grass had grown in the meandering
fissures that had opened in the paving of the forecourt. It
might have been thought, he said to himself, that nature
had found the villa repugnant. A noise made him start: the
girl had gone into the house and was now pulling up one of
the big roller-blinds that hung on each side of the door. So
he too went in.

He found himself faced by the living-room, which was
spacious and remarkably lofty, and of the same gloomy,
grey colour as the façade. The floor appeared to be covered
with minute pieces of rubble and dirt upon which the dust
had fallen softly like a shower of snow; at the end of the
room there was a huge brick fireplace, black and lifeless,
and, in front of the fireplace, a large sofa; no other furniture
was to be seen. Tommaso walked over to the sofa and then
discovered, between it and the fireplace, a little low table
upon which stood two glasses and a whisky bottle, un-
corked and with the cork beside it. The sofa was covered
with a material of a colour now unrecognizable, possibly
brown, possibly mauve, all split and ragged and with the

stuffing sticking out of the crevices. Tommaso took up the bottle : it was empty but looked as though it had dried up over the years, and the label was spotted with yellow; and on the table, grey with dust, there was now a clean circle. 'This is the living-room,' said the girl.

Tommaso had noticed that one of the walls had a fresco painted on it, and he went over to look at it. In a style characteristic of the period, it represented a social scene – a group of bathers on a beach. You could see the sea, and the sand, and a big striped umbrella. Round the umbrella, in varying poses, were grouped a number of men and women in bathing-costumes. The men were all muscular and athletic, with broad shoulders and small heads, and some of them wore monocles; the women were very buxom, with rotundities which seemed to be bursting out of their scanty costumes. The faces of both men and women were haughty, handsome, immobile. In the midst of these prosperous, naked people the puny figure of a manservant stood out prominently; he was dressed to look like a performing monkey, in a little short white jacket and black trousers, and he was handing round a tray of drinks. There was nothing indecent about this fresco; but Tommaso nevertheless had the feeling that he was looking at a pornographic illustration. Behind him, the girl said : 'They're comic, aren't they? Those were our fathers and mothers.'

Tommaso wanted to reply : 'You mean *your* father and *your* mother,' but he restrained himself in time. There was something, now, on the edge of his memory – just as one says sometimes that a word is on the tip of one's tongue. He seemed to recollect that the name of the girl's family was connected with a crime that had happened many years before, at about the time when the villa had been built. It was an old story now, and he had been a boy when it had happened; possibly he had heard it spoken of later. But if a crime had really taken place in the villa, that explained the modesty of the price and the strange, embarrassed off-handedness of the girl. Trying vainly to retrace in memory the name of the principal figure in the crime, Tommaso followed the girl, who now led him along a passage and showed him, one by one, the other rooms.

These rooms contained furniture in the same brutal, stark, 'twentieth-century' style in which the villa had been built – wardrobes, cabinets and bedside cupboards in the form of cubes, armchairs like boxes without lids, beds with enormous feet and square backs. All this furniture was in dark walnut – not solid walnut, however, but veneered; and the polish which had once disguised the fragility of these pieces that looked so massive had all vanished, and the veneer had an opaque look, was spotted with black stains, peeling off and in some places blistered and cracked. On a bed in one of these rooms there was still a sheet, thrown back and crumpled and with a large stain in the middle of it, of a faded, indeterminate colour somewhere between iodine yellow and greyish buff. On the bedside table was a small box. Tommaso read out the name of a laxative from the lid of the box, and then said: 'You might at least have made somebody sweep out the house, seeing that you want to sell it.'

'It's *I* who want to sell it,' answered the girl, meeting his look of disgust with an air of defiance. 'My brother and sister don't know anything about it. And I haven't had time to get the place cleaned up. I put the advertisement in the paper, and you're the first potential buyer.' She uttered these words in a tone of insulting haughtiness; then she went to the door of the bathroom and threw it open. 'This is the bathroom.'

Tommaso walked over and looked in, leaning cautiously forward. It was a normal bathroom; the white tiles were incrusted with dust and the taps green and lustreless. In the lavatory-bowl Tommaso saw something black sticking to the porcelain surface and, without a word, pointed it out to the girl. Disdainfully she turned her back upon him, went out of the room and opened a door in the passage. 'This is supposed to be the maid's room,' she said. Immediately something dark ran quickly away between their feet, there was a piercing scream, and for a moment Tommaso had the girl in his arms; she kept repeating, 'A rat, a rat,' and was trembling all over and digging her sharp nails into his neck. Tommaso said gently: 'Keep calm, it was only a rat.'

'Yes, I know, but I'm so terrified of rats.'

'Never mind, it's gone.'

'Thank you; I'm sorry.'

They went back into the living-room. At the moment when the girl had let forth her despairing cry, Tommaso, with a sudden enlightenment, had remembered the name of the family connected with the crime. It was not the girl's name; moreover the situation of the villa did not correspond. No crime, therefore, had been committed in the villa, although appearances certainly seemed to suggest it. All of a sudden the girl said nervously: 'Well, that's the villa, there's nothing more to see. You must admit that fifteen million is not a high price.'

'No, it's not a high price. But it's not the kind of villa I was looking for.'

'You don't like it?'

'No, it's built in a style I don't like at all.'

'We have a proposal to make it into a school or something like that. In the end I dare say we shall accept.'

'I think that would be a good solution.'

They left the villa and walked across the forecourt in a thin, stinging rain. 'What's the villa called?' asked Tommaso, just for something to say.

'It hasn't any name,' replied the girl, 'but the peasants have given it one which I can tell you now, since you're not going to buy it. They call it the house of the crime.'

The Alphabet

The appointment was at the other corner of a secondary road, where a muddy lane led away to the village between two hedges of elder. Girolamo turned into the road and stopped the car under the hedge. It had been raining all the morning, and the sky was full of dark, ragged clouds from amongst which a brilliant light shone out and was reflected brightly in the numerous puddles all over the road. Girolamo took the letter out of his pocket and read it again. As he read it he could not help saying to himself that, in telling Anna of his decision to leave her in writing rather than by word of mouth, he was committing an act of cowardice. But he justified himself with the thought that the blame lay in the girl's alarming character. Suddenly the door of the car was thrown open and Anna fell almost on top of him, saying hurriedly: 'Come along, get on, let's go!' Girolamo started the engine and off they went.

Girolamo turned into the secondary road and fell in behind a column of cars and lorries coming out of the town and going into the country. As he drove, he looked sideways at Anna as if to fortify himself in his intention of parting from her, and he again thought what he had thought the first time he had seen her: the face of a Madonna, of a delicate oval, but with two eyes which were far from gentle, which were, on the other hand, constantly agitated by some incomprehensible, unreasonable rage. In this expression of rage there was, nevertheless, a suggestion of unhappiness; and so Girolamo, every time he looked at her, could not but be conscious of an obscure feeling of pity.

He started at the sound of her voice asking harshly: 'Where do you keep your cigarettes?'

'In the dashboard locker.'

He saw her put out her small hand ('small hand, choleric hand' he recalled having read, some time ago, in a treatise on chiromancy) and fumble with the door of the locker, without succeeding in opening it. Then she turned red with anger, and said: 'Open this thing for me! Don't you see I can't manage it?'

'Impatience doesn't get you anywhere,' he said gently, putting out his hand and opening the locker; 'you're too impatient, you are.'

Swelling with anger, she gave a snort. 'Ugh, you and your lectures! You're just like my father. Now look, don't lecture me today, otherwise I'll ...'

'You'll what?'

'I'll open the door and throw myself out, at once.'

'May I ask what's the matter with you?'

'The matter is that my father's already been lecturing me this morning, and the result is that I've got a bump on my head.'

Girolamo knew that Anna's father, a builder's labourer, was a very patient and reasonable man; and he could not help being astonished. 'What, your father hit you?'

'No, of course not; if he struck me I'd kill him. No, I did it myself.'

'But why?'

'Out of desperation at his lecturing me like that. When he went on and on, I began shouting and then I took my head in my hands and bashed it against the wall. Feel here, what a bump I've got.'

She took his hand off the wheel and guided it up to her head, making him feel her skull beneath the thick, fine hair. He was conscious of the delicacy, the fragility, of this youthful head, and marvelled that such furious storms of rage could burst forth from it. 'Why, you're crazy,' he said.

'A little more and I'd have thrown myself out of the window.'

'But you can't control yourself; really, it needs so little!'

'Listen, I've already told you; don't lecture me, it's not a suitable moment.'

'All right, all right, provided you calm down.'

Girolamo said no more and drove on in silence. They were out of the built-up area now and were moving along a quiet country road between fields. After a long silence Girolamo started talking of indifferent matters because he wanted Anna to calm down and to receive the letter of farewell in a less disturbed state of mind. So he started talking about his work at the university, about his studies, his teachers, his companions. Then, still with the idea of keeping the conversation on neutral ground, he introduced the subject of a book he was reading, which he had at that moment on the seat of the car. Anna seemed now really to have calmed down; and, since Girolamo was speaking to her about this book, she asked him what kind of a book it was. Girolamo, pleased at this unhoped-for curiosity, without a word took up the book from the seat and placed it on her knee. It was a history of Italy, with the title in big red letters on the upper part of the cover. Girolamo watched the girl twisting and turning the book in her hands; then she asked: 'What is there in this book?'

'How d'you mean, what is there?'

'What's written in it?'

'Don't you see? You can tell from the title.'

The girl said nothing: she looked at the book in a hesitating sort of way. Girolamo added: 'It's a very good history. Really interesting.'

'But what of?'

'Really, you know, you're stupid! Why, of Italy, of course.'

In a flash, with her usual savage, frenzied suddenness, she blazed up in anger. 'Listen, don't answer me like that, because, as I said before, it's not the day for it. And now look, this is what I do with your book. Look!' Furiously she let down the window and hurled the book out of the car.

Girolamo, more astonished than angry, stopped the car and asked: 'What on earth is the matter with you?' – and, without waiting for an answer, got out and went to pick up the book where it had fallen. The road, at that point, ran along the edge of an airfield where a few aeroplanes were drawn up here and there on the runway, under the cloudy

sky. Some idlers who were looking at the airfield through
the fence turned to stare with curiosity at Girolamo as he
ran to collect the book. He stooped and picked it up; at that
same moment an arriving aeroplane passed above his head
with a deafening roar, and then, with the same suddenness,
it flashed into his mind that Anna's behaviour was
too strange not to have some significance. But what? Turning
over this thought in his mind he went back to the car, threw
the book on the seat and sat down again beside the girl.
But, instead of starting up the engine, he sat quite still, as
though meditating.

'Well, why don't you start?' she asked, with a hint of
repentance in her voice; 'are you angry with me? You
ought to be sorry for me. I'm made like that: either take
me or leave me.'

'Leave you,' Girolamo wanted to say. But he restrained
himself in time and replied: 'I'm not in the least angry. But
now you must oblige me by reading this letter.' He took the
letter out of his pocket and threw it into her lap.

He saw that she lowered her eyes towards the letter,
without touching it. Then she said: 'What is there in this
letter?'

'Read it. I wrote it just because I preferred not to tell you
by word of mouth what there is in it.'

'Won't you tell me what it is?'

'No, read it.'

Anna took the letter, drew the sheet of paper out of the
envelope and looked at it for a moment; then she said:
'Very well, I'll take it home and read it at leisure.'

All at once Girolamo longed for the whole matter to be
finished at once, without any more procrastinations. 'No,
you must read it here, in front of me,' he said; 'then you can
tell me what you think of it and we won't mention it again.'

He saw her turn red in the face with anger. 'I'll read it
when and where I please,' she said.

Girolamo, growing angry in turn, was on the point of
saying: 'But why don't you want to read it? Is it because
you're illiterate, perhaps?' – when suddenly he noticed that

Anna was holding the letter upside down, so that even if she had wanted to read it she could not. His anger abated, since it had occurred to him that possibly the girl really could not read. He said gently: 'Give me back that letter.'

'I'll give it back to you,' she said suspiciously and hesitatingly, 'only on condition that you tell me first what there is in it.'

He paused and then said: 'Nothing definite. I was just telling you I loved you.'

'And did you need to write me a letter in order to tell me that?'

'Well, to tell the truth, I wrote something else too.'

'What?'

'What you call a lecture. I told you you oughtn't always to be so excitable, so angry, in a rage with everybody and everything.'

'I've already said: 'I'm made like that.'

Girolamo started the car again and then, when they were once more moving along between fields, he said: 'That's no answer. You're made like that, it's true, but you could change.'

'I don't want to change.'

'In my opinion, the reason why you're always so violent is because there are so many things that you don't know, that you don't understand. And that infuriates you and makes you violent.'

'Who says so?'

'*I* say so. You threw that book out of the window because ... because in that book there is something that eludes you, something that you can't control.'

She made a gesture of impatience and then yawned ostentatiously. 'Oh well, that's enough lecturing. I'm hungry. Let's go and eat.'

'You'll give me back the letter, then?'

'Here it is.'

Girolamo took the letter and put it in the locker. They had now come out on to the road that circles round the lake of Castelgandolfo and were driving along past a row of gardens and villas that hid the lake itself. 'Just look at this map, will you?' he said, 'and see where one has to turn off to get to Nemi. See where it says *Via dei Laghi*.'

It was the final test. She took the map, unfolded it and then looked at it in embarrassment. 'I don't see this *Via dei Laghi*,' she said.

'And yet it must be there. What's written up there?'

'Where?'

'Up there at the top of the map.'

'I want to see now how she gets out of it,' thought Girolamo, not without a touch of cruelty. But Anna raised her head, looked out of the window and said suddenly: 'Why go all the way to Nemi? It's too far and I'm hungry. Look, let's go to that restaurant there; I've been there before, and the food's good.'

'There's a notice on that gate,' said Girolamo, 'and the notice says something that prevents us from eating at that restaurant.'

'What?'

'Closed for repairs.'

This time the girl said nothing. After a moment's silence, Girolamo went on: 'But on that other gate, away over there, there's a sign, and the sign says: "Restaurant Belvedere. Speciality: Game." Shall we go there?'

'Let's go anywhere you like, so long as we can eat.'

They reached the gate. Girolamo slowed down and turned the car into the garden of the restaurant, passing below the sign upon which, in big yellow letters on a green background, was written: 'Trattoria del Lago. Speciality: Fish from the Lake.'

The Room and the Street

Towards dawn Riccardo had a nightmare. He thought he was in a tunnel with a very low ceiling, like a tunnel in a mine, and that he was crawling on hands and knees in the direction of a way out; but it was impossible to tell whether this was near or far away, because of the pitch darkness and the suffocating closeness of the air. As he advanced on all fours, Riccardo hoped nevertheless to find a place where the tunnel widened and opened out; all at once, however, he realized that the ceiling of the tunnel was becoming steadily lower and lower, and that he was not, in fact, making his way towards the exit but into a blind alley where, presumably, the tunnel came to an end. He decided therefore to go back, but soon became aware that he had penetrated too far to be able to turn round : the narrowness of the passage made this impossible. This discovery filled him with a terrible anguish so unbearable that finally, with a prolonged groan, he awoke.

At once he realized that he was on hands and knees, as in his nightmare; and, from his contact with the smooth wall that he was feeling with both his hands, he understood also that he was not in his own bedroom but in a strange room which was unknown to him. But how on earth he found himself out of his bed, in a house not his own – this he was quite unable to comprehend. The sensation of the complete strangeness of the place filled him with uncontrollable agitation and panic; furiously he felt the wall with his hands, and the more he felt it the more unknown it seemed. Then his hands encountered something which seemed to him even more foreign than the wall – a flat surface, broad, upright, tall, slightly inclined towards him, soft and furry to the touch. Riccardo followed the contours of this armchair – for an armchair it was, and covered with velvet, into the bargain, an object that he remembered perfectly well *not* having in his bedroom; and finally his hand, reaching forward into the darkness, encountered the close, hanging folds of a curtain. Behind the curtain his fingers spasmodically discovered and seized upon the cord which worked the roller-shutter; he pulled it vigorously, and daylight flooded the room.

It was his own bedroom. By a kind of somnambulism from which he was aware that he suffered, Riccardo, while asleep, had risen from his bed and had gone and crouched down in the corner between the window and the armchair. As for the velvet on the armchair, which he recalled having always seen in a loose cover of snuff-coloured cotton, the explanation of this occurred to him immediately: the evening before his wife had taken off the loose cover, which was now dirty, in order to send it to be washed; and underneath the cover the armchair was, in fact, upholstered in green corduroy velvet.

But, now that he thought it over, he was struck, particularly, by the strong, precise feeling of strangeness which he had experienced for two or three minutes after he had awoken. Bewildered, he could not help reflecting that merely to wake up out of his bed, beside an armchair whose cover had been removed, had sufficed to give him the illusion of being in a new, unknown, strange and frightening place. Sitting on the untidy bed, Riccardo turned over this thought in his mind for some time without coming to any solution. Then he roused himself, remembering that he had to go to his office, and started dressing.

That day Riccardo's life went on as usual, that is to say, he had his usual thoughts concerning the life he led. In his office, where he spent two-thirds of his day, he could not avoid noticing, as usual, that his work did not interest him in the least. Something else he observed, not for the first time: on those few occasions when, in a moment of absentmindedness, he allowed himself to feel a passing interest in his work, he realized that, immediately afterwards, he experienced a feeling of remorse, as though he had been guilty of a betrayal. But what had he betrayed, seeing that he could not do anything else and had no vocation of any kind? Riccardo could not have said.

As always, moreover, he made his usual criticisms of his colleagues: they were coarse and vulgar, they were common-place, they were dreary and, into the bargain, they were unconscious of the by no means golden mean of their destiny; on the contrary, they were jovial and consequently given over to trivial departmental gossip and office jokes. With regard to these colleagues, too – although at the bottom of his heart he rejected them – it sometimes happened that Riccardo allowed himself to find them likeable, to laugh with them, to retail gossip and rattle off platitudes. And each time these mortifying surrenders occurred he experienced, as when he took an interest in his work, a feeling of remorse, as though he had betrayed something. But, again, who or what had he betrayed? Was this not his own social world? In what way was he better than his colleagues? To these questions, too, Riccardo found no answers.

Then, finally, his superiors. For them Riccardo harboured a limitless, though fundamentally unjustified, contempt. And with them the same phenomenon occurred as with his work and with his colleagues: it sometimes happened that he forgot his contempt and had a feeling of liking, of respect, even of admiration for them – only for a short time, however, and always, of course, with the usual accompaniment of remorse as if he had been guilty of a betrayal. In this case, too, he could not have said who or what he was betraying. These men were his superiors, there were no others, nor, so far as he knew, could there be.

At any rate, somehow or other, the day went by. When he finished work, Riccardo left with his colleagues and went to catch the usual bus that took him home in twenty minutes. He had been living for a couple of years in a new quarter, built on a hill. The road in which his home was situated wound round the hill and had two ways of approach, one at the bottom, from a big square where the bus stopped which Riccardo took every morning to go to his office, the other at the top of the hill, from another square where the bus finished its journey. Riccardo, odd though it may seem, had never seen this second approach. for the house in which he lived was very close to the lower square and he had never had any reason to go up the street as far as the upper square.

But on that day Riccardo was absent-minded and went past his usual bus-stop without getting out. At that moment he was annoyed, then he reflected that he could get out at the next stop and that this would perhaps be a good thing, for he would thus be forced to walk a little – something that he did less and less frequently nowadays. The bus, however, did not stop for some time; and when Riccardo finally got out, he realized that he was in a part of the new quarter that was completely unknown to him. A much more agreeable part, he immediately thought, much more attractive, more airy, more aristocratic than the part in which he himself lived.

Two rows of trees with very fine, spreading foliage – pepper-trees, possibly – leant over towards the centre of the street, thus forming a kind of tunnel of leaves. Through iron gates, in large gardens, there were glimpses, amongst trees, of the façades of luxurious villas. There was no one in the street; or rather, away down beyond all those spiked railings, there was one woman walking quickly along, dressed in a white blouse and a flame-coloured skirt. She was fair, and her hair, according to the fashion, was drawn up and puffed out in such a way as to form a kind of helmet; the back of her white neck was pretty and delicate, and upon it, even at that distance, could be distinguished a single golden curl that shone like a jewel. She had broad, full shoulders, a long back, a very slim waist enclosed in a wide leather belt. With every step she took, a vigorous, intense undulating movement was conveyed from her hips to the folds of her skirt.

The woman, as well as the street, seemed to Riccardo to be strangely attractive; and this was precisely because, like the street, she appeared to him to be a novelty of an untouched, surprising kind, like something never before experienced. Riccardo felt he must approach her, speak to her; and he felt also that his mistake regarding the bus had probably been providential: it sometimes happens that an entire life is changed in this way by a mere trifle. This thought caused him, indirectly, to remember his wife whom hitherto he had believed he loved, and his two children of whom he was very fond; and he realized, to his astonishment, that, if this woman really entered his life, he would not hesitate to throw his family overboard.

The woman had perhaps noticed that she was being followed; for all at once she stooped quickly and picked up an oleander flower which someone had pulled off and dropped on the pavement, raised it to her nostrils and then, after holding it for a short time between two fingers, with her arm hanging down, dropped it again on the ground. Riccardo quickened his step, picked up the flower and raised it to his lips. The woman was now walking more slowly, possibly to allow him to catch up with her, and every now and then she felt the back of her neck with her large, smooth, white hand, as though to make sure that her hair was in place, or smoothed out the folds of her blouse across her back. It looked, in fact, as though she knew she was being watched and was anxious not to appear untidy.

There was a bend in the street and now there were no trees on the farther side of it, and the street looked wider though no less attractive and no less new. Here there were no more villas with iron gates; a few imposing blocks of flats, five or six floors high and crowned with pent-houses, stood in a line along the pavements that sloped down the hill. Again Riccardo thought, almost involuntarily, that it would be far preferable to live in this street, with its air of elegance and aristocratic serenity, than in his own street which was so mediocre and so shabby. And it was the street, he went on to think, in which he intended to approach the woman in the red skirt; perhaps it was for that reason that it looked to him so much more attractive than the one in which he lived with his wife.

The woman slackened her pace again; Riccardo interpreted this as a tacit invitation and hurried forward in order to join her. Just at that moment she disappeared into the main door of one of the blocks of flats, with a last swirl, like a summons, of her red skirt. Riccardo hesitated and then followed her.

He saw her, at the far end of the hall walking towards the staircase, without making use of the lift – an indication, probably, that she lived on the first floor; it might be, on the other hand, that she was going up by the stairs so as to permit him to stop her and speak to her. Riccardo noticed that the hall, the lift and the staircase were, indeed, new to him, but in a curious sort of way – like certain landscapes which make us think that, though they are unknown to us, we have seen them in another life. Now the woman turned and disappeared again; Riccardo ran up the stairs two at a time and caught up with her, out of breath, just at the moment when she turned round and then said in a quiet voice: 'Ah, it's you.... Why did we fail to see each other?'

'And you – why on earth...?' stammered Riccardo. He wanted to add: 'Why on earth are you here, in this unknown building, at this time of day?' But he stopped in time, for he recognized, on the door in front of which they had stopped, the plate with his own name on it. This, then, was his own door, just as the street he had walked down shortly before was his own street, and the woman with the red skirt, his own wife. The latter, meanwhile, had put the key into the lock, and, at his question, she turned, smiling, and said: 'Why on earth am I a blonde? I got tired of being dark, that's all. What d'you think of it?'

Riccardo hastened to reply that her blonde hair, arranged in that way, suited her extremely well. They went in; his wife went to the kitchen to see if dinner was ready, and Riccardo to his own room, where he threw himself on the bed and remained there, flat on his back, in the gloom of twilight. He was aware now that there was a link between his nightmare of the previous night and his daytime illusion, but it was difficult to see what it was. There were many similar elements: his wife's hair that had ceased to be brown corresponded to the armchair that no longer had its loose cotton cover; the terror that had assailed him when he thought he found himself in a strange room, to the joyous hope he had felt when he had fancied that he was following an unknown woman along an unknown street. Furthermore there was, in both cases, one analogous, significant detail : both the room and the street had appeared new to him because he himself had been placed in a new position in relation to them. For he had not woken up in his own bed, but in a corner of the room; he had not entered the street by the lower approach, but at some unspecified point higher up. Seeking more and more wearily to follow the thread of these reflections, he finally fell asleep.

A Fine Sort of Love

They made their way along the path which they had trod-
den so many times six years before, quarrelling stubbornly
and harshly. 'But what d'you mean when you say we could
have been so happy? We were happy when we were able to
be happy, neither more nor less.'

'You never understand anything. You're so intelligent in
your profession, but in questions of love you're an idiot.'

'It's you that's the idiot.'

'What I meant was that we could have been so happy if
we'd only realized that those were our best years and that
we ought to make the most of them. Instead, we've spoilt
everything.'

'The usual ready-made remark! But I should like to
know what it is we've spoilt?'

'Our love. And not only our love: everything.'

'In what way?'

'You know in what way: quarrels, ill-humour, rudeness,
coldness, arguments, insults, blows.'

'No, not blows; I've never hit you.'

'Yes, you hit me that day when I shut myself in my room
and refused to come out. You banged me against a wall and
almost broke my head.'

'I didn't hit you. I broke open the door, and naturally, in
order to break it open, I pushed hard against the two
leaves. You were behind it and without meaning to, I
banged you against the wall.'

'It doesn't matter; what do the details matter? The only
thing I know is that we could have been so very, very happy
and we haven't been. And that those years, which could
have been the two best years of our lives, were spoilt,
miserably spoilt.'

'So very, very happy. . . . Spoilt, miserably spoilt. . . . Why
so many repetitions?'

'Oh, go to hell!'

They were half-way to their destination, now, walking between the low, mortarless walls of clean grey stones, over which, swarming and gesticulating, the prickly pears thrust their pale, thorny blades. Behind the prickly pears the slope of the hill was dry, bleak, barren, dotted with small, twisted olive-trees between which, in the distance, could be seen the sea, of a clear, luminous, smiling blue, tedious, almost, in its unvarying serenity. The young woman stopped suddenly and, gazing at the long line of the sea, cried in a sing-song voice like a prolonged moan: 'Oh, how happy we could have been! We were both twenty-two, we were just married, we had everything. Sometimes I wake up at night, while you're asleep – snoring, in fact – and I think of it and I start crying, crying, at the mere thought of the happiness we might have had and have not had.' She put such bitterness into her words that Silvio, influenced by it, could not help having a feeling of regret too. Supposing she was right? But he recovered himself quickly and inquired with irritation: 'And what ought this happiness of ours to have been like, in your opinion?'

His wife replied slowly, ecstatically: 'Loving each other, without ever stopping for one single moment, adoring each other, being not two people but one single person.'

'Your happiness,' said Silvio promptly, 'is vague and conventional. D'you know what it makes me think of?'

'What?'

'Of those picture postcards you see in tobacconists' shops, all glossy and coloured, with a sly-looking young man, dandified and flashily dressed, holding a girl with made-up eyes to his breast. And in the corner there's a beautiful pansy or a rose.'

'Idiot!'

'It's you that's the idiot – judging anyhow from the idea you have of love. Would you like to know what I, on the other hand, consider to be happiness?'

'I don't want to know anything.'

'But you've got to listen to me.'

'No, I don't want to know anything.' She put her hands

to her ears and gazed obstinately towards the sea. Silvio, in a rage, seized her by the wrists, pulled her hands away from her ears and, twisting her to one side, said hurriedly: 'Happiness is to be oneself, profoundly, truthfully, without any compromises, even at the cost of being unhappy. D'you understand? We had happiness during those two years because we loved one another, and love means that a man and a woman can be themselves without the conventionalities that you like so much. Just because we quarrelled and hit each other and insulted each other, we were happy. D'you understand?'

'Leave me alone.'

'And don't stop your ears when I speak to you, d'you see? Because you've got to listen to the intelligent things I say to you, just as I listened to the stupidities you said to me.'

'Leave me alone.'

Silvio kissed her on the corner of the mouth, whether in anger or affection, he did not know; then they separated and walked on as though nothing had happened. At last, at the end of the path, they saw the gate of the villa half-hidden in a cascade of creepers with minute leaves and little blue flowers. Above the gate could be seen the side of the house, white and simple, with a straight cornice, a drainpipe coming down to the ground, and two windows with green shutters. Silvio looked at these windows which, he knew, were those of the room in which he had lived for two years with his wife, and all at once he felt a pang in his heart: yes indeed, they had loved one another up in that room, and they had been happy, albeit in a violent sort of manner and not in the conventional way that she dreamed of. His wife said impatiently: 'Well then, let's go back again.'

'No, I want to go in.'

'But why?'

'Because I know that in this house we loved one another, and I want to see the place of our love again.'

'A fine sort of love.'

Silvio shrugged his shoulders; then he pulled the bell-rope and at once, on the other side of the garden, the well-known bell rang shrilly, with its harsh yet friendly voice. They waited a little, and then there was a movement behind the thick creepers over the gate, and the gate opened and there appeared a young girl of about fifteen, small and well-built, in a tight sweater too low at the neck and a very short skirt. Her face was the face of a grown woman; her long, bruised-looking black eyes had in them a gentle, ironical expression, and her lips were brown and full. 'What is it you want?' she asked. 'The Signora's not in.'

'Does the Signora still let rooms?'

'Yes, she does.'

'We'd like to see one of them.'

'But they're all occupied.'

'Never mind, we'd like to see them for when they're free.'

'Come in, then.'

Here again was the garden, old and overgrown and neglected; and here again the outside staircase, its steps of worn, flower-patterned tiles sprinkled with pine-needles from the branches bending over it. The girl said something about a pan on the fire and ran off. Silvio and his wife went up the staircase and through a door with coloured glass panes into a big room with two windows.

It was their room, and everything had remained the same – the spacious bed with the rust-coloured hemp-cloth bedspread, the English-style country furniture, the red-tiled floor, the bare white walls. The room was evidently inhabited by a married couple: masculine and feminine garments were to be seen hanging up here and there, and on the chairs; numbers of jars of face-cream and toilet articles were tidily arranged on the marble top of the chest-of-drawers; from under the pillow peeped a pink muslin chemise and a pair of blue pyjamas. Silvio, moved in spite of himself, said in a low voice as if talking to himself: 'And yet I know: we *were* happy here.'

His wife had a sudden access of fury. 'Why, stop it, will you? Look, this is what I think of your happiness!' She

Jealousy Plays Tricks

Ernesto was standing, one day, in the doorway of the sitting-room in his own home, watching, from a distance, his wife and the man whom he suspected of being his wife's lover, a friend of his called Luca. They were sitting on a sofa at the far end of the room, and were talking animatedly but in low voices about something which, it appeared, was of great interest to them. Ernesto was smoking furiously as he looked at them; for some time now jealousy had been keeping him awake at night and weighing him down with sleep in the daytime; and at that moment he could not have said which he would prefer – to go to sleep or to rid himself of the unconquerable anxiety which the thought of his wife aroused in him.

But in the end his fixed, malevolent stare seemed to annoy her. All of a sudden she jumped up, walked across the room to him and asked: 'Will you kindly tell me what it is that makes you stare at me like that?'

'No reason at all,' replied Ernesto, quoting a well-known English saying; 'it's no crime to look at you: a cat may look at a king.'

'Yes, but unfortunately I'm not a king. Luca wants to talk to me about his affairs. Go and wait for us in the study; we'll come and fetch you and we'll all go to the beach.' As she spoke, his wife pressed her hand lightly on his chest and pushed him out, into the bedroom. The door closed.

Instead of going into the study as had been so lovingly suggested to him, Ernesto, highly displeased, sat down in a corner of the bedroom and waited. But the second hand of his watch, on which he kept his eyes fixed, had scarcely moved five times round its circuit before the door opened and his wife, in her petticoat, with bare arms and stockinged feet, appeared in the doorway, threw her dress on to a chair and vanished.

Obviously she had not seen Ernesto crouching in his corner; but Ernesto had seen her only too well: the quick forward movement of her body in its transparent under-garment, the hurried gesture, the excited look on her face. And so, he reflected with a distress which was acute and at the same time bitterly triumphant, he now held the proof he had so long been looking for; his wife and Luca loved each other; in fact they carried their effrontery so far as to shut themselves up together in his own house, right under his nose. What should he do? Ernesto's first impulse, natur-ally, was to burst into the sitting-room; but he restrained himself in time, for there had suddenly flashed into his mind the revengeful notion of becoming in turn the deceiver after having himself been deceived. He would not burst in upon them but would play with them like a cat with a mouse; hitherto he had been ignorant and they had known; henceforward he would know and they would be ignorant.

In the meantime, however, in order to avoid making them suspicious, it would be wise for him to go into the study, as his wife, with treacherous foresight, had sug-gested. Ernesto made as though to rise from the armchair into which he had sunk, and then, as he made the effort to do so, all of a sudden he awoke.

He was – yes, he was in the bedroom; but there was no dress lying on the chair; and just at that moment the door opened and his wife, fully clothed this time, looked in and asked him if he was ready to go to the beach. 'So it was all a dream,' thought Ernesto as he followed her. Hitherto, in spite of his fatigue from sleeplessness, he had always man-aged to distinguish between sleeping and waking. Now, with a mingled feeling of alarm and astonishment, he be-came conscious that, without realizing it, he had passed from a dream which had some semblance of reality to a reality which had the absurdity of a dream. These thoughts filled his mind as they went down into the street. They got into the car. Ernesto placed himself at the wheel; his wife sat beside him and Luca behind.

Ernesto drove for some time without speaking. But as they turned into Via Cristoforo Colombo, he said: 'Just imagine, I went to sleep while I was waiting for you; and I had a really ridiculous dream.'

'What was that?'

'I dreamt that you were with Luca in the sitting-room and I was looking at you, and then you turned me out and shut the door in my face. After a little, however, you appeared in the doorway half undressed, threw down your dress on a chair and went back and shut yourself up with Luca.'

He saw his wife look at him sideways and then start laughing and laughing until her pretty, fair face became scarlet. Finally she stammered: 'But, my poor Ernesto...'

'Well, what's the matter?'

'My poor Ernesto, it wasn't a dream.'

'What? Did you really throw me out of the room, were you really shut up with him, were you really half undressed?'

'Now wait a moment, it was like this: Luca and I were talking and you irritated me, staring at me from the door, in the way you often do, like a bull that's just going to charge. So I asked you to go out of the room for a moment. But they came to tell me that the dressmaker had arrived with the new dress for me to try on, and so I asked Luca to leave the room too. After I had tried on the dress, which fitted me very well, I took it off and threw it on the chair in the bedroom, so that the maid could put it away. All this really happened. But at that point you fell asleep, and then, when you woke up, you thought it had been a dream.'

'But when I woke up the dress was no longer on the chair.'

'Of course not; you were asleep and you didn't realize that the maid had come in, put away the dress and gone out again. She said to me, in fact: "Signor Ernesto is asleep, shall I wake him up?" And I answered: "No, please don't, because he didn't sleep last night."'

'Thank you for being so considerate.'

'But what's the matter; are you angry with me?'

'No; if anything, I'm angry with myself.'

After driving along the Castelfusano road between the

dusty, tangled pine-wood and the harshly sparkling sea, they came to the bathing-establishment and the car park, with cars standing in a row all round it under the thatched shelters, their metal-work throwing out a blinding glare in the August sunshine. They went in and walked over to the hut, in a formation, and against a background, that seemed like those of a ballet in a theatre: on one side the green huts, all exactly the same, in a scalloped pattern against the blue sky and appearing to descend towards the sea; on the other, a procession of bathers, alternating according to sex, a man and a woman, a man and a woman, in single file, walking up the cement platform towards the way out. To accentuate the appearance of a ballet, the big umbrellas on the beach, against the background of the sea, were all yellow; while the almost naked figures standing out against the horizon were chestnut-brown. A large ball, black and green in segments, flew through the air, thrown back and forth by two players in red bathing-trunks. All this was secretly irritating to Ernesto. Just as, a little later, he was irritated at the sight of his wife when, after long preparations, she came out of the hut in a bikini.

It was, in fact, the most fantastically exiguous and symbolic bikini to be seen anywhere on the beach. Two thirds of her shapely bosom transcended the limits of her brassière, which was reduced to the width of an ordinary ribbon; from her breast to her belly, the eye could travel over an expanse of bare, blonde flesh, soft, supple, undulating, inviting, down to a triangle of flower-patterned material so small that, if you looked at her sideways, it was hidden by the golden-brown curve of her legs and she appeared to be entirely naked. In truth, thought Ernesto, his wife – rather like the Emperor in Hans Andersen's tale – was more naked, so to speak, than when she was really naked, inasmuch as, though she was in effect naked, she thought quite honestly that she was clothed and so had all the naturalness of someone who imagines he has nothing to be ashamed of. He said brusquely: 'Now look, do please go and cover yourself a bit more; this is really too much.'

'But this is the kind of bikini that's in fashion this year.'

'Put a handkerchief over yourself; this is really impossible. Don't you realize you're naked?'

'Well, and what if I was?'

'Just you go into the hut and put something on.'

'Ugh, how tiresome you are!' His wife turned, displaying to him, with unconscious irony, how naked she was when seen from behind also, and started off towards the door of the hut. Just at that moment, however, Luca, who had been waiting until she was undressed, went in. But this did not prevent her from going in with him. The door closed and Ernesto found himself alone.

The sun on his back was scorching, his face was burning with rage. Once again his wife had shut herself up with Luca and this time he could not possibly delude himself into thinking it a dream. What struck him most of all, as a particularly cruel feature of the matter, was that she should have shut herself up in the hut with Luca, making use of the pretext that he himself had provided – the scantiness of her bikini. Ernesto could not help feeling that by now the two lovers had lost all restraint; the intrigue was clear and transparent and perfectly obvious. From inside the hut there now came a sound of shuffling feet, a suppressed murmur of voices. Then, after an interval which seemed to him immensely long, the door opened and Luca appeared on the threshold, with an air of quiet satisfaction, fastening the belt of his trunks. Without hesitation Ernesto bounded forward and seized hold of him by the neck, shouting: 'That's enough, now.'

A confused scene followed. Luca and Ernesto, struggling together, finished up on the sand, in a cloud of dust; some of the bathers separated them, panting and dishevelled; then Ernesto's wife ran up, dripping wet from the sea, and, taking them each by one arm, dragged them off to the bar. They sat down in a corner. Luca was disturbed but calm, with the look of a man wrongly suspected; Ernesto was grim and gloomy; his wife, as usual, could not manage to keep serious: for her everything was a cause for hilarity.

Finally, after Ernesto had given an account of what had happened, she could no longer restrain herself and burst out laughing.

'There's nothing to laugh at,' said Ernesto gloomily.

'I'm laughing,' said his wife, 'because this time there's no doubt that the whole thing *was* a dream.'

'What d'you mean?'

'I went first into the hut, and when I came out you'd gone to sleep in the wicker armchair, on the platform. I went past in front of you and then on down to the sea, and you went on sleeping. Luca went into the hut, and you were still asleep. You dreamt therefore that you told me to wrap something round my hips, you dreamt that I shut myself up in the hut with Luca, and naturally, after a dream like that, as soon as Luca woke you up by opening the door, you went for him.'

'I'm sorry,' said Ernesto thoughtfully; 'first I mistook reality for a dream, and now I've mistaken a dream for reality. My nerves have gone all to pieces, for some time now, and I don't seem to understand anything.'

'But how,' exclaimed his wife, 'could you possibly think that I would shut myself up in the hut with Luca – right under your nose, into the bargain?'

'I thought so because this morning you really did shut yourself up with him in the sitting-room.'

'Yes, but it was the sitting-room and I wasn't in a bathing-costume.'

'You were in your petticoat.'

'But when I was in my petticoat, Luca wasn't in the room.'

'How was I to know that? All the same, it seemed to me so outrageous that I thought it must be a dream. Perhaps that was why, when the thing repeated itself in a dream, I believed it was true.'

'Well, let's go and have a bathe now. Are you coming with us?'

'You go on,' said Ernesto sulkily; 'I'll join you later.'

'The water's marvellous,' cried his wife, as she went off

on Luca's arm.

Ernesto watched them as they walked away down the cement platform towards the sea. Someone at a table close by said loudly: 'How happy they are together, those two. You can see they're in love.'

Questions

We went and sat down at the café, at the far end of a long row of little tables which by now were almost all deserted. Next to us, in a recess, sat a customer of whom nothing could be seen but his legs. It was very late, and along the street, uselessly bespangled with neon signs, there now passed very few cars, which slowed down in front of the depopulated cafés and then slid away again, as if in disappointment. There were no crowds, now, on the pavements; nothing but a few hurrying couples on the way home, and groups of men ambling slowly along, talking in loud voices. Then, suddenly, the neon lights went out, all at the same time, leaving only the white lights from the row of lamp-posts underneath the dark façades of the buildings. The street, put to shame by commonplace night, then appeared as it really was – a street like any other street.

I said to Lucio: 'I'm going to get the papers.'

'What papers?'

'This evening's papers.'

'You mean yesterday evening's.'

'Please order me a coffee. I'll be back in a minute.'

I went to the kiosk. The newsvendor, a fat man in blue trousers tied at the ankles and a jersey with the name of an American paper on the chest and back, was taking down the frames holding the illustrated magazines and piling up bundles of unsold newspapers. In a leisurely way, pausing to read the headings and look at the photographs, I bought an evening paper, then a literary review, then a weekly, and finally another newspaper. When I went back to the table, Lucio was already talking to the customer who was sitting by himself. I tried to see who he was but was unable to do so because he was hidden by the corner of the building. Lucio, evidently pursuing a conversation already begun, asked: 'I'm sorry, I don't understand, haven't you a light-switch beside the door?'

'Yes, I have,' answered the other, in a quiet, patient voice which I seemed to recognize. 'But it's the switch for the ceiling-lamp, and that, alas, has been broken for some years and I can never make up my mind to get it mended. So, in order to turn on the light in the room, I have to make my way in the dark over to the bed and turn on the standard lamp on the bedside table. Since I've been doing this for years, I go unhesitatingly, straight as a die. But the unexpected can happen: a chair fallen on the floor, for instance, like yesterday evening. And then I bark my shins and hurt myself, and I get in a rage and swear like a trooper.'

'And once you've turned on the light, what do you do?'

'I undress in order to go to bed. Strange, isn't it?'

'Very strange indeed. D'you mind my asking you questions?'

'No, I don't mind at all.'

'Then tell me, in order, how you undress.'

There was silence; the other man appeared to be reflecting. Then he replied: 'I take off my jacket.'

'And where do you put it?'

'I put it, together with my trousers and shoes, on a movable clothes-stand and push the whole thing out of the room, into the passage, so that Giuseppe ...'

'Who's Giuseppe?'

'My manservant. Giuseppe finds it there in the morning, and brushes and presses the suit and cleans the shoes, for when I get up.'

'Well, now you're in your socks and drawers and shirt. What d'you do next?'

The other man started laughing in the darkness. 'I do a strip-tease. We all do a strip-tease every evening without realizing it, just as Monsieur Jourdain, when he spoke, created prose.' He laughed, pleased with his literary allusion, and then went on: 'You won't believe me. I take off one of my socks, my tie and half my shirt ...'

'*Half* your shirt?'

'Yes, I take it *half* off. And then I start reading, sitting in the little armchair at the foot of the bed.'

'What d'you read?'

'The first thing that comes to hand. Generally something that doesn't involve thought. For example, yesterday evening I read a few pages of the railway time-table. All the lines in Sicily. Another time, perhaps I read the telephone directory, pages and pages of names all beginning with the same letter. Or again, a newspaper. But not the political or cultural articles. I read mostly the business announcements – sales, bargains, property deals, etc. But I also like the police notices about dairymen who water their milk, and the arrivals and departures, and the weather forecasts...'

'And how long do you read?'

The other man started laughing again. 'Why do you laugh?' asked Lucio.

'I laugh because you make me think of myself, and I realize that there *is* something to laugh at. Well, I read until I begin to feel cold. Usually I start sneezing and then I know it's time to go to bed.'

'That's all very well in the winter, but what d'you do in summer?'

'For the summer I've found another system. I sit on my foot, which is bent back in a certain way. When I begin to get pins and needles, I stop reading.'

Lucio was now reflecting for longer and longer intervals between asking his questions. It was as though these questions were becoming more and more profound and conclusive; whereas in reality, so it seemed to me, they were as insignificant as could be imagined. Finally he said: 'You stop reading, then, and you go to bed. What happens next?'

'Nothing much happens. When I stretch out my feet under the covers, I disturb my cat which at that time is asleep at the foot of the bed. Invariably, he takes a jump and goes and curls up in the armchair and stays there all night.'

'What sort of a cat is he?'

'He's a cat of the most ordinary kind, a grey, striped tabby.'

'And what's he called?'

The other man started laughing once more. 'You'll think

it strange; I've given him my own name, Maurizio.'

'Why in the world?'

'It's like this: since I have rather a habit of talking to myself, when this happens I pretend to myself that I'm talking to the cat. I say, for instance: "Maurizio, today you've been a beast". Or: "Maurizio, you're lazy, you do nothing but sleep". True statements, as you can see, which apply to me as well as to the cat.'

'Very ingenious. And once the cat has established itself in the armchair, what do *you* do?'

'I select a point in space and contemplate it.'

'How d'you mean?'

'I remain for half an hour or an hour with my eyes wide open, without thinking of anything, as it were stupefied, motionless, gazing into the air. Then, all of a sudden and for no reason, I turn out the light and lie down.'

'Ah, you lie down. In what way? – I mean, how d'you place yourself?'

'I lie on my left side, always.'

'But where d'you put your left arm?'

'Down my side.'

'And your right arm?'

'Folded, with the hand on my left forearm.'

'And d'you fall asleep at once?'

'No, I think of something to calm me down and send me off to sleep.'

'What d'you think about?'

'The moon.'

'How d'you mean – the moon?'

'Perhaps because there's been so much talk for some time about astronautics, I imagine that I find myself on the moon, entirely alone, amongst all those craters and deserts. At other times I imagine myself flying towards Mars. Or descending upon Venus. I imagine these things once, twice, three times, always in the same way, and in the end I fall asleep.'

'How long d'you take to fall asleep, thinking about the stars?'

'Goodness knows. Once I turned on the light again when I was already falling asleep and looked at the time. Between the moment when I had turned out the light and the moment when I turned it on again I had gone – in my mind, of course – all the way to Saturn, and had come back again, and the whole thing took only ten minutes. Faster than any *sputnik*.' At this point he rose and came out from behind the corner of the building. I recognized him at once as Maurizio M., a very well-known journalist, a specialist in foreign politics. Stretching himself, he said to Lucio: 'You know, with all your questions you've really made me feel sleepy. Good night.' He walked off at a quick pace and very soon disappeared at the far end of the street.

I allowed a few minutes to pass and then asked Lucio: 'Will you please tell me why you bombarded him with all those insignificant questions?'

Shrugging his shoulders, he replied: 'What would you have liked me to ask him? His opinions on the world political situation? I can always read them in the newspaper tomorrow.'

'But why did you ask him those questions?'

'I don't know; probably because he was sitting near me. That is, for no reason at all.'

I said nothing, and started thinking. Lucio had, in fact, behaved like those people who, when walking along a street, if they come across a couple of workmen busy digging a hole, will stop and remain there, perhaps even for hours, gazing at the empty hole which gets deeper and deeper and in which there appears to be nothing but earth. I said so to him. 'That may be,' he answered. 'But it's always better to gaze at an empty hole than a hole at the bottom of which a couple of drainpipes are sticking out, perhaps, or an electric cable, or some other contrivance. An empty hole is at least really and truly empty.'

'Antique statues have been found at the bottom of holes.'

'That never happens. When it did happen, in the past, they were always copies of the Alexandrian period. I tell you, nothing genuine.'

The waiter came up and said: 'Gentlemen, we're closing.'

'Oh, by the way,' said Lucio as he walked away with me towards the car, 'what do *you* do when you go to bed?'

They sat down at the table, facing one another, without speaking. Once they were seated, Riccardo raised his eyes and noticed that his wife had an odd expression on her face which he now saw for the first time since they had been married: a smile – or was it perhaps not a smile? – a meaningless and, in some sort of way, stupid smile hovering on her lips and giving her white, delicate face an unusually plump appearance, as though she had toothache or had filled her mouth with water. But her fair hair was very carefully arranged; and her blue eyes, unmoving and expressionless, revealed nothing.

The maid came in with a dish of *hors d'œuvres*; Riccardo watched his wife help herself generously to three slices of ham and three figs, and he had a feeling of disappointment, tempered however by the thought that she had been suffering, shortly before, from nervous exhaustion and therefore was in need of nourishment. He waited until the maid had left the room and then, with a painful mental effort, tried to assume a free and easy expression and said, in a voice as cheerful and ringing as he could manage: 'Tell me everything.'

Now it so happened that, just at that moment, his wife put into her mouth half a slice of ham carefully wrapped round half a fig. Her face blown out and smiling, she nodded, as much as to say that she could not speak because she had her mouth full. Riccardo wondered what there could be behind that smile and again came to no conclusion. Then he said, impetuously: 'I know what you're thinking.'

He saw her glance at him expectantly, without speaking, her mouth full but unmoving. 'You're thinking,' he said, 'that I'm frightened, distressed, agitated, and that I'm making an effort to put a good face on it, as they say. Nothing could be more wrong.'

His wife said nothing but started chewing again. Riccardo went on: 'I spent the whole night thinking and thinking and thinking. Naturally I was thinking about what had occurred, that is, about the facts. And the more I thought about it, the more I despaired. Then, all of a sudden, something happened to me that I can't explain. Perhaps I had got tired and given up trying to understand; perhaps it was that I had really understood. It was like going behind the scenes at a theatre and seeing that the landscape that forms the background to the stage isn't a real landscape but a structure of sacking and plywood. I went, so to speak, behind the facts and discovered that, in reality, they were merely words, that is, sounds without significance. So then, instead of thinking of the facts as facts, I began thinking of the facts as words and I realized that everything was settled, everything.'

This time his wife did not reply because the maid had come back into the room and was changing the plates. Instead, she asked the maid, in a normal voice: 'Has Baby had his dinner yet?'

'He's having it now.'

'How's he getting on? A good appetite?'

'Oh,' said the woman with a laugh, 'he always has a good appetite. He's a real wolf, he is.'

The maid went out and Riccardo resumed: 'Yes, everything. And I asked myself: supposing I were being made unhappy simply by words, that is, by sounds? Why then don't I start behaving as if they were really nothing but sounds, and be done with it?'

His wife was in the act of raising her fork to her mouth; at these words from Riccardo, she held the fork in mid-air and looked at him in silence. She still went on smiling; only her smile now was oddly concentrated entirely at the left corner of her mouth, and consequently her left cheek was more swollen than her right. Riccardo said: 'Take for instance the word "sequestration". As long as I thought of sequestration, last night, I was in despair. I saw the van carrying off the furniture, the house empty, etc., etc. But as soon as I went behind the facts, I realized that it was merely a word, that is, an absurd sound and nothing more. Indeed, just to take an example : sequestration or no sequestration, this chair remains a chair, nothing changes. I tell you it's a word, nothing more nor less.'

It seemed to him that his wife was looking at him with astonishment; or perhaps it was his own astonishment at talking like this which he was attributing to her. 'I can imagine the objection you would make,' he resumed hurriedly; 'the chair remains a chair, it is true, but, once sequestrated, it is no longer mine. This, also, has no significance. Mine, yours, his – all these are sounds without significance. One cannot possess anything, just as one cannot sequestrate anything. An object is an object; it is neither mine, nor yours, nor his; today it is here, tomorrow it will be there, the day after, somewhere else.' Riccardo now had a feeling of intoxication, as if he had regained some kind of freedom after long servitude. Nevertheless his wife's smile, so meaningless, so inopportune, was disquieting to him. Hurriedly he added : 'Am I wrong or is there a sort of pitying look in your eyes now? Perhaps you're thinking that grief has affected my brain. Well, don't deceive yourself : I'm not in the least distressed, as you can see.' Suddenly he burst into a fit of noisy laughter which, to himself, appeared frank and gay, and in which he felt he was expressing the whole joy of freedom regained at last. 'Tell me now, is that the laughter of a man in anguish? Yes, I ought to be in anguish, according to the general opinion; but I'm not. I've discovered that I was tormenting myself over words, that is, over sounds, and that in consequence I don't need to torment myself any longer, never again.'

'Margherita,' said his wife in her calmest voice to the maid who had come in again, 'tell Nurse to bring Baby here as soon as he's finished his dinner : I want to see him.'

'Yes, Signora.'

'Let's consider another unpleasant fact : arrest. Yes, if I think of arrest as a fact, I don't deny that it's enough to make one despair. But if I think of it as a word, everything falls into place. Perhaps you would like to know how I

manage to transform arrest into a sound. Perfectly simple:
by applying the word to myself and seeing what happens.
What happens? Nothing absolutely nothing; with or without arrest I remain as I was, exactly the same. And I
remain as I was, precisely because arrest is a word without
significance, a mere sound.'

His wife started smiling again, but this time with the
right-hand corner of her mouth. Riccardo, emboldened,
concluded: 'Of course, many people will tell you that I am
in fact changed, but what does it matter? They would have
to prove to you, in the first place, that an arrested man is
different from a non-arrested man.' He was well launched,
now, and was becoming more and more elated, with the
intoxication of an acrobat who successfully performs a
number of dangerous feats, one after another. His wife
looked towards the door, then pressed the bell under the
table with her foot. The maid reappeared. 'Baby?'

'Yes, he's just coming; he's being dressed.'

As soon as the door was shut Riccardo said: 'And here
are some more senseless words – deficit, trial, prison and so
on. All of them sounds which leave things as they are, with
no more effect than the sound the wind makes as it travels
through the trees. Mere sounds: why suffer, then, if they're
no more than sounds?'

He looked at his wife and, all of a sudden, a disturbing
idea flashed through his mind: that forced, meaningless,
foolish smile that puffed up her face – was it possible that it
resembled the smile which he himself, as he felt, was trying
continually to maintain on his own face while he was
speaking? But he had no time to examine this question, for
the door opened and a country girl, rustic and smiling and
dressed all in white, came in holding in her arms a magnificent fair-haired baby with a perfectly round head, two
thirds of it plump cheeks and one third fine golden hair.
Elegantly dressed in pale blue, the white flesh of his wrists
and ankles bursting out from sleeves and trousers that were
a little too tight, serene, curious, turning his eyes towards
the ceiling as if to observe the world about him, the baby

suffered himself to be handed by the girl to his mother. His mother took him in her arms and kissed him on the brow, smoothing back his hair, then on each of his little fat hands. 'Giorgio, how are you, Giorgio?'

The baby laughed and said: 'Bla, bla, bla.'

'Have you had your dinner, Giorgio?'

'Bla, bla, bla.'

'It was good now, wasn't it?'

'Bla, bla, bla.'

His mother gave the girl some instructions and then handed back the baby to her. Again this time the baby allowed himself to be passed from hand to hand with complete indifference, turning his eyes up to the ceiling and towards the farthest corners of the room, as though to reconnoitre the world in which he had been for so short a time. The girl gave a slight bow and left the room.

Riccardo waited until the door was shut and then said: 'There you are! The things that torment us have the same significance as the words, or rather the sounds, that the baby was making just now. Bla, bla, bla. Why torment oneself, then?'

His wife looked at him; the smile which had puffed out her face disappeared suddenly, for the first time since they had sat down at table; and her eyes filled with tears, which made them look ugly and small. She put down her napkin on the table and went out of the room.

Riccardo, after a moment, also rose; he went over to the window and looked out. Since the flat was on the first floor he could see the pavement shining in the mild noonday light; the green and brown trunk of a tree; a parked car, sand-coloured; the black, dry asphalt of the street; the houses opposite, yellowish. He became aware that all these things, in themselves insignificant, had for him, at that moment, a painful significance, undoubted even if obscure. He recalled then how the baby had turned his eyes all round the room, and he longed to be able to look at reality himself in that same way, so that his wife's tears, the asphalt of the street and everything else might become mere meaningless objects, as they would certainly have seemed to the baby if he had looked at them. In the meantime, however, he had to go on living. He rested his forehead against the window-pane and closed his eyes.

Nothing

At five in the afternoon, as he entered his flat which was already filled with the grey shadows of twilight, Giovanni felt overcome by loneliness. Without turning on the lights he rid himself of his waterproof in the hall, then went into his study and sat down on a small chair by the door, like a timid visitor, his legs crossed, his arms folded, his eyes staring into the darkness. His painful feeling of loneliness was now mingled with vague surprise: he had been alone all day long but had not suffered from it, and only now did he realize, with excruciating suddenness, how lonely he was – like a sleepwalker on the edge of a roof who awakes and discovers all at once that he is hanging in space. In order to calm himself, he tried to analyse his feeling, to break it asunder by thought. He told himself that it was a kind of panic and that this panic originated in turn from dismay at feeling himself insufficient, cut off, incomplete and therefore anxious to complete himself, in other words to find companionship. Moreover it was above all a physical distress, like thirst and hunger; and, like thirst and hunger, it could be allayed only by a remedy which was also physical, that is, by the presence of a person.

He recalled that he had found himself alone in his flat on other occasions: it often happened to him because he had come to Rome only a short time before and hardly knew anybody. But on the other occasions there had been a difference: he had known that in an hour, in two hours, in the evening, even perhaps next morning, he would see somebody. This time, on the other hand, he expected to see nobody, absolutely nobody, neither that day, nor the day following which was Sunday, nor, probably, on Monday. Perhaps, he thought, panic had come upon him because he had suddenly perceived, in front of him, this desert of endless solitary hours.

In the meantime, however, he had to do something to

alleviate the anguish which was oppressing him at this moment. In the end he could find nothing better than to make up his mind to telephone someone. Still in the dark, he left the study and felt his way into the bedroom, where the telephone was. It was a small room in which the bed faced the window and the window faced a building opposite his own on the other side of the street. On top of this building there was an illuminated advertising sign, with gigantic letters alternately red, green, violet and yellow. The lighting of the sign was turned on every day at this time and remained on until midnight. But, from his bed, Giovanni could see only one of the letters, an enormous 'U' which, he knew, was the seventh letter of the word 'calzature'. He went into the room and, although he was accustomed to it, stood for a moment amazed: like a huge butterfly with transparent wings, the intense, vibrating green light of the sign was fluttering its rays between the four white walls. Overcoming the feeling of cheerlessness that it produced, Giovanni lay down flat on his back on the bed, took the telephone from the bedside table, placed it on his chest and then, slightly raising his head, painfully dialled a number.

It was the first and only number that came into his head and it was, in fact, the number of the only person to whom, as he realized, he ought not to telephone: a beautiful, disagreeable girl, gifted with a malicious kind of intelligence, quicker to notice other people's defects than their good qualities, who regarded the love-relationship as a treacherous contest in which the aim of each of the two adversaries was to try and wound the other one at the most vulnerable point. Giovanni had started a flirtation with this girl; and then she, inexplicably, had severed the relationship and he, having been made to look ridiculous, had sworn to himself that he would never see her again. Instead of which it was to her, of all people, to whom he now turned for comfort in his loneliness.

She answered immediately, at the first sound of the telephone, as if she were not merely close by but with her hand actually on the receiver, ready to lift it. In a low, affectedly calm voice she asked: 'Who is speaking?'

Giovanni gave his name and added, in a tone of forced jauntiness: 'And what are you up to?'

'Nothing. And you?'

'Nothing, also.'

Giovanni had been guarded in his reply because he knew that the girl snatched at any sort of pretext for saying something malicious. And indeed, after a moment's silence, she said: 'Yes, but between my nothing and yours there's a difference.'

'What difference?'

'I'm doing nothing because I haven't any desire to do anything. My nothing is voluntary. It's a nothing which does not trouble me, in fact it pleases me; I intended it, I enjoy it, I relish it. It's a nothing that's full of all sorts of things. Your nothing, on the other hand, is an empty nothing that you don't like, that you didn't intend, that vexes you, that you'd like to get rid of.'

'What a bitch,' Giovanni could not help thinking, admiring, almost in spite of himself, the girl's perverse perspicacity, yet at the same time hurt and offended. Reluctantly he asked: 'What makes you think that?'

'Oh, quite simple – the tone of your voice, especially when compared with mine. We both used the word "nothing", but we said it in a very, very different way. I said it with the whole of myself, so to speak; you said it with the edge of your throat. My voice was deep, full, calm, sensual, relaxed; yours was strangled, hesitating, despairing, thin, trembling, strained. Isn't that so?'

So, indeed, it was; and to such a point that Giovanni, as he listened to the perfidious voice describing his own state of mind, was again conscious of a feeling of loneliness even more acutely depressing than before. With an effort, however, he protested: 'What reason have you to think it's so? You might even be wrong, don't you think?'

'In the first place my ear, which is very sharp, tells me so. And then, from the sound of your voice, I reconstructed your situation.'

'And what is that?'

'That you went home all alone, that you were frightened of solitude, that you didn't expect to see anyone either today or tomorrow or even the day after, that you got into a panic, that you searched feverishly for somebody to telephone to, that you couldn't find anyone better than me, and that, in the end, you made up your mind to ring me, saying to yourself: "Let's telephone Alice. She's a bitch but she's better than nothing." Isn't that so?'

He tried to make a joke of it. 'The only true thing in all that is that you're a bitch, a real, genuine bitch.'

'No, that isn't true, it's the rest that's true.'

Giovanni thought it was time to bring the discussion to an end. 'D'you know what I think?' he said.

'What?'

'That in reality you suffer from loneliness neither more nor less than I do. That we both find ourselves, as it happens, in exactly the same situation: I'm alone, you're alone. And that your "nothing" is just like mine.'

'What is it that makes you think that?'

'If nothing else, the fact that you were so quick to answer the telephone. And so I have a suggestion to make to you: that we should go out and have dinner together, and talk about solitude in some restaurant.'

He was answered by an unpleasant laugh. 'You see how wrong you are. You always *are* wrong. I don't feel in the least lonely, and actually I'm not alone. D'you know how many people there are here, all round me, listening to your interesting telephone conversation?'

Giovanni felt himself blushing. 'What, you're not alone?'

'I never told you I was alone. I merely told you I was doing nothing, which was the truth. But one can do nothing even in company.'

Giovanni's hand was on the telephone; slowly he lowered the receiver and hung it up. Then, for a moment, flat on his back with the telephone on his chest, he stared at the luminous 'U' of the advertisement, which was now violet and filled the room with amethyst vibrations. Then all at once the violet changed to red; and the room turned into a little blood-red inferno. Giovanni lifted the telephone from his chest and put it back on the table; then he rose from the bed and went out of the room.

He felt he was going mad; and that the feverish vibration of the light had communicated itself to his thought, which was now fluttering its wings inside his head like a large imprisoned butterfly. He felt his way back along the passage, went into the study and sat down again on the small chair by the door. Just at that moment, suddenly, the telephone started ringing.

He rushed back into the bedroom, which was now gleaming with yellow light and looked like a gilded cave, threw himself face downwards across the bed and took off the receiver. A woman's voice assailed him: 'It's me, Carla, but you seem to have forgotten that we were to meet today, an hour ago, already, has something happened to you? – I've been waiting more than an hour, I telephoned but first there was no reply and then the line was engaged, I have the impression you forget everything, you ought to write down your engagements,' etc., etc.

Giovanni listened with immense astonishment to the stream of complaints; then he asked for the name of the café where the girl was waiting, said he would come as quickly as possible and hung up the receiver. Only to take it up again immediately afterwards, as the telephone rang again.

This time it was the voice of a man, one of his University friends called Mario. 'About the appointment for tomorrow morning, everything remains as before except that, instead of going in one car, we're going in two, so you'll be able to be alone with Giulia, as you wanted. I'm going with Fulvia and Renzo in the other car.'

This call, too, was hurriedly brought to an end. Afterwards Giovanni put down the receiver and sat on the bed, legs dangling, amongst the frantic vibrations of the advertisement which had now gone green. And so, he could not help thinking, he had felt lonely, desperately lonely, both in respect of that day and the day after, whereas in reality he had a sentimental engagement for the evening and an outing in gay company next morning. How had he managed to forget? It suddenly flashed across him that he could now telephone the malicious Alice and prove to her that she had been wrong and that he was not lonely, on the contrary. But, after a moment's reflection, he gave up the idea, telling himself that perhaps, after all, Alice had been right. In fact, he thought, a man is not lonely because he is alone; he is lonely if he feels alone.

Don't You Feel Better?

He had been sitting in the dark for an hour, beside the little table upon which stood the telephone. At first he had waited in a normal manner, lolling in an armchair, with the lamps lit, turning over the pages of a magazine. Then he had realized that the light only served to make his suspense more painful, doubling the discomfort of it, it seemed to him, by the sight of furniture which was laden and, so to speak, impregnated with anxiety, disappointment and anger. He wanted, above all, not to see the telephone, so black and so dumb, which obstinately denied him the sound of the beloved voice. So, in the end, he had turned off the lights and had then discovered to his surprise that darkness brought him immense relief, as though the chairs and tables, the sideboard and the sofa had indeed, up till that moment, been waiting with him, and he himself, by causing them to vanish in the darkness, had in some way reduced the anguish that oppressed him. The discovery irritated him; after all, the furniture was merely furniture, and it was absurd to attribute to it his own feelings. Finding some distraction in this thought, he waited another half-hour. Then the door-bell rang. Giacomo remembered the tiresome visit which he had not had the courage to avoid; he rose to his feet, felt his way into the hall and opened the door. 'What, in the dark?' asked Elvira as she came in.

'I'm sorry, I was in the dark so as to have a rest.'

He saw that she was making her way towards the sofa and hurriedly went on: 'Look, I think it would be better for you to sit here,' indicating a chair near the telephone table.

She cast a glance at the telephone and said: 'You want to be close to the telephone, you're expecting a call?' – and then, without any transition: 'Well, I have news, plenty of news.'

'What is it?'

'Not good, alas.' Elvira sat down, took her enormous bag

on her knee and began fumbling in it, plunging her little thin arm into it up to the elbow. Giacomo noticed that her round, childish face was haggard underneath the bright make-up, and that her large eyes looked as if they were devouring her wasted cheeks. Small and very slim, she was almost eclipsed by the lowered brim of her conical hat and the folds of her too ample waterproof. Resigned to his role as confidant, Giacomo inquired: 'Why not good?'

Elvira blew her nose and then replied, as if resuming a half-finished conversation: 'Let's take things in order. Yesterday morning, after I left you, I really had the intention of following your advice – that is, to be patient and wait for him to get into touch with me. But when I went back to that flat of mine which is so terribly sad, it was too much for me...'

'Why sad?' Giacomo asked suddenly, almost against his will.

'Sad because he's no longer there, and yet his coats and his books and his pipes are still there, which, without him, are dreadfully sad.'

Giacomo moved on his chair, threw a glance at the telephone and then said: 'It's you who are sad, not the flat or the pipes or the coats or the books. The flat is a flat of a certain size, with a certain number of rooms, arranged in a certain way; the coats are made of wool or some other material, of different colours and patterns; the pipes are of briar or meerschaum; the books are of different formats and colourings; what is there sad about all that?'

'That he is not there.'

'But it's you that feels sadness, not the coats and pipes and books. These objects have nothing to do with you and your sadness, just as you have nothing to do with them, anyhow. There's no connexion between you and these objects, or rather there's a connexion of ownership, which doesn't amount to much. What I am saying will seem even more obvious to you if in place of a pipe or a jacket you put a dog or a cat or even a child, that is, a living creature upon which you could not, however, impose your own sadness, just as you do not impose it, for example, upon me. Then you would see how inappropriate your language is.'

Elvira looked at him in surprise and then said hastily: 'Oh well, as you like. Anyhow, it was too much for me and I decided there and then to go and find him. So I took the car and started off for Ostia. It was a positively funereal day and . . .'

'Why funereal?'

Again she looked surprised. However, she said: 'It was pouring with rain, the sky was filled with low, dark clouds, there was a strong wind – in a word, it was funereal.'

'Allow me,' said Giacomo; 'let us say, rather, that it was a day of bad weather, with wind, rain, low cloud, poor visibility. In short, nothing funereal about it.'

'Oh, very well,' she said with a sigh, 'it was a day of bad weather, just as you please. So I arrived at Ostia in streaming rain which inundated my windscreen till I could hardly see. Can you imagine Ostia at this season? The desolation of the bathing-places with rows of closed and deserted huts along a dark, wet beach, with an angry sea in the background? The dreariness of the asphalt roads along by the sea – black, smooth, shining, empty as far as the eye can see? The melancholy look of the avenues, with piles of dead leaves, yellow and red and glossy with rain, under the bare trees? Well, imagine me then, going to look for a man who doesn't love me, in the midst of all this sadness, and you'll have the complete picture.'

The telephone rang, at last; Giacomo lifted the receiver to his ear and a coarse voice with a local accent inquired: 'Is that the dairy?' Giacomo put down the receiver again and then said: 'A false picture. You keep repeating yourself. Ostia is neither sad nor gay, it is what it is, a small seaside town where few people stay in the winter. In the same way the bathing establishments are not desolate but merely closed, the asphalt roads are not dreary but merely empty, the fallen leaves under the trees are not melancholy, merely dry and then soaked with rain. All these things, on the other hand – Ostia, the bathing-places, the roads, the leaves – have an existence of their own, a problematic nature of their own, of which you know nothing and which does not concern you in the least.'

Elvira finally burst out: 'Will you kindly tell me what's wrong with you today? Why d'you interrupt me continually?'

'In order to console you,' said Giacomo. 'Don't you in fact realize that if, instead of saying the bathing-places were desolate, you said they were closed, you'd already feel a bit better?'

'I don't need consolation; I simply want you to listen to me. Well then – I looked for his house, and in the end I found it, at the far end of the road along the sea, a filthy house.'

'Why filthy?'

'Ugh – let's say, then, an old house that hasn't been done up for at least forty years.'

'Good. Let's say that.'

'Well, I went upstairs and knocked at the door of a certain Signora Zampichelli, which was opened to me by a thin, shrivelled little old woman with spectacles; with my heart in my mouth, I asked if he was at home. She told me he wasn't; then I said I was his sister and asked if she would allow me to wait in his room. She led me inside; I asked, in a casual sort of way, whether he saw many people, and she said she didn't know anything about that but it was true that she was hardly ever at home because she kept a draper's shop. Then she went away and I looked round. Imagine a bare, positively naked room...'

The telephone gave a half-ring; Giacomo waited for it to ring again, but in vain. 'The line's crossed,' said Elvira sympathetically.

'Without any drawers or socks or shirt?' said Giacomo, irritated.

'What the hell d'you mean?'

'The room was naked, that is, it wasn't clothed, that is, it had no socks or shirt or drawers.'

'Very well then, let's say it contained only the indispen-

sable pieces of furniture, a bed, a table, a chest-of-drawers.'
Elvira was silent; then, becoming excited again, she went
on: 'He had told me he wanted to try living alone, without
me, in order to collect his thoughts, to meditate, to think
things over. I, on the other hand, am convinced that he
went to Ostia to see a woman. And indeed, look at this!'
She fumbled in her bag and pulled out a small white paper
package which she placed on the table.

'What is it?'

'A revolting feminine comb.'

Giacomo took the package and opened it: it was in fact
a sham tortoise-shell comb, very light in colour, such as a
fair woman might use. 'Why revolting?' he asked.

'Because it belonged to goodness knows what filthy slut.'

'All I see is a comb,' said Giacomo, 'made of pale,
sham tortoise-shell, which has obviously been used; a bit
dirty, that's all.'

'But what d'you think about it? D'you think that comb
might really have been left there by some woman he's
seeing at Ostia?'

'Where did you find it?'

'Under the bed.'

'It might,' said Giacomo slowly, 'it might be a comb
belonging to someone who inhabited the room before him.
You know, these furnished rooms are never very carefully
swept.'

There was silence. After a little, Elvira went on: 'Let's
hope you're right. But I assure you that at the moment I
thought I should have died. I remember getting up from the
bed on which I was sitting, going over to the window and
looking in a dazed sort of way at the sea. The sun had come
out, and the sea was smiling in the sunshine, and I, comparing that smiling sea with the feeling that ...'

'The sea doesn't smile,' said Giacomo suddenly.

'Ah, yes! Can't I even say that? And why?'

'Because the sea hasn't a mouth. A mouth smiles, but in
fact, among all mouths, only the mouth of a human being.
The sea can do plenty of things, but smile – certainly not.'

The telephone rang again, this time continuously; Giacomo took up the receiver and held it to his ear. In a few words the voice, well-known to him, of the maidservant informed him that the Signorina had gone out of Rome on a trip and therefore would not be telephoning or coming to see him that day. 'But where has she gone?' Giacomo demanded; 'One moment – why?' Then he heard a click as the call was cut off; he slowly replaced the receiver and sat motionless, his eyes fixed on the telephone. At last, however, he seemed to become aware of an indefinable strangeness in the profound silence that had succeeded his words of disappointment. He slowly raised his eyes and saw that Elvira was watching him intently with eyes full of intense, vindictive irony. 'I know what you're thinking,' she said suddenly.

'What?'

'You're thinking of the telephone, and you're cursing it, and it seems to you a malign and fatal object from which comes nothing but bad news. Instead of which' – and her voice rose to a tone of shrillness – 'instead of which, just as the sea can't smile because it hasn't a mouth, so the telephone is neither fatal nor malign but simply an ordinary everyday object, black, not so very large, made in a certain way, with a dial, some numbers, wires, etc. Don't you feel better now?'

Passing the Time

The doorbell and the telephone both rang at the same moment. Ernesto thought he ought first of all to run and open the door because it was the most important: it was in fact three o'clock and at that hour Alina would be appearing on the doorstep, as she did every day. As for the telephone, he would let it ring, perhaps he would not even answer it: it was sure to be some bore or other, or anyhow something entirely unimportant, since the only thing that was really important to him, the arrival of Alina, would have already happened.

All this he thought as he rushed from his study to the front door. He upset a stool on which were piled some engineering note-books and, out of breath, with the telephone still ringing, threw open the door.

It was not Alina, however, on the doorstep, but the boy from the bar, a youth with red cheeks and a close-cropped head, with some bottles of liquor that he had ordered shortly before, on his way home. 'The bottles,' said the boy.

The telephone continued to ring with a persistence which all at once seemed to Ernesto to be significant. His mind filled with disappointment and presentiment, he said to the boy: 'Put them down here; thank you,' and ran to the telephone. It was, in fact, Alina's voice which said to him at once: 'At last!'

'What is it? You're not going to tell me you can't come?'

'Yes, or rather, no. I can't come at the usual time.'

'At what time can you come?' Ernesto asked with relief.

'At five o'clock. In two hours.'

'But why?' asked Ernesto, irritated, already forgetting his relief of a moment before.

'I'll explain. Expect me; see you in two hours' time.'

'But what am I to do in those two hours?'

'You've plenty of things to do: you can read, listen to music, work. Good-bye then, till later.'

Ernesto looked at the receiver, as though he would have liked to say something more; then he put it down and went back into his study. Alina was right, after all: he had many things to do. So he went over to the bookshelf and took down a novel which he had not yet read; then he put a disc of classical music on the record-player; finally he sat down in the only armchair in the room and, as he sank down on its old creaking springs, even went so far as to try and heave a sigh of satisfaction, like someone preparing to spend a couple of hours in a quiet, pleasant, instructive manner.

But it was a false sigh, he reflected almost immediately. He realized, in fact, that while his eyes mechanically followed the printed words on the page from left to right, his mind was elsewhere and was not grasping the meaning of what he was reading. Furthermore, the sound of the violin coming from the record-player, twisting and twining through the air like a sap-filled tropical plant or a rutting snake, tickled his ear-drums indeed but did not go beyond them, so that it remained mere sound and did not reach the point of becoming music. He still persisted for some time in reading and listening; then he slowly closed his book and equally slowly rose to his feet, went to the record-player and stopped it.

His eyes fell on the table which he habitually used for drawing. It occurred to him to follow Alina's advice once more, and work. Perhaps, he thought, work would engross him more than reading or music: a more active, more venturesome participation was required in work than in relaxation. But when he had turned on the lamp over his drawing-board and was bending over the table, he felt a strange and disagreeable sensation – that he was no longer a single person but two people: one of them had remained down there in the armchair, the other was bending over the drawing-table. And the one that was in the armchair was the more important, the more real; while the one bending over the drawing-board was merely a bad actor playing his part badly. He lit a cigarette to give himself confidence, then turned off the light and moved away from the table.

It occurred to him that in order to pass the time it was advisable, in the first place, to keep to the conventional divisions of time as inscribed on the face of the clock. The times devoted to reading, to music, to work were regulated by psychology, by feeling, and were long or short according to the interest of the moment. But time according to the clock, conventionally divided into seconds and minutes, was what it professed to be: an occupation which was regulated according to this clock-time would last exactly as long as it ought to last. An occupation of this kind, however, which excluded all participation on the part of the person devoting himself to it, must be completely mechanical. He had, therefore, to transform himself into a machine in order to make the time pass, abrogating any sort of mental activity, any sort of impulse of feeling, and reducing his presence to the repetition of the same identical gesture.

Casting his eye round the room, which was untidily crowded with a variety of objects, he noticed a large parcel on a chair and remembered that it contained two books which he had acquired a few days before. They were French books which had to do with his engineering studies, and he recalled that they were unbound and had their pages uncut. He went and fetched the parcel and undid it; and there, in fact, were two big volumes of seven hundred pages each. The leaves were folded in such a way that it was necessary to cut them not only at the top but also along the sides; the paper was so thick that the pages could not be cut four at a time but only one at a time. He sat down in the armchair and made a rapid calculation: at fifteen seconds a page it would take a minute for every four pages, that is, more than two hours for each book. Even admitting that fifteen seconds was too much and reducing the time by half, it would nevertheless take him over an hour for each book. He looked round for a paper-cutter, then remembered that he did not possess one. So he took from the drawing-table a razor-blade which he used for sharpening pencils, went and sat down again and started cutting the pages of the first volume. It was not easy; the blade, too small and too pointed, went astray every now and then and tore the page; every now and then it slipped from his fingers and got lost inside the book. However he went on cutting calmly and methodically for some minutes, finding a certain pleasure in running the little blade up the side of the book and feeling the paper opening like a flower. Then, as he made a wrong movement, the blade slipped out of the crease and cut half the page clean away. Ernesto rose and went to look for some gummed paper; he tore off a piece of the same length as the page and stuck it together. But, as he was about to resume the operation, he discovered that the razor-blade had disappeared. He might now have continued with a kitchen knife, with a piece of cardboard, with a pencil; but he felt he had lost all desire to do so. It was true : while he had been cutting the pages his mind had been absent, his feeling quiescent; but he had been increasingly conscious, in his arm and hand, of a profound disinclination, and there had indeed been a sort of muscular ill-will throughout his body which had caused him to look with dismay at the hundreds of pages that still remained to be cut. He took up the two books and went and placed them on the bookshelf, amongst the others which had been already cut and read.

He felt, nevertheless, that the business of cutting the pages was not truly decisive. Cutting the pages of a book one has just bought was one of those things which, at the right moment, one did with curiosity, with impatience, with enthusiasm. It was natural therefore that, if the eagerness to read was lacking, disinclination should make itself felt. No, he went on to think, it was necessary to do something absolutely mechanical and absurd, something that demanded no participation at all, even of the smallest kind. After a few minutes' reflection, sunk deep in the armchair, he said to himself that a completely mechanical, absurd action was difficult to find, for the simple reason that man is not a machine and does not willingly do absurd things. Then, suddenly, it seemed to him that he had found a solution. He got up and left the room.

In the little kitchen, overcrowded with pots and pans, on a small table by the window there was a big paper bag which he had brought home from the grocer's that same day. It was a bag full of coffee-beans, weighing half a kilo; for Ernesto had a habit of drinking a great deal of coffee while he was working. It would be a mechanical, absurd act, he thought, gazing hopefully at the paper bag, to count the coffee-beans one by one and put them into a tin. Perhaps counting the beans, even from a bag weighing half a kilo, would be a quicker thing than cutting fourteen hundred pages; but, to make up for that, it would indeed be an entirely mechanical, absurd thing to do. Moreover, once he had counted the coffee-beans, he could do a number of other things of the same kind in order to pass the time: for instance, he could cut up a complete newspaper into so many little strips and strips into so many little squares. Now that he had discovered this combination of the mechanical and the absurd, he realized that there were infinite things one could do with a reasonable assurance that they would serve to pass the time.

So he took a chair, sat down and upset the paper bag on to the table. The coffee-beans were scattered over a wide area, their rounded, greasy surfaces sliding across the marble table-top, and then, as he continued to empty the bag, forming a little brown, pyramidal heap. Ernesto took a round tin which had once contained biscuits, opened it and placed it at a short distance from the pyramid of beans. Then he picked up the first bean, said 'one' in a loud voice, and threw it into the tin, where it fell with a modest tinkle. He continued thus, counting and throwing; the beans fell one after another into the tin; his fingers became greasy. Then, suddenly, he seemed to see himself, all alone, sitting on a kitchen chair, in the act of counting coffee-beans, and he felt he had gone mad. This thought of madness at once brought him to a halt. For in fact, if a machine were conscious of being a machine, it would undoubtedly think it was mad. And consequently it would cease, precisely because of this thought, to be a machine, would refuse to go on acting as a machine. The tin was still nearly empty. Ernesto threw in a few more beans, munched a couple of them, then rose and went out of the kitchen.

Once he was back again in the study a fearful thought flashed across his mind: perhaps the two hours would never pass, in which case he could do nothing, absolutely nothing; and if he really did nothing, time would be suspended, at least with regard to himself, and the two hours would not only seem, but would actually be, eternal. He would have gone outside time, owing to the absolute impossibility of making time pass. On the other shore, Alina would hold out her arms to him, but in vain: time that does not pass – that is, eternity – would separate them for ever.

He thrust his hands into his hair, terrified. Then, all of a sudden, he heard Alina's well-known, unmistakeable ring at the front door. He rushed to open it and, to his wonder and delight, there she was, smiling in the doorway. 'I'm early,' she said. 'I finished before I expected.'

'But what did you have to do?'

'Just imagine, an intolerable thing: I had to stay at home and see to the plumber who was mending my bath. He seemed to go on for ever; then, all of a sudden, somehow or other, he told me he had finished and was going away.'

'And what did you do while you were waiting?'

'It seemed an enternity. But then I discovered a very good way of making the time pass. Guess what I did.'

'What?'

'I thought about you.'

Ernesto followed her into the study. As he followed her, he found himself wondering with astonishment: 'Why didn't *I* do the same thing, why didn't *I* think about *her*?'

Measurements

After he parted from his wife, Giacomo went to live in a three-roomed top-floor flat in the old part of the town. He made the largest room into his engineering office, with the drawing-table facing the window. He took to leading the same life as when he was living with his wife: work from nine till one, then lunch, then a rest, then work again from four until eight, and afterwards some form of relaxation such as the cinema, dinner in a restaurant, conversation with friends. Nothing was changed, except that his wife was not there and he lived as a bachelor. But he never thought of his wife. In his heart, where once there had been her image, he seemed now to have nothing but a dull, compact lump. In the same way a wall, when you tap it, reveals dead areas where a cement girder, part of the internal structure of a house, passes through it.

He was conscious, however, that he was working unwillingly and that sometimes he sat doing nothing for as much as an hour, perched on his stool in front of his table, his eyes fixed on the window. Opposite his flat, on the other side of the narrow street, was an old *palazzo* which had been built, probably, during the first half of the nineteenth century. It was a yellowish building, with a façade studded all over with small rectangular bosses, with neo-classical window-frames and brown shutters. But above the level of its flat, parapeted roof this cold and rather mean regularity gave place to an architectural disorder which, in a haphazard manner, made up a townscape chaotic and bizarre to the point of absurdity. On this flat roof, in fact, there had been built, at various periods, innumerable superstructures both large and small – pavilions, huts, walls, balustrades, steps and staircases, loggias and chimney-stacks. These structures fascinated Giacomo without his being able to explain why: possibly because they constituted a kind of conundrum in masonry, inasmuch as it was generally diffi-

cult to guess their origin and purpose; or possibly, he sometimes thought, because ugliness, as opposed to beauty
which always has limits, is unlimited and inexhaustible.

Straight in front of his window was the balustrade,
composed of round iron shafts in a floral style such as was
in use seventy years ago – that is, with ornaments in the
shape of closed corollas at each end and in the middle. The
balustrade was broken at regular intervals by square, grey-
plastered pillars surmounted by copings of grey stone,
possibly tufa. This balustrade was the simplest and most
insignificant thing in the world; yet Giacomo could not
help persistently staring at it, making a mental note of its
measurements and carefully studying its different aspects.
Thus he calculated that the distance between one pillar and
another was about two metres, that the shafts were eighty
centimetres high and the pillars one metre. He also observed
that the balustrade was painted white but that the white
was now dirty and streaked with rust; that the grey plaster
of the pillars, thanks to sun and rain, had turned delicately
and richly mauve; and that green patches that looked like
moss were visible at the bases of the pillars, at the point
where you could see a row of terracotta boxes, filled with
earth but without any sign of flowers or plants, along the
lower part of the balustrade. In all there were seven pillars,
two metres distant from one another, which brought the
length of the whole flat roof to about fourteen metres or
slightly more.

Behind the balustrade rose a chaos of structures which
fascinated Giacomo. The tallest, high against the sky like
the bridge of a ship, was a kind of masonry box, coloured
yellow and entirely enclosed except for two cruciform air-
holes or peep-holes. It was probably the tower containing
the water-tanks. Giacomo, as usual, calculated its measurements: two and a half metres in height for the front wall,
three for the back wall; it had a steeply sloping tiled roof.
There could not therefore be more than six tanks, placed in
two rows, three in each row; finally the depth of the tower
was about one and a half metres or perhaps one metre

eighty. On the left side of the tower rose a tall, thin, rusty chimney; against its right side stood a flue-pipe surmounted by a crooked and corroded tin hood. Higher up, like spiders' webs against the sky, rose a number of television aerials. Giacomo counted a good fifteen of these aerials, which were arranged in varying ways, some higher and some lower.

From the water-tower – as, indeed, from the bridge of a ship – you descended to the flat roof by means of a small iron staircase, also in floral style and painted white like the succeed in doing so because it was a corkscrew staircase balustrade. Giacomo tried to count the steps but could not and turned round on itself, and the steps were hidden by the spiral railings following its twists and turns.

At the foot of the staircase, on the flat roof, there was a profusion of chimney-stacks constructed in the following manner: a brickwork base of more or less conical shape, very wide and heavy, supporting a tall, slender chimney, rusty and blackened and surmounted by a hood and a ventilator, both of them movable. The brickwork bases, he noticed, showed that the chimney-stacks had been built at different periods: the plaster was of varying colours, from the chalky whiteness of the most recent limewash to the purplish grey of that of fifty years ago. The chimneys belched forth a dark smoke that varied in density, all of which helped to blacken the spiral staircase and the water-tower.

Farther along, right in front of Giacomo's window, there were three structures. First of all, in the middle, stood a kind of tall, narrow sentry-box, deep yellow ochre in colour, with a little door almost like the door of a safe, painted a delicate pearl grey. It had no windows, and Giacomo never succeeded in understanding what purpose it served. To the left, on the other hand, was a bizarre structure that spoke for itself – a room, obviously unauthorized, with four walls and even a window but no roof. Clearly the owners had not had time to cover it over before the authorities intervened to stop the building of it; so they had resigned themselves to making it into an enclosed terrace; and it was in fact possible to see, through the window, that it contained a group of white-painted iron chairs and a little round table, also of iron, of the kind to be seen in gardens. The walls of this unauthorized room were painted a dark Pompeian red, and this had flaked off in several places showing the dead whiteness of the plaster underneath.

To the right was a square structure, broad and squat, surmounted by a low cupola of iron and glass which, to all appearances, served to cover the well of the interior staircase. Through the little panes of glass, dirty with the dust of almost a century, it was just possible to see the vague shapes of the wheels and ropes of a lift and, if you looked carefully, you could even see the wheels going round and the ropes quivering whenever the lift itself was in motion. The lower part of this structure was painted yellow and was all spotted with mauve patches of damp; the iron parts of the cupola were painted white, and in style it followed the floral manner of the little iron staircase and the balustrade.

Behind these three structures, the sentry-box, the un-authorized room and the cupola, rose other mysterious excrescences, sited in varying ways, decked out, also, with small staircases and balustrades and painted in different shades of yellow and red and grey. Giacomo gazed at this townscape for many hours a day, with obstinate intentness, as though he wished to discover its intimate, its most secret essence. But he was conscious of understanding nothing about it, and that it was precisely because he understood nothing that he went on gazing at it. The thought sometimes occurred to him that in reality these things formed the fixed, incomprehensible background of every life: as long as life went on, they were not noticed; as soon as life stopped, they revealed themselves.

But he was annoyed that, during his observations of the flat roof opposite, he was unable to help mentally calculating its measurements: so much in height, so much in width, so much in depth, so much in length, in linear

metres, square metres, cubic metres. This irresistible inclin-
ation to measure everything contributed not a little towards
endowing his contemplation with a character of absurdity.
Why, indeed, should he have to measure, for instance, the
height of the cupola or the length of the flat roof? No one
had asked him for a surveyor's report or a plan for the
superstructure or any other calculation connected with his
profession. He was, in fact, providing himself with measurements of which he had no need and which were not
made necessary by anything.

Amongst the few works of literature on the shelves of his
bookcase, side by side with his engineering manuals, was a
volume entitled: *My Flight from the Piombi Prison*, by
Giacomo Casanova. This was an extract from the memoirs
of the famous adventurer and contained only the episode of
his escape from the prisons of Venice. One day, being unable to work and wishing to distract himself from his contemplation of the roofs, Giacomo took down the book and
opened it. His eye fell upon the following description:
'These prison cells are situated under the roof at the two
sides of the palace: three on the west side, among which
was mine, and four on the east side. The drain-pipe from
the roof on the west side goes down into the courtyard; the
one from the roof on the east side, on the other hand, goes
down perpendicularly into the canal which is called Rio di
Palazzo. On this side the cells are very light and you can
stand upright, which is not possible in the cell in which I
found myself and which is known as "the cell with the
beam" because of the enormous beam which deprives it
of light ...' Giacomo went on reading with interest:
Casanova was planning his escape, and to give the reader an
impression of the difficulty and danger of this he gave
plentiful visual details as well as measurements and topo-
graphical information. Giacomo noticed that there was a
certain resemblance between Casanova's minute, precise observations and those that he himself was making every day as
he gazed at the flat roof opposite. There was just this one
difference: Casanova's observations had a purpose – his

escape otherwise the adventurer would never have thought of turning his attention to matters so humble and insignificant; whereas his own were purposeless, inexplicable, absurd. Casanova's life had run its course to the very end; his own life, on the other hand, appeared to have stopped.

He went on reading the book for a short time, then threw it down and went back to look at the roof opposite; more chaotic and absurd than ever, beneath an overcast, whitish, sirocco sky. The thought came to him that he must at all costs find a means of tearing himself away from the stupid contemplation to which his life had gradually become reduced in recent times. But what was he to do? For a moment he thought of taking pen and paper and writing a long letter to his wife, explaining that, ever since they had parted, he had spent his time gazing at rusty chimney-stacks and old pent-houses and that this was undoubtedly a proof that he still loved her and could not live without her. But he gave up the idea, partly because it seemed to him that it would be too sentimental a letter, partly because he knew for sure that his wife would not understand and anyhow would not answer. In the end, after long reflection, he took a pencil and started to draw, on a large sheet of paper, the outline of the structures on the flat roof opposite, beginning with the water-tower.

Insomnia Together

Girolamo was already in the doorway when his wife called him back. 'Wait!' she said.

'What is it?'

She was sitting up in bed with her back against the disordered pillows and was looking at him with a doubting, bitter expression, her lips twisted. 'Why don't you sleep with me?'

'You know why: I'm suffering from insomnia and I shouldn't let you sleep a wink all night long.'

'But I don't like being alone at night. It's so good to sleep together. Stay here with me tonight.'

'It's good to sleep together, but not to suffer from insomnia together. Insomnia together: it sounds terrible.'

'It doesn't matter. I'll stay awake too. But I don't want to sleep alone.'

'It won't always be like this. I'll get over my insomnia. Then I'll come back and sleep with you.'

'But I don't want to sleep alone.'

'Good night.'

He saw a disconcerted look on her face and then, as though recovering herself, she smiled at him and waved her hand in farewell. Girolamo opened the door and went out.

He went into his study where, for four months, he had been sleeping, or rather lying awake, on a divan bed. He undressed in haste and lay down under the sheets with his usual aggressive determination to go to sleep, which served no purpose at all, as he very well knew. Before putting out the light, he glanced at his watch: it was one o'clock. His sleep was heavy and dreamless. Suddenly he sat up in bed with a jump, with a feeling of suffocation. His heart was beating violently; he thought he heard a sound of breathing, as of a crouching animal, close beside him. He put out his hand, encountered something long and warm and bare, and at the end of this arm – for an arm it was – a hand which immediately grasped his own hand and caused it to travel slowly upwards in the opposite direction until it reached a pair of lips which imprinted upon it a devoted kiss. 'It's me,' said his wife's voice out of the darkness; 'go to sleep now, try and sleep.'

Girolamo turned on the light and remained in a sitting position. His wife was lying beside him, at the edge of the divan. Through the transparent, faintly green material of her nightdress he could distinguish the long, relaxed lines and scarcely suggested curves of her pale, thin, adolescent body. Her face, too, was pale and long, her hair black and smooth, her nose rather large, her lips thick and shadowed with down. She gazed up at him, her dark, narrow eyes glistening; then asked him: 'What's the matter?'

Girolamo's head felt feverish and lucid – like a street on a January night, he thought, with a cold, violent wind blowing. With this feeling of lucidity there could be no question of turning out the lights and trying to sleep. In an intensely bad temper, he said: 'All right then, what do we do now?'

'We stay awake together.'

'But what do we *do*?'

'What d'you usually do when you can't sleep?'

'I don't do anything, strictly speaking. I just lie in bed. Or else I get up and do something or other.'

'What?'

'Oh, I don't know; I might, for instance, go to the window and look out.'

'Very well, let's go to the window and look out together.'

They went over to the window; she put her arm round his waist and flattened her nose against the pane, beside him. Their flat was on the top floor of a modern building, in a suburb, and looked out on to a huge open meadow, very rough and steep and full of holes and hillocks. At that hour the meadow, faintly lit by the light from infrequent lamp-posts, was a boundless, shadowy quadrilateral, with whitish scraps of waste paper here and there, the grassy depressions black and the hillocks paler because they were bare. On the far side of the meadow, a long way away, like a glacier-front above an amphitheatre of moraine, could be seen a barrier of houses, their façade dark and dead save for one top-floor window which shone with a solitary, brilliant light. Over the houses, in the misty sky, hung a little yellow sickle of a moon surrounded by a dim halo. At that moment an air liner crossed the sky diagonally above the moon, showing alternately the red lights on its wings and the green lights on its tail.

'Look,' said the girl, 'an aeroplane.'

'Yes, an aeroplane.'

'Where d'you think it comes from?'

'Goodness only knows.'

She was silent for a moment and then went on. 'They throw the rubbish of the whole quarter into this field. Children play there in the daytime, in the evenings couples make love there. And at night?'

'At night it's haunted by cats.'

'D'you think they'll build houses there some day?'

'Yes, undoubtedly.'

'Then they'll take away our view and it will be better for us to move.'

She pressed against his hip with her own bony hip and, all of a sudden, made a sentimental gesture: she laid her head on his shoulder. But she corrected herself almost at once and said: 'Look, over there, in that building opposite, there's a lighted window. I wonder who it is?'

'Somebody who's not asleep.'

'Thanks for the explanation. Is that window lit up every evening?'

'I think it is.'

'Perhaps it's someone who's afraid of sleeping in the dark.'

Without a word, Girolamo left the window and walked off towards the door. His wife ran after him: 'Where are you going?'

'Into the kitchen, to make myself some orange squash. My sleeping pill didn't make me sleep but it has dried up my mouth: I'm dying of thirst.'

'I'll make the squash for you.'

They went out into the passage. It was a small flat, four rooms in all, two on each side of the passage and then a little entrance-hall. His wife uttered a cry: 'Look, oh look!'

Girolamo looked down: on the shiny, yellow, imitation marble floor numbers of big black cockroaches were fleeing from every direction towards the corners, trying to find a dark place. A couple of these cockroaches, dazzled, perhaps, by the light, were circling giddily round and round in a kind of frantic dance. Girolamo's wife cried out again: 'There are such a lot of them! How disgusting, how disgusting!' She went in great haste into the bathroom and came back holding a cone-shaped tin with holes at the top. 'Look, *you* kill them,' she said, 'they make me sick.'

Methodically Girolamo started chasing the cockroaches, unloading little clouds of yellow insecticide powder on to them. The tin, as he shook it, made a tiny rumbling sound which to the insects, he thought, must sound terrible, like the explosion of an atomic bomb to human beings. The cockroaches still went on walking for a little, more and more slowly, their black backs veiled with yellow; then they stopped and turned over, feet in the air, dead. Disgusted, Girolamo finally gave back the tin to his wife, saying: 'There, that's enough for tonight.'

'But where do they come from? It's a new house.'

'From the kitchen sink, probably.'

He opened a cupboard at the end of the passage, took out a broom and with meticulous care swept all the dead cockroaches together into a single heap, in a corner. Then he went into the kitchen. Standing at the table, her belly pressed against its marble top, his wife was zealously and vigorously squeezing four bisected oranges into a tumbler. Girolamo went and sat down behind her and contemplated with indifference her pure, slender back which, each time she twisted and pressed down the half-oranges to squeeze out the juice, made a slight rhythmical movement like the movement of a dance. Without turning round, she said: 'Would you like me to pass the juice through a sieve?'

'No, I prefer it like that, without being strained.'

'Here you are then.'

Girolamo rose, took the glass and slowly drank the fresh, thick juice, standing beside the refrigerator. The kitchen, with its dazzling white light multiplied by the whiteness of the tiles, suddenly made him think of his own head, dazed with insomnia. His wife came over to him and timidly asked him: 'Are you sleepy?'

'No.'

'Not even a little?'

'No, not even a little.'

'What time is it?'

'Twenty to four.'

'Are you bored with me?'

'On the contrary, tonight we've done a whole heap of interesting things: we've looked out at the meadow, we've seen an aeroplane in the sky and a lighted window in a building, we've had a cockroach-hunt, we've made some orange squash.'

'I've an idea: let's go along to my room and put on a record and listen to some music.'

'What music?'

'Something gay – a Twist, for instance.'

'We shall wake up the whole building.'

'No, no, we can play it quietly.'

They went into the bedroom, which was extremely untidy: feminine garments strewn all over the place, stockings and shoes on the carpet, the bed rumpled, the wardrobe doors hanging open. She went to a corner in which the gramophone stood and put on a record. As soon as the music started, she came back into the middle of the room and held out her arms towards him: 'Let's dance.'

'You know I can't dance.'

'I'll teach you the Twist; then at least insomnia will have served some purpose.'

'No, I don't want to.'

'All right, then I'll dance for you. I'll do as the Oriental women do for their lords, in the harem.'

He watched her as she stretched her arms out in front of her with closed fists, then gradually bent her knees, swaying her hips from side to side as she did so. It was a kind of concertina movement: now her body shrank in on itself down to the floor, now stretched itself upwards towards the ceiling as she raised herself on the tips of her toes. She danced with complete absorption, her knees close together, her feet turned outwards, her head bent forward with her hair hanging down. Then, suddenly, she ran straight towards Girolamo who was sitting on the bed, fell on top of him with a little cry and panted out: 'That's enough of dancing, now. I'm tired.'

Girolamo, with a touch of irony, suggested: 'Why don't you try and sleep a bit? You must be sleepy, aren't you?'

'If you stay here with me, I'll sleep. But please don't leave me alone.'

'Very well.'

His wife was silent for a little, then she murmured in a sleepy voice: 'D'you know, I do love you so very much,' and pressed herself against him. She must have dropped off to sleep at once, for Girolamo, almost immediately, heard her breathing deeply and regularly like someone fast asleep. He waited a few minutes, then very slowly disengaged himself from her, laid her down in the bed, pulled the coverlet over her and went out of the room.

He went back into his study, took a pair of binoculars from a drawer and walked across to the window. Every night he looked through his binoculars at the distant lighted window far away on the other side of the meadow, in the hope – a hope which was always unfulfilled – that he might see who it was that was awake at that hour. But again this time the sleepless inhabitant of the lighted room failed to appear. In the end Girolamo grew tired of watching; he went and lay down on the divan and turned out the light.

All Right

They entered the lift. Nora retreated into a corner, holding between them the bunch of mimosa which Sandro had just given her. She put out her large, smooth, white hand and pressed the button; and as soon as the lift started going up, she said: 'Now mind, I'm letting you come up, but only on one condition: that as soon as he telephones, you go away.'

'All right.'

From behind the blue-green, yellow-starred sprays of mimosa, Sandro saw a sudden look of anger on her beautiful face with the untidy locks of fair hair straggling across it; her big red mouth was twisted, her pale blue eyes contracted. 'No,' she said, 'it's not all right because I know in advance that, once you're up there, you'll start talking to me about the great love you have for me and then you'll refuse to go away and I shall have to fight to get rid of you. And I don't want any fights.'

'But why are you angry?'

'I'm angry because you won't understand.'

'Understand what?'

'That I don't love you and shall never love you.'

'All right.'

'You always say "all right". But what is there that's all right for you about me? Nothing. So why d'you say "all right"?' She was flying into a temper again now as she spoke. 'What you ought to be saying is "all wrong, all very wrong indeed".'

Sandro bent his head and said: 'I'm sorry. One says "all right" just as one says "I agree".'

'But we don't agree and we never shall.'

The lift came to a stop and Nora hurried out impetuously, passing in front of Sandro and smearing his whole face with mimosa pollen. She went to the front door of the flat, then turned and cried: 'Come on, what are you doing in there? You wanted to come up, so come on in.'

Sandro came out of the lift and followed her. As soon as the door had closed behind them and as they paused for a moment in the darkness, immediately the telephone began ringing in an adjoining room. Sandro heard Nora rush forward in the dark, knocking blindly into the furniture; then her voice said breathlessly: 'Hullo, who is it? Hullo'; and then immediately afterwards, falling, as it were, into the relief of a sudden tenderness: 'Ah, it's you, my love.'

The telephone conversation was brief. Nora answered: 'Yes, no, yes, no' as though she were afraid that Sandro might understand what was being said to her from the other end of the line. Then, in an anxious, docile, imploring, melting tone, she exclaimed: 'One moment, wait, tell me . . .' But there was only the click of the receiver being replaced and then a profound silence.

After a few seconds, as he stood in the darkness of the entrance-hall with his back against the door, Sandro heard the sound of a tap dripping in the bathroom or possibly the kitchen, the confused music of a radio in a neighbouring flat, the small, remote voice of someone telephoning on the floor below; but nothing that might indicate Nora's presence in the apartment. Or rather – yes – he seemed to be aware, suddenly, of the faint rustling of garments, of the tread of bare feet. Finally he made up his mind and asked: 'Well?'

Nora's voice, half suffocated, replied: 'Listen!'

'Yes?'

'You like being here with me?'

'You know I like it.'

'Then do what I tell you: don't light any lights, not even a match, come into my bedroom until you reach the armchair at the foot of the bed, sit down there and stay still and quiet.'

'But why?'

'I've undressed and gone to bed. In the state of mind in which I am, I'd rather be alone. But since it gives you such pleasure to be with me, I'll allow you to stay. On condition, however, that you don't light any lights or speak.'

'Couldn't I hold your hand?'

'No, for goodness' sake; if you touch me I'll scream.'

'What am I to do?'

'Nothing; you're not even to exist – just as the chairs and the chest-of-drawers and the other pieces of furniture don't exist, in this darkness.'

'But if I don't exist, what am I to do?'

'You like being with me? Well, be content, then.'

Sandro was silent; very slowly he felt his way to the arm-chair. When he reached it, he put his hand on the cushion before sitting down. His fingers caught in some soft, thin material, possibly a stocking; then he felt, under his palm, the two little domes of a brassière. So, then, she had really undressed, after that anxious conversation on the tele-phone. He removed all the things from the armchair, let himself down between the two arms and then remained motionless.

A very long silence followed. Sandro, after a little, care-fully slipped his hand into his pocket, sought and found a packet of cigarettes and some book-matches, and was on the point of lighting a cigarette. But he suddenly remem-bered Nora's injunction: 'Don't even light a match' and gave up the idea. Not a sound came from the bed; even the music from the radio in the neighbouring flat and the voice telephoning on the floor below had stopped. The silence was complete, and its very completeness made it intoler-able. Then, to his relief, Sandro again heard a rustling sound, as of sheets being thrust aside; and then Nora's voice, quiet and close beside him, saying: 'Say something to me.'

'Where are you?'

'I'm in bed.'

'Aren't you still under the bedclothes?'

'No, they were stifling me. I'm lying across the bed, with my feet on the pillow and my head hanging down. My head is not far from your knees, in fact I could touch them with my mouth, and my hair just reaches the carpet.'

'D'you want me to put on the light?'

'No, I'm naked; if you do, I'll turn you out.'

Sandro very gradually moved his hand along his knees. Cautiously he put out one finger and indeed felt, at his finger-tip, a slight but lively tickling sensation from a soft lock of hair. 'What d'you want me to say to you?' he asked.

'Something that will distract me, that will make me think of other things.'

Sandro said slowly: 'I don't know what to say.'

'What, you tell me you love me and you don't know what to say?'

'I can tell you I love you.'

'No, no, please, don't talk to me about love.'

'Well then, what am I to talk about?'

'Talk to me about something you like.'

Sandro thought for a moment and then said: 'I like the sea. Shall I talk to you about the sea?'

'Yes, talk to me about the sea.'

Sandro was silent for a little, then he began: 'I like to go rowing on the sea, in the early morning, in springtime. The sea has a fresh smell of green seaweed, and there are white butterflies flying over it, two by two, as there are over the fields in the country. The sea is smooth and of a glassy blue, and I row slowly; I go close inshore and start rowing near the rocks. From time to time I stop and look. The water rises and falls according to the ebb and flow; when it rises it makes a slight gurgling sound as it penetrates into the cavities of the rocks, when it falls it makes a different, harsher gurgling sound as it comes out of the cavities. Green and brown seaweed clings to the rocks, and brilliant red sea anemones and purple sea urchins and dark-coloured limpets. If I look down into the water, I can see that it's transparent to a great depth, and I can distinguish tiny little fish swimming about, this way and that, in the brightness of the sunlight, going in and out of the cavities, wagging their tails; they're silvery, with a black stripe inside their transparent bodies and eyes like little black balls in their heads.'

There was a sudden cry of: 'That's enough, that's

enough.'

'Why is that enough? Don't you like me to talk to you about the sea?'

'You're an idiot, you'll never understand anything; you've been talking about the one thing you ought *not* to have talked about.'

'But why not?'

'Because *I* like the sea too, and I liked it especially when I went there with *him*, and by talking about it you've given me a longing for it. You should have talked to me about anything rather than the sea.'

'What, in your opinion, should I have talked to you about?'

'Oh, I don't know. Stamps, football, shooting.'

'But I don't collect stamps, I'm not fond of football, and I never go out shooting.'

'Oh, be quiet, be quiet, be quiet, please!'

He heard her moving again, and this time he was quite unable to make out where she had gone. Then her voice, low and furious, reached him from the entrance-hall: 'Now I'm going to lock myself in the bathroom, open the window and throw myself out.'

'For God's sake!' Sandro rose and ran in the darkness into the hall, but at the same moment the bathroom door closed and the key was turned in the lock. Sandro beat with his fist on the closed door, calling out to her; then he ran back into the bedroom, went, still in the dark, to the window and threw it open. The white light from a sky covered with fleecy clouds dazzled him after the prolonged darkness. He leant out over the window-sill but could not manage to see the bathroom window, which was hidden in a recess in the façade of the building. He looked down: six floors below could be seen the roofs of cars and the larger roof of a bus moving slowly and laboriously along the street. Suddenly, behind him, the telephone rang loudly.

Sandro had barely time to turn round before Nora had come out of the bathroom, rushed to the telephone and taken off the receiver. She had a bath-towel wrapped round her, and he could not help wondering, with astonishment, how she had even managed to find the time to cover herself.

Nora, in a breathless voice said 'All right' once; then she repeated 'All right' in a joyful manner, then listened for a moment and, for the third time, still joyfully but now conclusively, again said: 'All right.' Finally she put back the receiver and turned towards Sandro. 'I'm sorry,' she said, 'but I must remind you of our agreement. You must go: he's just coming.'

'I'm going; all right.'

'You know what you might do? Telephone me later on.'

'At what time?'

'Oh well, I don't know, about eight.'

'All right.'

'Shut the door.'

'All right.'

Mere Objects

'It's two streets further on, one of these turnings going across from Via Flaminia to the Lungotevere.' Livia seemed anxious to reach the street in which the flat was – too anxious, thought Ciro, even if it *was* a question of the flat in which they would live after they were married. Wondering what reason there could be for this excessive anxiety and failing to find any, Ciro drove along in the grey, fine rain over the shining asphalt of the Lungotevere till he came to the second side-street, and then turned into it. It seemed an ordinary kind of street, neither ugly nor beautiful, neither old nor new, with two rows of biscuit-coloured buildings, cars parked along the pavements and no shops. A quiet street. On one of the front doors hung a red placard announcing 'To Let'. 'That's it,' said Livia, with a burst of joy in her voice.

Ciro stopped the car; they got out and went into a modest entrance-hall with a brick floor and two rows of plants in terracotta vases. In the lift Ciro asked his fiancée: 'How did you come to find it?'

'I came past here this morning and saw the placard. That's the best way to find a flat – to go round and look at placards.'

'Did you go up?'

'No, but I asked the porter about it and he said the flat could only be seen between two and four. I made him describe it to me: it's just exactly right for us.'

'But what's the matter, are you agitated?'

'I'm not in the least agitated. I'm pleased. After so much looking, here we are at last.'

The lift came to a halt and they got out. They found themselves on a landing upon which only one door opened, a door of rustic type, of rough wood with iron hinges. Ciro looked at the brass plate and read: 'Ippolito'. He said grumpily: 'Whatever sort of a name is that? Ippolito, just like that and nothing else.'

'Well, what's strange about it? His name is Ippolito.'

'But hasn't he a profession, a trade? Isn't he a doctor or a lawyer or something? Ippolito's the surname. Hasn't he a Christian name?'

He saw her shrug her shoulders; and he had a sudden feeling of jealous possessiveness for her beautiful, thin face with its big eyes, its aquiline nose, its small red mouth. He said impetuously: 'Give me a kiss.'

'But we must look at the flat.'

'Give me a kiss.'

'No, not now.' Livia went and pressed the bell just at the same moment as Ciro pulled her to him and kissed her. Almost immediately the door was thrown open and there appeared in the doorway a young man whose appearance put one in mind of a bear: he was tall but with a look of sturdy, massive indolence about him; his head was large and round, his hair curly and very thick, there was a sleepy expression in his eyes, his nose was short, his lips full. Ciro and his fiancée at once drew apart from each other, Livia, apparently, somewhat confused, Ciro defiant but content. The owner of the flat considered them for a moment and then asked: 'What can I do for you?'

He had a harsh, deep bass voice; and Ciro was suddenly conscious of a feeling of apprehension and danger. As though apologizing, but really in order to assert his own relationship with Livia, he said: 'You must forgive us, we're engaged to be married and we were kissing right in front of your door before we rang the bell. In point of fact, we've come to look at the flat.'

'Allow me, my name's Ippolito,' said the young man, putting out his hand, without commenting in any way upon Ciro's explanations.

'How d'you do? This is Livia.'

'How d'you do?'

They went in. Ciro, urged on by a sudden need to make clear, in front of Ippolito, his own position as fiancé, said to Livia: 'Sorry, but have I got lipstick on my mouth?'

Ippolito, who was closing the door, turned and looked at him but said nothing. Livia blushed and then said, in a colourless voice: 'No, you haven't anything.'

'But I feel as if I had something.'

'No, there's nothing; I didn't have any lipstick on my mouth.'

'This is the entrance-hall,' said Ippolito, his remark cutting short the squabble between the engaged couple.

The entrance-hall was small and monastic, with white-washed walls and vaulted ceiling, a sixteenth-century chest and high-backed chairs, a wrought-iron lamp. 'Are you ... a student?' Ciro asked Ippolito.

'No, I work for the films, I'm a script-writer.'

Livia, with sudden interest, inquired: 'Are you a director too?'

Ippolito turned his dull eyes upon her for a moment before answering. Then he replied in a deep voice: 'Certainly one day I shall shoot my own film. For the present I'm getting my hand in with script-writing.'

Not knowing how to give vent to the hostility he felt towards Ippolito, Ciro said: 'Everything's easy, or anyhow seems easy, in the cinema.'

'And you, what do you do?'

'I'm studying engineering.'

'This is the bedroom,' said Ippolito, throwing open a door in the passage. The bedroom was small, with a window opening on to the terrace that ran all round the penthouse flat. Through the panes could be seen the grey, opaque sky of a wet day. A big double bed blocked up the whole room. The bed, too, was in rustic style, its head consisting entirely of curly pieces of wrought iron. Handwoven stuffs, iron implements, small pictures of Sicilian carts adorned the walls. 'A double bed?' said Ciro. 'Then you don't live alone?'

'Yes, I live alone, but I like to have plenty of room when I go to bed.'

'And this flat – d'you rent it furnished?'

'Furnished and not furnished.'

'It's rather small,' said Ciro, looking at the bed and try-ing to define to himself the persistent feeling of danger and jealousy which Ippolito aroused in him.

'*I* say it's ideal for us,' said Livia, with an emphasis that appeared to Ciro both excessive and unseemly.

'It's small, yes,' answered Ippolito slowly, 'but it's just the thing for two people who are fond of each other.'

'And we two are fond of each other,' said Ciro, suddenly taking Livia round the waist, 'it's true, isn't it, Livia, that we're fond of each other?'

Ippolito looked at them without speaking: he had a persistent, heavy, sleepy, truly bearish manner of looking, which irritated Ciro. The latter, without reflecting, went on: 'Give me a kiss' – and at the same time kissed Livia on the neck. 'Excuse me,' said Ippolito, 'the telephone's ring-ing'; and he hurried out of the room. The other two re-mained in each other's embrace: Livia did not repel, in fact she seemed to favour, Ciro's caresses. But, as they sep-arated, she said coldly: 'You have no shame; one doesn't kiss in front of a stranger.'

'You're my fiancée, soon you'll be my wife.'

'Never mind, one doesn't do it.'

Ippolito came back, saying: 'If you'd like to see the living-room . . .' and led them along the passage. Ciro tried to take Livia's hand, but she pulled herself violently away from him. Throwing open the door, Ippolito said: 'The bedroom's small, but, to make up for it, there's a big living-room.'

The living-room was indeed large, and, partly owing to its long windows, was reminiscent of the saloon of a ship: the uncarpeted floor was of light-coloured, glossy wood; the furniture, of Swedish type, was of black iron and teak; there were detachable bookcases made of steel; and red and black leather sofas and armchairs. On a table near the window stood a typewriter swamped by a surge of white sheets of paper. On the floor, notebooks and film scripts were piled up in heaps. 'Yes,' said Ciro, 'the living-room is large.'

'To me it seems stupendous,' said Livia with enthusiasm.

'Where is the telephone?' asked Ciro. He explained to Livia: 'I must warn them at the boarding-house that we shan't be in to lunch.'

'The telephone's in the passage,' said Ippolito.

Ciro went out into the passage with the feeling that he was doing wrong in leaving Livia and Ippolito alone, even for a moment. The telephone was on a shelf behind the door. Ciro noticed to his satisfaction that a mirror hanging opposite the telephone reflected the whole of that part of the living-room in which Livia and Ippolito were standing. He dialled the number of the boarding-house; and then, with a sickening sense of inevitability, saw, in the mirror, Livia go up to Ippolito, place the palm of her hands on his chest, gazing fixedly up at him, and then give him a strange, stealthy kiss, as swift and angry as the peck of a bird. They separated almost at once, black against the background of grey sky through the windows. Ciro abandoned his telephone call and went back into the living-room, saying: 'We must go back at once. There's someone waiting for me.'

With his usual sleepy indolence, Ippolito showed them to the door. As they went out, he said: 'I have a good many applicants; let me know something by the day after to-morrow. I would let you have the flat rather than anyone else.'

'Why?' demanded Ciro, turning round in a hostile manner.

'I dunno. I like you better than the others.'

'Good-bye, Signor Ippolito,' said Livia; 'we'll telephone.'

Back in the car, Ciro drove without saying a word as far as the Lungotevere, then went and stopped beside the parapet. The rain was still falling, grey and thick, on the black asphalt: the cars, as they passed, threw up fans of dingy water. 'Why are you stopping here?' asked Livia.

Ciro pulled up the handbrake, turned off the engine, then looked at her and said in a choked voice: 'So the whole thing was a trick.'

'What d'you mean, a trick?'

'You'd come to an agreement with your lover to palm off his flat on me. God knows why: just out of sadism, probably.'

'What *are* you talking about?'

'D'you think I didn't see you kissing?'

There was silence. Then she asked quietly: 'So you imagine that there's a liaison between me and Signor Ippolito?'

'Why d'you call him Ippolito? Call him by his name.'

'What name?'

'Ippolito's his surname. He must be called Paolo, Pietro, Giovanni, something or other. Or perhaps, in your intimacy, you call him Cocò, Pepé, Lulú . . .'

He saw her smile. She said quite simply: 'But I can't call him anything because I don't know his name.'

'Really, you mean to tell me you don't know your lover's name?'

'But I'm not Ippolito's mistress.'

'What d'you mean? How about the kiss?'

Again there was silence. Then Livia, reasonably and calmly, continued: 'Not merely am I not Ippolito's mistress but I had never seen him before today. When he opened the door and saw us kissing on the landing I dare say he perhaps imagined that I was a loose woman. So, when we went in, without your noticing it he squeezed my hand. I was indignant and was on the point of telling you we must go away. Just at that moment you took it into your head to kiss me in front of him. So then, when you went to the telephone, I threw my arms round his neck.'

'But why did you do that? I don't understand you.'

'Because you insulted me, you'd treated me like a mere object. At that moment, if Ippolito had been a decrepit old man, a leper, a monster, I would have kissed him just the same. I didn't do it for Ippolito's sake – he means nothing to me; nor did I do it because of you: you're what you are and there's nothing to be done about it. I did it for my own sake.'

'For your own sake?'

'Yes, so as to get back the feeling of not being an object, a mere chattel.'

Ciro started up the car again and moved off very slowly beneath the rain which was now falling more heavily. 'But are you going to see Ippolito again?' he asked after a moment.

'Why should I see him again? I made use of him just as you had made use of me. I shan't ever see him again.'

Renzo went home carrying a small portable radio which he had acquired that afternoon. From the front door he went straight into the bedroom, turned on the light, sat down on the bed and placed the radio on the bedside table beside the telephone. From a leather box he took a cigarette and lit it; then he turned the knob of the radio. Out came the loud notes of a dance tune; Renzo listened to this for a little, then turned the knob again; this time it was a sports commentator. After the commentator there was classical music, violins and a piano, and then again a voice explaining something or other. Renzo was now looking at, rather than listening to, the radio, with a more and more absent-minded expression. All of a sudden he leant forward, turned off the radio and quickly dialled a number on the telephone. As soon as he heard his wife's voice saying 'Hello' he asked: 'How are you?'

'I'm all right.'

'What are you doing?'

'I was just going to bed.'

'I telephoned you because you said I might.'

'One says all sorts of things; you shouldn't take me so literally.'

'So I oughtn't to have telephoned you?'

'I'm not saying that, I'm only saying it wasn't really an invitation to telephone me. It was just a polite remark, that's all.'

Renzo was silent, then he went on: 'Are you already in bed?'

'No, not yet.'

There was silence again. Suddenly Renzo said: 'I'm coming to see you.'

'Don't think of such a thing, I'm already undressed.'

'Oh well, then, that means we'll sleep together.'

'Sleep together? Are you mad?'

'Why should I be mad?'

'We've been separated now for three months, I don't love you and you don't love me, we've nothing in common with each other – and you want us to sleep together!'

'I said sleep together, nothing more.'

'What does that mean?'

'It means that I'll come, lie down beside you and go to sleep at once. What does it matter to you? Come on!'

There was silence. Then his wife said: 'How absurd! Anyhow I'm dying to go to sleep and I couldn't even come and open the door to you. I shall be asleep in five minutes.'

'Let's do it like this,' replied Renzo. 'You put the keys in the flower vase on the right, outside your front door. When I get there I'll come in and lie down beside you without waking you up. In the morning, again without waking you up, I'll go away. Is that all right?'

'I don't know what pleasure you can get out of it.'

'Never mind about me. Tell me if you agree.'

'Well, all right. But I warn you, you'll find me asleep and you're not on any account to wake me up.'

'All right. See you soon.'

Renzo hung up the receiver, lit another cigarette, turned the knob of the radio and sat smoking on the edge of the bed, his legs crossed, listening to the music. When he had finished his cigarette he turned off the radio, got up and went to the bathroom. It was a long, narrow room with a window at the far end, through which could be seen the façade of the block of flats opposite, of a chemical blue with numbers of balconies with silver-painted balustrades. Renzo opened a small lacquered cupboard and started putting what he needed for the night into a leather bag: brush and comb, toothpaste and toothbrush, electric razor. Then he took down his pyjamas from their hanger, rolled them up and pushed them with some difficulty into the bag, afterwards closing the zip fastener. With his bulging bag under his arm he went back into the entrance-hall and turned off the electricity supply. There was a moment of darkness. Then he opened the front door and went out on to the landing.

As the lift, with a monotonous hum, went down floor by floor Renzo, as usual, read the maintenance instructions with careful attention: 'See that the doors are properly closed; anyone using the lift does so at his own risk', etc., etc., as well as some obscene words which someone had scratched on the shiny wooden surface. The lift stopped, Renzo crossed the hall and went out into the street. Below the balconied blocks of flats, their windows all unlit, the parked cars seemed smitten with paralysis, some of them placed crookedly, some in herring-bone fashion, some the wrong way round. No one went past; the street was almost in darkness. Renzo, before getting into his own car, looked at his wrist-watch and saw that it was a quarter past one.

It was possible to go from the quarter where he lived to his wife's flat without passing through the centre of the city – a journey through street after street each similar to the last, with the same balcony-laden blocks of flats, the same rows of cars untidily abandoned along the pavements. Renzo started to drive at a high but methodically controlled speed from street to street, taking the turnings without slowing down, with a piercing screech from the wheels. He came at last to the square where his wife lived, a kind of well made of cement with five enormously high blocks of flats towering over a minute lake of asphalt. Each of these blocks had a little garden in front of the main door, with a pair of vases full of geraniums at the entrance. Renzo found the keys and went straight through the hall to door number 3, on the ground floor. The door opened gently and he crept into the dark flat, standing still for a moment and holding his breath.

There was deep silence; nevertheless the darkness seemed to be animated by a presence, invisible yet living. Renzo stopped, took off his shoes and started making his way in the dark towards the bedroom. The flat was in every way similar to his own, as he knew from having been there a couple of times when discussing the separation with his wife; the only difference was that he himself was on the fifth floor and his wife on the ground floor. The bedroom door was ajar; Renzo went in and listened: the sound of deep, irregular breathing showed him that his wife was there, and was asleep.

He recalled that the bed, a large, almost a double, bed, stood with its head against the wall on the right: he still had to discover on which side his wife was sleeping. Very slowly, holding out his hand in front of him, Renzo advanced in the darkness until his shin came in contact with the edge of the bed. Then he bent down towards the pillow and finally felt her hair tickling the palm of his hand. His wife, then, was sleeping on the side nearest the door. Renzo tiptoed round the bed, put down his bag on the floor, pulled out his pyjamas and his phial of sleeping-pills, undressed, put on his pyjamas and put the phial in one of the pockets, lifted the bedclothes and slipped into bed.

For a short time he lay still, flat on his back, keeping to the edge of the bed, holding his breath and listening. His wife's breathing was harsh, violent, almost angry, the breathing of a young woman who each night, greedily and without difficulty, finds refreshment after the fatigues of the day. In what position was she sleeping? Renzo put out his hand till it encountered the body of the sleeping woman: she was curled up, her chin almost meeting her knees. But just at that moment, all of a sudden he heard her heave a sigh, a noisy, impatient, anguished sigh. Then, with an almost furious violence, she turned round and threw herself upon him, embracing him closely.

She was now on top of him, her leg resting on his legs, one arm across his waist and her head on his chest. But her breathing, which had returned to its normal rhythm, excluded any possibility of her consciousness. She was asleep; and the desperate, yearning affection of her embrace was automatic. Renzo placed one arm round her shoulders and folded his other arm behind the back of his neck.

He lay still for a long time, listening to his wife's heavy, child-like, exhausted and, in a way, painful breathing. Every now and then he heard her sigh deeply, or felt her press her body more closely against his but both sighs and movements were mechanical, with no intention behind them. An hour, perhaps, passed in this way; then Renzo realized that, if he wanted to sleep, he must change his position: one of his wife's feet was pressing hard on his ankle, cross-wise, right on the bone; her leg, weighing heavily on his, had ended by causing an acute, fixed cramp. And her head, lying oppressively on his chest, seemed as heavy as lead.

But when he started trying gradually to extricate himself without awakening her, the sleeping woman, with the same blind violence with which she had clung to him, disengaged herself from the embrace and threw herself over to the other side of the bed, still remaining, however, with her back against his. This movement, too, apparently so de-liberate, had been automatic and unconscious. He heard her, in her new position, sigh two or three times in a dis-tressed manner, and then, after a little resume her former irregular, angry breathing.

She stayed for about an hour flung across the bed in this way; and in the end Renzo dozed off, into a light, trans-parent sleep, however, in which the presence of the woman at his side continued to preoccupy him. Then, all of a sudden, there was a renewed, furious movement beneath the bedclothes and this time the embrace was much more intimate than before: body against body, her face close against Renzo's neck, her hands joined on his chest. He heard her mutter some harsh, snarling word, a word that seemed appropriate to her harsh sleep; then, strangely, mechanically, she reached out to find his hand and clasped it tightly. But in this handclasp, as in her embrace, Renzo was aware of a complete absence of consciousness, of its pure automatism. Anyhow this very intimate attitude did not endure for long. Suddenly a new convulsive jerk hurled his wife away from him, on to her back this time, with her head buried in the pillow beside his own. The hand that was clasping his remained inert, and finally slid away from his fingers.

Renzo, at this point, looked at the luminous dial of his

watch and saw that it was now four o'clock. In the course of two hours his wife had embraced him twice and had twice drawn away from him – all of them things which, in their waking hours, had not happened for a long time. But he felt that he must sleep. He took the phial of sleeping-pills from his pocket, unscrewed the lid, dropped three tablets into the palm of his hand and swallowed them. His wife gave a double sigh almost like a sob and sought his hand again. Renzo closed his eyes.

He awoke four hours later and saw that the place beside him in the bed was empty. But from the bathroom next door came the sound of rushing water from the shower. The room was still in darkness but threads of light filtered through the slats of the shutters. On an armchair at the foot of the bed his wife's clothes were scattered untidily, just as she had taken them off the evening before, her skirt and jacket at the bottom of the heap, her more intimate garments and stockings on the top. His own clothes were strewn on the floor, on the bedside rug.

Renzo jumped out of bed and started dressing hastily. The sound of water from the shower had now ceased and, in the silence, noises from neighbouring flats could be heard through the thin walls – babies crying, telephones ringing, voices on the radio, arguments and shouts. Renzo went to the bathroom door and knocked twice.

'I can't open the door,' cried his wife from inside.

'I wanted to say good-bye to you.'

'Good-bye, then. Good-bye.'

'Thank you for last night.'

'Nothing to thank me for. But please . . .'

'Yes?'

'Please don't telephone me again.'

Renzo stared for a moment at the closed door, then shook his head vigorously and left the flat. In the hall downstairs he ran into a man in a blue blouse who was carrying a sack full of rubbish on his back. The little square with the tall, narrow blocks of flats all round it was obstructed by a number of empty buses, for which it served as the terminus; the conductors and drivers were chattering in a group in the middle of the square. Renzo got into his car and, looking at himself in the driving-mirror, did his best to smooth back his hair which was still rumpled after the night. Then he started the engine and drove away.

The Poet and the Doctor

Their appointment was at the obelisk in the Foro Italico. It had rained the day before; the sky was of a crude, fresh blue, like new paint; grey, cotton-wool clouds rimmed with purple were driven across it, swollen and heavy, by an impetuous wind; the splendid sunshine made scrub-covered Monte Mario look black behind the pale gold pinnacle of the obelisk. Giovanni stopped his car near the obelisk, pulled up the handbrake, then got out and began undoing the fastenings and unhitching the hooks of the hood. It was blazing hot, presaging, perhaps, another thunderstorm, and he felt happy, his blood coursing vigorously through his veins. Soon the girl would arrive, and they would go out into the country, to some lovely green place, and there they would remain until the evening.

But the hooks refused to be unhitched without someone, at the same time, pulling back the hood. As he was vainly fumbling, he heard a voice suggesting: 'Would you like me to help you?'

He turned and saw a young man of his own age, thin and dark, with a fine, delicate face, gazing at him with sparkling eyes beneath thick black eyebrows. Before he had time to thank him, he had already grasped the handles of the hood. In a moment the hooks and fastenings were undone and the hood was lowered. Giovanni got into the car again and offered the unknown man a cigarette. He expected that he would take it and go away, but this did not happen. The young man, after lighting his cigarette from Giovanni's, pressing the latter's hand with both his own which, as Giovanni noticed with surprise, were trembling visibly, then leant against the car with one arm on the door, raised the cigarette to his mouth, inhaled the smoke, blew it out through his nostrils, spat out a particle of tobacco which had stuck to his lips, and finally, with extravagant banality, said suddenly: 'A lovely day, isn't it?'

Giovanni realized to his surprise that he did not mind the young man staying and talking to him; on the contrary. He attributed this state of mind to his own feeling of happiness and answered promptly: 'Yes, it's really magnificent.' He paused a moment and then, for some odd reason, it occurred to him to add: 'If it wasn't for this wind, it would be perfect.'

Looking into the distance, the young man said: 'On a day like this, it's good to get into the country, don't you think?'

There was a softness in his voice, a softness which was, however, sombre and almost threatening; and, Giovanni noticed, every now and then he lapsed into a slight stammer that was not without charm. Giovanni felt a sudden liking for him and replied with conviction: 'Yes, on a day like this it really is good to get into the country.'

The other man shook his head and went on smoking, for a moment, in silence. Then he resumed: 'On days like this I should like to get out of the city, walk into a field and lie down amongst the corn. You can lie among the tall corn-stalks as if you were in a green alcove, with corn-stalks for a bed and corn-stalks for walls and the blue sky for a roof. You can take an ear of corn and crush the grain between your teeth; it's tender and full of milk, and you can suck out the milk as you lie looking upwards, into the sunshine. Lovely, don't you think?'

Giovanni reflected that the young man spoke well, even a little too well, perhaps, and in a manner that might have seemed irritating to him if he had not been defeated by this inexplicable liking that he felt for him. In order to bring the conversation back to a less lyrical tone, he asked: 'If you think it's so lovely, why don't you go into the country?'

The other man inhaled the smoke of his cigarette and replied: 'I'd like very much to go.'

'Well then, I repeat, why don't you go?'

'I don't want to go alone.'

Giovanni answered cordially: 'Well, you must find yourself a girl. Why don't you do that?'

The young man made a curious, almost convulsive movement with his hand and his head, and said nothing. Giovanni persisted: 'Anyhow, *I've* found a girl. I'm waiting for her at this moment.' He thought he had spoken thus in order to let the young man understand that he would soon have to leave him. But that was not the only reason: it was perhaps also from vanity and secret satisfaction.

The young man turned unexpectedly, seizing hold of the door with both hands and staring at Giovanni with brilliant eyes. Giovanni felt sudden resentment: 'What is it? Why d'you look at me like that?'

He noticed that the other man became immediately confused, in an extravagant, impetuous way. 'I'm sorry,' said the latter, 'I always do that with everybody, I look at people in an insistent sort of way; I'm sorry.'

'Oh, never mind, I was just wondering. It's always embarrassing to have someone staring at you.'

The young man said nothing; but he did not move. Giovanni looked at the clock on the dashboard: the girl ought to have arrived by this time. But he was surprised to find that, secretly, this lateness did not displease him at all. 'Are you a student?' he inquired.

'Yes.'

'What are you studying?'

'Letters.'

'I'm studying medicine.'

'Two very different subjects,' said the other, with a gloomy, thoughtful expression.

'I ought to have known that you were studying letters,' said Giovanni, 'from the way in which you spoke about the country.'

'What way?'

'Oh, I don't know' – Giovanni suddenly realized that he was blushing from some unexplained feeling of shame – 'I don't know: a kind of literary, poetical way.'

'I do in fact sometimes write poetry,' said the other drily.

Giovanni replied, conciliatingly: '*I* love poetry, too, I often read it. I try to keep up to date, although I don't have very much time, especially when the examination period approaches.' He wondered whether he ought to name the two or three poets whom he preferred; but fear of being thought badly of prevented him. After a moment the young man inquired, in a soft, sad, caressing voice: 'D'you like poetry so very much?'

'Yes; perhaps I don't understand it very well, but certain poets I really do like. They give me a sense of life, of – of things.' Giovanni realized that he was stumbling over his words and again fell silent, in embarrassment, looking up at his companion and half fearing to see him smile pityingly. But he had remained serious and did not seem in the least inclined to make fun of him. Instead, he asked: 'Which poet d'you like best among the moderns?'

Taken unawares, Giovanni realized that he could not remember the name of any poet. Then, by chance, one name floated up to the surface of his memory. 'I've read, for instance, some poems by Garcia Lorca and they seemed to me very fine.'

'Which ones?'

Giovanni was now conscious of an almost insurmountable shyness. Finally he said: 'Well, at the moment I don't remember their titles but I remember that I liked them very much indeed; that I read and re-read them. Ah yes, there was one about the death of a bull-fighter.'

'Yes, and what other one?'

'I don't remember.'

In an exaggeratedly gentle voice, the young man asked: 'Have you many books?'

'As I said, I try to keep up to date.'

'Have you a bookcase?'

'I have two fairly big bookshelves. In one I keep my medical books. In the other, books for what I may call relaxation.'

'What books are they?'

'Oh well, I don't know – books of poetry, of course, and then novels, short stories, essays, a bit of everything. But alas, I don't have much time to read.'

'When d'you read?'

'Well, in the evening, if I stay at home and have nothing better to do.' He saw that he had made an incautious remark which might be interpreted as a sign of insufficient interest in reading, and he broke off, humiliated. But the other man did not seem to have noticed, or even to have heard, his clumsy statement. So he corrected himself hurriedly. 'What I mean is – if this girl that I'm waiting for doesn't telephone and ask me to go out with her. After all, life – don't you think? – is more important than books.'

'You mean that the girl – is life?'

'In a sense, yes.'

'D'you go out together in the evenings?'

'Just when it so happens.'

'And what d'you do?'

'We go to the cinema, generally.'

'You like the cinema?'

'Yes, I do.'

'What sort of films d'you like best?'

'I don't really know – good films.'

'But surely you must like some films better than others?'

'Yes, of course. French films, for instance.'

'Which ones?'

'I don't remember now.'

'And of the film directors, which d'you like best?'

'Directors – of what country?'

'I don't know – Italian directors, French, German, Japanese, American.'

Giovanni realized all at once that the young man was speaking in a more and more absent-minded, mechanical fashion, with the indifference of an automaton whose mechanism has gone wrong. Then he stepped back from the car, asking: 'And d'you like the Russian directors?' – and then, without waiting for an answer, walked away. Giovanni looked up into the driving-mirror. He could see the young man walking along on the white marble paving-stones, in the direction of the bridge, and at that same moment, coming towards him and recognizable from a long way off by her black, green and red tartan skirt, was the girl Giovanni was expecting. It all happened in a minute, so that it did not even occur to Giovanni to get up and intervene. The young man and the girl met, they spoke to each other for a few seconds; then the young man seized the girl by the waist and tried to drag her away. The girl reacted violently, tearing herself free. The young man raised his hand and gave her a slap on the cheek. The girl started running towards the car. The young man also started running, but in the opposite direction.

Then she opened the door and sat down, breathless and uneasy, beside him. 'How are you?' she said.

Giovanni looked at her sideways: on the dark girl's pale cheek the red mark of the blow still remained; it had the shape, almost, of an open hand. In silence he lowered the handbrake, started the engine and began backing cautiously into the square. 'I'm all right,' he replied.

She settled herself more comfortably on the seat, spreading the folds of her skirt round her as the car moved off. 'Where are we going?' she asked.

'We're going into the country. We're going to go and lie in a cornfield, amongst the corn-stalks.'

The Swollen Face

For a long stretch of the Via Appia they walked in silence along the grassy verge, passing the gates of villas one after another, the cypresses and pines at the roadside appearing discoloured and dust-covered against a sirocco-darkened sky. The grass, burnt up by the sultry weather, seemed to crumble beneath their feet; waste paper, tins, newspapers left behind by picnickers covered the ground wherever there was the agreeable shade of a big tree or the picturesque presence of a ruin. It was the hottest and most deserted time of day; only a few cars went past, bumping over the big stones of the Roman pavement. Livio, looking sideways at his wife, said suddenly: 'What's the matter with you? Your face is swollen as though you had toothache.'

It was true: his wife's round, pretty face had a swollen appearance, a congested, inflated look; and this not only in its shape but also in its unhealthily flushed, dense colour. 'There's nothing wrong with me,' she said, her teeth clenched; 'what's come into your head?'

But by now they had reached the rustic gate of the villa in which the film-star lived, and the low wall with railings along it covered with climbing rose-trees with little yellow flowers. 'Here we are,' said Livio, and turned off into a field, along the boundary wall. It was a piece of waste ground, with scattered rubbish-heaps that must have been still fresh, for they threw out, in the heat, a strong, acid smell. Far away, beyond the edge of a precipitous slope, could be seen a pale line of distant concrete buildings, with a livid light upon them beneath the dark sky. Livio followed the wall to a point where it turned at right angles, then stopped, put aside the branches of the rose-trees so as to make an opening for the lens of his camera, adjusted the sights and then said: 'From here you can see the open space in front of the house. She's bound to come out. Of course she'll come out.'

'Supposing she doesn't?'

'She's bound to.'

From one of the rubbish-heaps Livio took an old petrol-tin, turned it upside down and sat on it, his camera on his knees, his face at the opening, between two bars of the railing. His wife, behind him, asked: 'How many times have you been here already?'

'This is the fifth time.'

'You're determined, aren't you, to get this photograph?'

Livio noticed something malicious and provoking in his wife's question, but he attached no importance to it and, without taking his face away from the opening, answered: 'I'm determined because it will sell very well.'

'Or for some other reason?'

Beyond the garden and the gravelled open space, Livio could see the façade of the red-painted villa, the row of vases planted with lemon-trees along the terrace, the door framed in white marble under a tiled porch. Slightly to the right of the door could be seen the front part of an enormous American car, black and with dazzling chromium plate, very like a hearse. In the dull sirocco light the fine gravel of the drive seemed to be pulsating with a swarming life of its own which made one feel dizzy. Livio turned his face from the opening and inquired with sudden irritation: '*What* other reason?'

His wife was now wandering about round the heap of rubbish on which he was seated, in a state of feverish, menacing agitation like that of a wild beast in a cage. She suddenly whisked round. 'D'you really think I don't understand?'

'But *what*?'

'That you want to get this photograph of her so as to have an excuse for approaching her and visiting her and then, by degrees, becoming her lover.'

In his astonishment Livio, for a moment, found nothing to say. Finally he pronounced slowly: 'Is that what you think?'

'Certainly,' she said, in an irresolute yet stubborn tone of voice, as though she too were aware of the absurdity of the accusation but had nevertheless privately made up her mind to maintain it at all costs.

'D'you really think that I, Livio Millefiorini, a shabby, down-at-heel photographer, would aspire to become the lover of a film-star who is famous all over the world, who is a multi-millionairess, and who, into the bargain, is well provided with a husband, not to mention a number of suitors?'

His wife's round, childish face, more swollen-looking than ever, expressed at the same time both indecision and obstinacy. At length she said impudently: 'Well, yes, that's what I think.' She took a kick at an empty tin and went on: 'D'you think I didn't notice your disappointment today when I said I wanted to come with you? And your delight, on those other days, when I said I *wouldn't* come with you?'

'But, Lucia ...'

'You want to have an excuse for getting into touch with her. You'll take a photograph and then you'll telephone her and so you'll meet and make love.'

Livio looked at her; then with sudden haste he put his eye to the opening: he thought he had caught sight of something moving on the open space. It was not the film-star, however, but two large poodles, of a dirty white not very different from the colour of the gravel, which rolled about, nibbling at each other, and then rushed off round the corner of the villa and vanished. Livio turned round again and said with profound conviction: 'You're mad. Now I understand why you have a swollen face today. You're swollen with jealousy.'

'No, I'm not mad. And I'll take this opportunity of telling you: I'm fed up, fed up, fed up.'

Livio wondered whether it would not be a good plan, while he was waiting for the invisible film-star, to take some interesting photograph in the meantime. He suddenly noticed something glittering, on the top step in front of the door. He put his eye to the lens and saw that it was two glasses and a bottle of whisky. Perhaps, he thought, the star and her husband had sat on the step, possibly the evening before, to have a little tipple and look at the full moon as it appeared behind the cypresses of the Via Appia. 'A glass of whisky in the moonlight, sitting unceremoniously on the doorstep: that's the title,' thought Livio as he took the photograph and at once re-loaded his camera. Behind him, he heard his wife repeat: 'Yes, I'm utterly fed up.'

'Fed up with what?'

'With everything, and in the first place with you. If you even loved me.... But you don't love me; it's barely two years since we were married and you're running after all the women.'

'But when, when ...?'

'You run after all the women, and therefore certain things which I might have put up with if you loved me have become unendurable.'

'But what things?'

'What things? Well listen, I'll tell you them all. The furnished room with the window on the courtyard, with no separate entrance and with the "use" of a kitchen. Buses and trams. Meals standing up in a snack bar. Third-rate cinemas. Television at the dairy. And look here – look!'

Livio looked; there was something compelling in the tone of the exasperated voice. Standing on the rubbish-heap, his wife had pulled up her skirt a little and was showing him the patched edge of her under-garment and the long darns in the stockings on her thin legs. 'Look!' she said; 'my underclothes are in tatters, I wear stockings like spiders' webs and shoes down at the heels, and this dress is two years old. And the baby is wrapped in rags and has a drawer for his cradle. Isn't that enough for you?'

Livio frowned and tried to reason with her. 'I started only a short time ago. I had to spend all my money on fitting up a studio. Now I shall be beginning to earn.'

But by this time his wife was no longer listening to him. 'Besides,' she said, 'I must also tell you, I don't like your profession.'

Livio once again put his face to the opening among the rose-bushes. The glass door under the tiled porch had now opened and a manservant in a white jacket appeared. The man stopped, took the whisky bottle and the two glasses and vanished. Livio took a photograph of this also, reloaded his camera and then turned round and said, with intense irritation: 'So you don't like my profession? Why ever not? It's just as good as any other, isn't it?'

'No,' she cried angrily, 'it's not just as good as any other. It's a despicable profession. You spend your time annoying people who have done you no harm and whose only fault is that they are well-known. You persecute them, you're ruthless with them, you won't leave them in peace. You're incapable of love yourself and you spy upon the love of those who *do* love, you have no real life of your own and you try to portray the lives of those who *do* have real lives, you're a penniless wretch yourself and you photograph the luxury and the amusements of those who have money. And I tell you, too, that when certain things happen – like the thing that happened the other evening at the door of that night club, when the actor started kicking you – then I'm ashamed of you. Because, instead of standing up to him, all you tried to do was to get as many photographs of him as you could, and I really believe that, if you'd been able to, you'd have actually photographed his foot at the moment when it was kicking your behind, and then you'd have been happy.' She laughed, came down off the rubbish-heap and stopped at a short distance from him. Livio took a quick glance through the opening, saw that the space in front of the house was still deserted, then turned round and cried: 'You'll be sorry for these things that you're saying to me.'

'The hour of truth has arrived,' she said with some solemnity; 'I'm fed up, fed up. Fed up with your photographs that nobody buys, fed up with hearing you talk about your contemptible exploits, fed up with hoping for better days. You would photograph anything in the world if it could be useful to you, even our own private life. In fact you've already done so.'

'What d'you mean?'

'Yes, you've done it, you took a photograph of me at the seaside, in a bikini, standing in front of a hut at a deserted bathing-place, and the picture was published with the title: "Rainy May. But some people are already thinking of sea-bathing."'

Livio shrugged his shoulders. 'But you were perfectly willing to be taken.'

'Yes, and I caught a cold.'

'But will you please tell me what you want of me?'

He saw her look disconcerted for a moment; then she said: 'I want you to give up lying in wait in this stupid way, and then we can go.'

'Are you still convinced that I want to become the film star's lover?'

'Yes.'

'Well, I'm not going to give in to you. I've decided to get this photograph, and get it I shall.'

His attention had been distracted while he was speaking. But now he turned and saw, through the tangle of rose-trees, that there was something going on, over on the space in front of the house: in fact the star herself opened the glass door under the tiled porch and appeared in the door-way. Livio recognized the straw-coloured hair, the plump, thickly powdered face, the large, heavily made-up eyes, the big red mouth, the celebrated enormous bosom which peeped out above her bodice in two closely-pressed swell-ings. She lifted her bag up to the level of her bosom, fumbled in it, drew out a pair of dark glasses and put them on. Then she raised her arm and gave a shout. At once a dark shadow rushed across the lens: it was her chauffeur. She looked down, then walked out towards the car. She was dressed in a ridiculous way, like a doll, in a tight, pale-blue bodice and a wide, flower-patterned crinoline skirt which revealed legs of a chalky whiteness.

Now or never, thought Livio. He lifted the camera and started following her with it as she walked across the open space, ready to take the photograph at the moment when she was getting into the car. But all of a sudden he felt some shapeless, massive object come crashing down upon him, causing him to fall off the petrol-tin on which he was standing. When he got up again, he saw his wife running away over the field towards the Via Appia, clutching his camera in her hand.

For a short while he stood still, angry and disappointed, his eyes filled with tears. Then, resigned, he walked away slowly towards the road. But he was brought to a halt: the star's long black car was passing, at that moment, right in front of him; here was another photograph that his wife had prevented him from taking. The car went off into the distance; he looked up and saw his wife coming towards him, holding the camera. Her face was no longer either swollen or red; she had given vent to her feelings; and she was smiling at him. As she came up to him she said: 'Now you can take a photograph of *me*. It's a very long time since you promised to, but you can never make up your mind.'

It Was an Adventure

The woman had telephoned him several times with a persistence which was at the same time both proud and pathetic, a mixture of urgent entreaty and haughty dignity that in the end had aroused his curiosity. He felt it could lead either to an adventure, or anyhow to something unusual and eccentric; and that in either case it was worth taking the risk. And so, at the fifth telephone call, he said: 'All right, then. Where d'you propose we should meet?'

'D'you know the bar-restaurant "The Lotus Flower"?'

'The one on the E.U.R. motorway?'

'Yes, that's it. I'll be at the bar, with a magazine in my hand. I'm dark, and I'll be dressed in black.'

'Why in black?'

'I'm in mourning for a relative.'

When, on the day arranged, he reached the bottom of the bare hill on which the 'Lotus Flower' restaurant stood solitary, Lorenzo slowed down his car and looked upwards: pale and round as a sacramental wafer, an enormous full moon hung in the greenish sky of twilight, behind the black outline of a kind of pagoda. The windows of the pagoda were all lit up with a yellow light; and the road which wound spirally round the hill was pricked out with red lanterns. It looked like a Japanese print – but of the most commercial type; and the contrast with the row of bluish skyscrapers opposite, on the motorway, was positively irritating. Lorenzo pressed down the accelerator, and the car moved rapidly up the slope and came to a stop on an open space, amongst other cars, in front of the pagoda.

A screen with a design of lotus flowers in red and gold stood just inside the entrance-door. Lorenzo walked round the screen and, as soon as his eyes had grown accustomed to the semi-darkness, he saw a low room with a ceiling of red cross-beams, little black-lacquered wooden tables, bamboo chairs and painted lanterns. Many couples were sitting at the tables, most of them girls and young men of modest circumstances, such as might well be attracted by the coarsely exotic quality of the place. Other couples, in the centre of the room, were moving in a slow, absorbed manner to the rhythms of a juke-box. Under a staircase leading to the upper floor, with a balustrade also in the Chinese style, could be seen the bar, with its chromium-plated coffee-machine and its rows of bottles. A woman was sitting there, all alone, on one of the high stools, and in her hand, conspicuously against her black skirt, she was holding a rolled-up magazine. Lorenzo went across and, before speaking to her, looked at her carefully.

As he came close to her, he saw that she was very young and not without a certain rustic beauty of her own. Her face was round, with a noble, authoritative expression, her hair thick and puffed out; she had rather piercing eyes, a small aquiline nose which looked like the beak of a bird of prey, and a big, arrogant mouth. The clumsy, smudged make-up on her lips stood out like a wound against the pallor of her face. Her black eyes, following the fashion, were circled with black. Lorenzo thought, automatically: 'It's an adventure.' Then he put out his hand, saying: 'Good evening. My name's Lorenzo.'

'And mine's Assunta.'

Taking her by the elbow and indicating a secluded table, Lorenzo said politely: 'Shall we go over there?' She got down at once, obediently, from her stool, showing herself to be small but graceful and well-made, and again he thought, with cheerful assurance: 'Yes, certainly this is an adventure.' They sat down on the uncomfortable bamboo seats, in the blood-red light of a paper lantern. As soon as the waiter had taken their orders and gone away, she said resentfully: 'D'you know I've been waiting for half an hour already?'

Her voice was like her outward appearance, rustic and aggressive. Lorenzo smiled and said: 'I'm sorry I'm late. But now I'm completely at your service until...' – he looked at his watch and then added: 'let us say anyhow for two hours.'

The two chairs were very close together and their knees were touching, but she did not seem to notice it. Lorenzo thought once again that this was certainly an adventure, but this time with, as it were, a kind of premature satiety. Then she said brusquely: 'Perhaps, however, it would be best for you to know, in the first place, who I am.'

'Yes, tell me.'

'I come from P.' – and she mentioned a small town not far from Rome – 'and I've been married for a year. My father-in-law was a landowner and he died last year. My husband and I then decided to move to Rome.' She paused for a moment, then went on rather sombrely: 'I'm in love with my husband and I wouldn't be unfaithful to him, for all the gold in the world. Let that be quite clear.'

Immediately, and almost with relief, Lorenzo thought: 'It's not an adventure. Let's see then what it is.' He asked her with some curiosity: 'Why d'you tell me this?'

'Because you city young men have strange ideas about women.'

Smiling, Lorenzo replied: 'Let's leave criticisms aside and come down to facts. Tell me in what way I can be of use to you.'

She pointed to the magazine which she had put down on the table. 'In this magazine it says that you're a very social kind of man.'

Lorenzo glanced at the magazine. It was a popular illustrated production which specialized in society gossip; and in a small photograph he was shown dancing at a night club, amongst a number of other couples. 'I'm not a social person,' he said. 'This magazine passes me off as something that I'm *not*.'

She did not appear to have heard him. 'My husband and I know no one here in Rome,' she said. 'Since this magazine speaks of you as being a man who knows a great many people, I telephoned you to ask you a favour.'

'What is that?'

'To help me to get to know some people. To introduce

me into your circle.'

'This is not an adventure,' thought Lorenzo, 'it's just a piece of folly. But it may be amusing.' Nothing of these reflections was visible on his unmoving face. In order to gain time, he inquired: 'Is it possible that you know nobody, absolutely nobody?'

'Yes, it's true,' she answered ingenuously; 'here in Rome we have neither relations nor friends. We're all alone.'

'Where d'you live?'

'We live in the Parioli quarter, in quite a big flat, with a very large living-room, but nobody ever comes there.'

'And what d'you do all day long?'

'Nothing.'

'What d'you mean, nothing? You must do something.'

'In the mornings I'm busy in the house; I have a cook and a maid. Then we have lunch. After lunch we sleep. In the afternoon we go out, or rather *I* go out, because my husband doesn't like going for walks. I go out and walk about the town.'

'Alone?'

'Yes, alone.'

'And what d'you do?'

'Nothing. I wander round the streets and look at the shop windows and the people. Then I go home, we have dinner, and in the evenings we either go to the cinema or we watch television.'

'But your husband must have a profession and must know people in his profession.'

'My husband hasn't any profession. He's a landowner, like his father. Once a week he goes to the country and he knows people there, of course. But in Rome he knows no one.'

Finally, as though to conclude his cross-questioning, Lorenzo asked: 'And what sort of people would you like to know?'

'Nice sort of people, with whom we could enjoy ourselves and have a pleasant time.'

'What does that imply?'

'Oh well, the usual things: going for walks, going to the cinema together, going out to dinner, perhaps even playing cards. My husband likes playing cards.'

'What sort of type is your husband?'

'He's young. He's rather fat.'

'Yes,' thought Lorenzo, 'this is a piece of folly, just the kind of thing that happens to me.' He said gently: 'Forgive me, but a favour of the sort you're asking of me is something that one does only for a woman one loves, or with whom one has ties of deep friendship. In our case, what reason is there why I should do what you want? We're not in love, we barely know one another ...'

He realized that she had not foreseen so obvious an objection; for she remained silent, her eyes wide open. He continued, with the feeling, nevertheless, that he was saying the wrong thing: 'You're a stranger to me; what pretext should I have for introducing you, as you say, into my circle?'

She said suddenly: 'I'm sorry, evidently I made a mistake.'

'What d'you mean?'

'Seeing your face in that magazine, I thought you were a kind sort of person and that you would do me this favour without asking anything in exchange. But I made a mistake. I'm sorry.' Abruptly she rose to her feet.

Lorenzo again revised his ideas. 'It's not a piece of folly,' he thought. 'Perhaps it's really an adventure.' Rather feebly he said: 'Wait. I haven't said everything yet. Sit down again for a moment and let's talk.'

But she seemed now, in her disappointment, to be anxious only to cut the matter short. 'No, no, let me go.' She turned her back on him and walked towards the door. Lorenzo followed her.

Once outside, she hesitated for a moment, and Lorenzo took advantage of it to catch up with her and say: 'At least let me take you home.'

'No not home. Just as far as the first taxi rank.'

'But why? I can perfectly well drive you home.'

'No, no, I tell you; not home.'

In the meantime, however, she had quite calmly got into the car and sat down beside Lorenzo, spreading out her wide skirt partly over his legs. While the car was going down the road round and round the hill, she asked, all of a sudden: 'Who's that girl you were dancing with, in the photograph? Is she your fiancée?'

'I haven't a fiancée. She's just – some girl or other.'

'No,' she answered, with strange, sudden jealousy, 'I'd be willing to swear that she's not just some girl or other.'

'Why d'you think that?'

'From the way you're dancing with her.'

'Why, what way?'

'Cheek to cheek.'

By this time they had arrived at a taxi-rank. 'Here we are,' she said; 'let me get out here.' And Lorenzo could not but stop and open the door. He saw her turn her head for a moment as she added: 'Once more, you must excuse me'; and then she walked away, proud and erect, into the darkness of the evening. Then it crossed his mind again that probably it was, in truth, an adventure. But this seemed to him a fatuous notion and he corrected himself: 'It was a piece of folly.'

After the effusive expressions of the previous evening at the night club where he had met the two girls, the voice on the telephone seemed to Girolamo, in some inexplicable way, to be reluctant and almost hostile. 'To lunch? You want us to go out to lunch in this heat?'

'But yesterday evening we agreed that we'd have lunch together today.'

'One says all sorts of things in the evening after one's had something to drink.'

'Really, if you remember, it was you yourself who suggested that I might telephone and arrange about lunch.'

'*I* did? Obviously I must have been drunk.'

'Anyhow, what d'you want to do?'

'Wait a moment.'

Girolamo heard the click of the girl's heels as she walked across the floor, and then the sound of an agitated, disagreeable argument; but he could not distinguish the words. And then the voice again: 'Come in an hour's time.'

'Are you coming by yourself?'

'No question of that. My friend's coming too.'

Feeling very disconcerted and wondering whether it was possible to find some excuse and extricate himself from the engagement, Girolamo spent an hour driving about from one suburban avenue to another, in the shade of big plane-trees laden with summer foliage. The two girls lived in the Parioli quarter; and when he stopped in front of the block of flats, he was surprised at the modern luxury of the façade, all glass and marble: they had appeared to him to be in quite modest circumstances – a couple of office-workers, perhaps. But when he went into the entrance hall, he discovered that their flat was in the semi-basement. He went down the stairs, in darkness found the door and rang the bell. The same ungracious voice shouted to him from inside to go and wait in the street. Girolamo reflected that the girls probably had only one room available and that the room was in a state of great untidiness. He climbed the stairs again and went and sat in his car, in front of the main entrance.

He waited a long time, the coachwork of his car becoming red hot in the sunshine; at last they appeared. They were very different: the younger one small and pretty; the elder, tall and ugly; but they had in common the same corpse-like powder on their pale faces, the same funereal circle of black make-up round their eyes, the same anaemic lipstick, the colour of mucus, on their mouths. Their clothes, too, were similar: two green tulip-shaped skirts and two diaphanous blouses of stiff, transparent material through which — as if they had been made of cellophane — could be seen their sturdy brassières, tightly stretched and close-fitting and of a dark pink colour. The hair of both of them was a straw-coloured blonde which contrasted with their black eyes and eyebrows. They came over to him and the smaller of the two put her face in at the window and said: 'Let's go and have lunch, then. But I warn you, we have things to do in half an hour's time, three quarters at the most.'

'What a hurry you're in,' said Girolamo, annoyed.

'I'm sorry, but either that, or we go home.'

Asking himself what could be the reason for this crude behaviour, but feeling almost more curious than offended, Girolamo drove them rapidly to a restaurant not far from the Ponte Milvio. But when they went into the garden they saw only a number of empty tables in the hot, scanty shade of the acacia-trees. 'There's no one here,' said Girolamo; 'it's the August holiday, of course. D'you want to stay here, or would you rather try somewhere else?'

The smaller one answered rudely: 'We didn't come out to show ourselves off but to eat. Let's stay here.'

They sat down, the waiter came, the smaller one started reading the menu. 'Lobster. Can I order lobster?'

'Of course,' said Girolamo, astonished; 'what a question!'

'One never knows. Did you count your money before you invited us?'

The waiter, notebook in hand, waited patiently, with the air of a man who knows such situations and is not surprised. Girolamo, with a laugh which concealed his irritation, said: 'Yes, I counted my money: you can go for the lobster.'

'Lobster, then,' said the waiter. 'And what wine?'

The smaller girl again inquired: 'Can I order a bottle of wine? Or shall I say the ordinary draught wine?'

'You can order what you like,' said Girolamo, bored.

'Don't get angry,' said the taller girl; 'we're doing this for your sake. So often people invite us out and then haven't enough money.'

The waiter went away; and the smaller girl asked rudely: 'By the way, I don't even know what your name is.'

'My name's Girolamo.'

'I don't like the name Girolamo.'

'And you two – what are your names?'

'She's called Cloti,' said the taller one, 'and I'm Maia.'

'But those are diminutives, aren't they?'

'Yes, her name is Clotilde and mine is Marianna.'

'What diminutive d'you suggest for me?' Girolamo asked Cloti.

'None,' replied the girl brusquely.

'Well, you've got to call me something. And seeing that you don't like Girolamo ...'

'What d'you want me to call you?' answered Cloti. 'In any case we part in half an hour and shan't ever see each other again.'

'Are you sure of that?'

'Oh yes, perfectly sure.'

The waiter came back, and they started eating the lobster in silence, looking at empty tables upon which big sparrows in search of crumbs came and perched from time to time, fluttering down from the boughs of the acacia-trees. Girolamo observed Cloti stealthily and was confirmed in his opinion that she was very pretty and that she attracted him. Her eyes were black and bright and slightly prominent, and she was snub-nosed, her nose being tiny and uptilted, with conspicuous nostrils; her mouth was capricious, pouting, fleshy, the lower lip curving downwards over an almost non-existent chin. Her head was set on a very beautiful neck, round and white, smooth and strong. At last Girolamo said: 'D'you know you have very beautiful eyes?'

'It's no use your paying me compliments,' Cloti snarled at him. 'Kindly remember: I'm not grist for *your* mill.'

'For whose, then?'

'That has nothing to do with you.'

Girolamo turned towards Maia. 'Will you do me a favour?'

Maia had a plump, circular face from which a long, pointed nose stuck out like the beak of a bird. 'What favour d'you want me to do you?' she asked.

'Tell your friend to be a little more polite.'

She turned and repeated, like a parrot: 'D'you hear, Cloti? Why aren't you more polite?'

'You wanted me to come out to lunch, and I've come. But don't ask anything more of me.'

'But, Cloti . . .'

'Oh, leave me alone.'

Girolamo said with a sigh: 'Let's talk about something else. How d'you come to be in town over the holiday? Aren't you going away?'

'What about you?' replied Cloti. 'Why haven't *you* gone away?'

'I like Rome in the summer.'

'Well, *we* like Rome in the summer, too.'

'We're office-workers,' explained Maia; 'we're not going on holiday till the end of the month.'

'Where d'you work?'

Cloti quickly intervened. 'What's that got to do with you? Have I asked *you* where you work?'

'If you asked me, I'd tell you.'

'But I'm not asking you, it doesn't interest me.'

'Why, Cloti,' said Girolamo affectionately, 'may I know why you're angry with me?' He put out his hand across the table and placed it on top of the girl's small, pretty, slightly puffy hand. Cloti immediately pulled her hand away, crying: 'Don't touch me!'

'But what's the matter with you, Cloti, what's wrong?'

'Besides, don't call me Cloti.'

'What am I to call you, then?'

'Call me Signorina Clotilde.'

'Well, really,' said Girolamo, losing patience, 'if you didn't want to come, you might have said so. But, once you've accepted, it's your duty at least to be polite.'

'Duty? You're crazy. Why duty? Just because you're giving me lunch?'

'Really, Cloti,' said her friend.

'You be quiet,' cried Cloti; 'it was you who made me accept this absurd invitation. In fact, seeing that it was you, you can stay here with him. I'm going. Good-bye, good-bye.' She rose and hurried away between the tables, towards the gate.

'And now,' said Girolamo as soon as Cloti had disappeared, 'now you must do me the favour of explaining your friend's behaviour which, to put it mildly, is incomprehensible to me.'

He saw her shake her head. 'It's my fault,' she said, 'because I insisted on her accepting. She didn't want to come.'

'But why didn't she want to come?'

'Don't be offended. It was because she doesn't want to waste any more time with penniless young men.'

'But I,' said Girolamo in profound astonishment, 'I'm not penniless.'

'You're not penniless?'

'No, I'm not by any means penniless.'

'Strange; Cloti had that impression. And so did I – don't be offended – I would have sworn it.'

'But what made you think that?'

'I don't know; everything in general.'

Girolamo sat silent for a moment, then went on: 'But, since Cloti has these ideas about men, why, before treating me like that, didn't she make certain, why didn't she ask me? I would have told her the truth – that I'm not penniless; then she might have been polite and we should have got on well together.'

'You must forgive her. It was from fear.'

'But fear of what?'

'Fear of getting mixed up with one of the usual paupers. You must understand us: we're both of us poor, so what wonder that we try and get to know men who have some means?'

'Yes, but do at least find out.'

'Life is a jungle,' said the girl philosophically. 'Cloti tries to defend herself, that's all. You find it easy to be rational; but a person who is afraid isn't rational.'

Girolamo said no more. The waiter brought the bill and he paid it. Finally the girl said: 'If you like, we could go to the sea tomorrow. I'll speak to Cloti about it.'

'No,' said Girolamo, 'I don't think we can go.'

'Why? Are you offended?'

'No, but now you've made *me* afraid.'

'Afraid of what?'

'Life is a jungle,' said Girolamo, rising to his feet.

Head Against the Wall

Tarcisio finished the scandalous story amid complete silence from the group of friends to whom he had been speaking; and then, after a moment, bending forward, he added in a low, intense voice: 'How disgusting, how disgusting! And this is the man that the young men follow and admire, that they all call "Maestro". How disgusting! I tell you truthfully, when I see him pass I feel my blood boil. And a great desire comes over me to confront him and tell him to his face what I think of him and then give him a couple of good clouts.'

The café waiter came up and said in a loud, sing-song voice: 'Closing time, gentlemen!' But interest in the truly disturbing story told by Tarcisio was so strong that no one noticed him. 'If I were you,' said a woman's voice, quivering with indignation, 'if I were you, I should do it. I should go up to him, tell him the truth to his face, and punch him on the nose.'

A soft, insinuating male voice which Tarcisio did not know, said: 'But why violence? There are other more civilized means for making the truth known. After all, we're not savages. We have the Press, for instance, at our disposal. No need for slaps in the face. The written word is enough.'

Tarcisio listened with bent head to these comments and did not speak. Finally he said: 'I want to do all the harm I possibly can to that man. I must find the way. And I shall find it.'

The waiter persisted: 'Closing time, gentlemen!' And now, partly, perhaps, in order to dissipate the uneasiness which Tarcisio's very open and very violent passion had aroused, the whole company rose and each one paid for his own drinks. Then the customary farewells rang out in the quiet of the night: 'Good night, till tomorrow, good-bye, good night!' Tarcisio was starting off alone when the man who had been the last to speak, the man with the soft, insinuating voice, a dark young man with a big hooked nose and small, bright, black eyes, came up to him, saying: 'If you'll allow me, I'll drive you home.' Instinctively Tarcisio would have liked to refuse, for he did not find the young man sympathetic; but he reflected that after all it would be convenient for him, since he lived a long way away, so he got into the unknown man's little car. The latter introduced himself, holding out his hand and saying: 'Allow me, my name is Livi'; and then, after the car had started off at a moderate speed through the deserted streets of the nocturnal city, he continued, without looking at Tarcisio: 'The story you told interested me very much. I want to make a suggestion to you.'

'What is that?'

'I'm a contributor to a magazine which you no doubt know' – and he cited the name of a partly social, partly political magazine which in reality was very little known – 'and for some time we've been collecting material against this personage that you were talking about. I suggest that I might come and see you and take down the whole story. What d'you think?'

'I think – well, it's an idea,' said Tarcisio hesitatingly.

'Of course,' continued the young man, his habitual calm slightly tinged with self-satisfied, judicious falsity, 'of course the story is not true. But untrue stories can be divided into two categories: those that appear true and those that do not. Yours, however monstrous, has a look of truth. That's enough for us.'

This time Tarcisio protested: 'You don't think it's true? It *is* true.'

The other man remained unruffled. 'Is it? Well, let's see: were you present when L— did those things? Did you see them with your own eyes?'

'No, I didn't see them with my own eyes.' Tarcisio fumbled in his pocket, pulled out a packet of cigarettes, feverishly lit one and went on: 'However, they were told me by someone who *had* seen them.'

'Excuse me – who was it?'

Tarcisio told him the name. The other knit his brow slightly, above his big aquiline nose, and said: 'I know him. He's an unbridled, a positively pathological liar. You can't rely on *him*.'

Tarcisio inhaled a mouthful of smoke, then a second, then a third: his throat was dry, and the smoke, as he drew it in, scorched it with a parching heat. He repeated, in a strangled voice: 'He's a liar?'

'The biggest liar there is. But that doesn't matter. As I have already said, we want to destroy L—; and your story, whether true or false, will come in handy to us. So that's understood, I'll come and see you tomorrow.'

Tarcisio threw away his cigarette, which suddenly seemed very bitter to him, and answered with an effort: 'No, now I think it over, it's better not.'

'But why? Do you hesitate because perhaps you're afraid that L— will come to know it was you who told the story? In that case you can set your mind at rest. By this time L— already knows everything.'

Tarcisio took out the packet of cigarettes again, extracted one with trembling fingers, then put it back into the packet. 'How?' he said.

'Didn't you see, in the group at the café, a middle-aged man, bald and fat and serious-looking, who was listening to you and not saying a word? D'you know who that man was?'

'Yes, I know.' Tarcisio said the name.

'But perhaps you don't know that he's a friend of L—, one of his most intimate friends. By this time he has already telephoned to L—, has already told him everything.'

They had now arrived. The car slowed down and came to a stop in a wide, tree-lined street, in front of the huge but modest entrance-door of a suburban block of flats. 'We're going to do this article, then,' said the young man, pulling up the handbrake and turning towards Tarcisio. 'I'll come tomorrow morning; I'll jot down the whole thing in an hour. Of course, if you like, I'll let you see it in proof...'

'Leave me alone, good-bye, good-bye.' Tarcisio scrambled out of the car with almost hysterical haste, went to the door, stuck his key into the lock, entered and closed the door again. All this he did without turning round, without looking back at the little car and the dark young man.

He rushed up four flights of the narrow, dark staircase; halted a moment, panting, on a landing on which three identical rubbish-bins stood beside three doors, also identical; then opened the door of his flat and went in. The cold, stale smell of cooking increased his feeling of despair. Feeling his way in the darkness, he went to the bedroom, turned on the light and looked in: the big double bed occupied almost the whole of the little room; his wife's black head showed up prominently between the white of the sheets and the white of the pillow. Her back was turned towards him, and she appeared to be asleep. Furiously he flung himself across the bed, seized his wife by the shoulders and shook her: 'Clelia, Clelia!'

She sighed, moved slightly, and then started to curl up again under the bedclothes. So he shook her again, crying: 'Wake up, come on, wake up!'

This time she awoke completely and turned over, showing her face, which was neither young nor beautiful, with too long a nose and a hurt expression. Keeping her eyes closed, she said in a drawling, mournful voice: 'I was asleep. What on earth d'you want? Aren't you content now with leaving me alone all day long, d'you also want me not to sleep at night?'

'You're my wife, aren't you? It's your duty to listen to me.'

'But what d'you want me to do?'

'A very unpleasant thing has happened to me. I want you to tell me what you think about it.'

'Let's hear it, then.' Clelia pulled herself up till her thin bust showed above the bedclothes and stared at him with eyes that were vague and half-closed with sleep. 'I'm your wife. I'm listening.'

Tarcisio sat down on the edge of the bed and gave an

account of all that had happened that evening: the scandalous story about L— which he had told at the café; the mute presence of a friend of L—; the journalist's proposal; the conversation that had followed. 'What d'you think?' he concluded anxiously; 'd'you think I did wrong? After all, I had been assured that the story was true. D'you think it'll do me harm?'

His wife was now sitting up in bed looking at him with a stupefied expression in which, nevertheless, there was a glint of a kind of malicious awareness. Finally, with eyes lowered, and in a monotonous, sleepy voice, she replied: 'I think your principal weakness is envy. Actually your greatest weakness is your insensibility towards me, which is quite inhuman. But that is a thing which concerns only myself. Your enviousness concerns the whole world.'

'But I'm not envious.'

'You *are* envious. You're a failure, you feel yourself a failure, you'd like not to be a failure. And so you envy all those who are not failures like you. L— may be a monster – I'm not denying that – but you're up against him simply and solely because he's not a failure like you. It was envy that made you tell a story like that, which even a blind man could see was not true.'

'You – you, my wife – say this to me?'

'You asked me what I thought and I've told you.'

'I asked you for an opinion, not for insults.'

'You call them insults? My opinion is that they're the truth.'

'And you, my wife, speak to me like this?'

'Yes, I speak to you like this because it's the truth. And now you can be quite sure that that man, the friend of L— who was present, has already told him everything. And L— will get his revenge.'

'How d'you mean – get his revenge?'

'I don't know,' said his wife confusedly, as though she were suddenly feeling sleepy again; 'L— is a powerful man and you are not, and he'll do something to get his own back. The story you told could lead to a prosecution. But L— will get his revenge in some other way.'

'And you, my wife, you speak to me like this?'

'I don't know what to say to you. You wanted me to speak and I've spoken. Now let me sleep.'

Tarcisio suddenly seized his wife by the neck and shouted again: 'You, my wife, you speak to me like this?' Then, pushing her away violently, he clasped his head in his hands, got down off the bed and began wandering round the room, knocking his head against the wall. His attention was attracted by the wardrobe, with its straight corner sharp as a knife-edge; with furious, deliberate violence he went and banged his head against it. It was a hard blow but Tarcisio scarcely noticed it: he was thinking of L— and of how he would have come to know of his slanderous story; he was thinking of how L— would get his revenge; he was at the same time both frightened and ashamed; and he was also in despair because his wife had said unpleasant things to him and he feared that these things might be true. After banging his head against the corner of the wardrobe he went over to his wife, staggering and holding his hand to his head where he had knocked it, and felt a wetness in his palm, and when he took his hand away he saw that it was red with blood. In a trembling voice, he said: 'Look at all this blood. I think I've hurt myself.'

His wife uttered a cry and jumped out of bed; she took Tarcisio by the arm and led him to the kitchen. On the way, as she walked beside him, she kissed his bloodstained hand in an agonized frenzy, rather like a dog licking its master after barking at him.

Within the four narrow walls of the kitchen, Tarcisio, standing in front of the grey cement sink full of dirty dishes, held his head under the tap. He felt his wife's hand softly, gently, lightly, lovingly, wiping the wound with a little wad of cotton-wool; and at the same time he was conscious of the sour smell of the dish-water: his wife's body was close to his; every now and then her side lightly touched his, as she kept saying, in a troubled voice: 'It's nothing ... It's just a little cut.' Then, with bowed head, Tarcisio started to weep, letting the tears fall on the greasy surface of the bottom of a saucepan which lay upside down in the sink.

The Good Life

The house was reached by an unpaved, muddy road at the end of which could be seen the blue-green, undulating countryside growing paler and paler until it melted into the white sky. On each side of the road there were houses under construction, and everywhere there were lime pits, scaffolding, barrels with the bottom knocked out, rafters; but, since it was midday, work had stopped, and the workmen, sitting on the low walls, were eating their sandwiches without speaking. No one went past; there was a great silence. 'We shall find them at lunch,' Marco said to me as he stepped cautiously over the puddles, 'but, on the other hand, that's the only moment when one can be sure of finding that woman.' I asked him what she did, and he replied that she had a milliner's shop in town and that it was there that his sister, looking for a job, had become involved in this tyrannical friendship. 'She's a kind of business woman,' he concluded, passing his gigantic hand, broad as a shovel, not over his brow but over his whole face; 'anyhow you'll see her now.'

The flat was on the ground floor of a small building with pink walls and pistachio-green shutters. The door was opened by a young servant-girl, who left us for a moment in a tiny sitting-room, a plain little room notwithstanding its few cheap, coquettish ornaments, and who came back almost at once, saying that we could go through into the dining-room. As Marco had foreseen, the two women were still at table. A great light flooded the bare room; the wide stretch of country visible through the curtainless window had a curious effect, as though it were the sea. What struck me most of all, together with the smell of cooking which tainted the air, was the untidy and extremely uncouth appearance of the table. The cloth was stained with wine, crumbs and dirty plates were all over the place; the crockery was coarse and greasy with oil and tomato right up to its edges; instead of a bottle there was a crooked flask in a straw casing.

I looked at the two women who, somewhat embarrassed, had stopped eating. Dora, Marco's sister, would have been beautiful if she had not looked so pale and haggard: she was fair-haired, bloodless, white as wax, with big blue eyes, deep-set and dull. Signorina Vercelloni, on the other hand, was quite the opposite: broad and thick-set, she wore her hair short and had the fleshy, blunt features of a boy; her eyes were black and calm, with a slow way of looking that was not without a certain unconscious majesty; her lips, which were not painted, were shadowed by a slight down of a decidedly dark colour. I noticed also that, while Dora sat erect and composed on her chair, her friend, either because she had drunk a little too much or because she did not care, sat crosswise, lounging against the back of her chair with her table-napkin tucked into the collar of her masculine shirt. She was dressed in grey, with a jacket of masculine cut and a narrow skirt, and a bright-coloured tie hung down on to her chest.

She did not appear surprised by our visit, but slightly annoyed, as though she considered it an interference at the same time both indiscreet and useless. We sat down; and, without any delay – just as if Signorina Vercelloni had not been present – Marco, bending his big body forward on the narrow chair, began urging his sister not to persist in living away from home any longer, but to return to the bosom of the family. His arguments were both sound and moderate; he alluded skilfully to their mother's displeasure, without saying a word against Signorina Vercelloni; obviously, notwithstanding his resentment, he wished to appear moderate and objective. But, as she listened, there was an expression of extreme obtuseness on his sister's face. 'No,' she replied finally, in the tone of someone repeating a lesson, 'I'm not coming with you.... Up till now I've been too kind, I've sacrificed myself, but now I've come to understand that I ought to be valued according to my merits.... Besides, I want to enjoy life.'

Signorina Vercelloni, who had displayed no anxiety, smiled calmly and unostentatiously, showing her fine, regular teeth which were as white as milk. 'Poor Dora,' she said in a sonorous voice; 'it's understandable that she doesn't want to go back home.... At over twenty-eight you kept her shut up in the house all day long, you made her wash the dishes and cook and sweep the floors...' With superior, protective calmness she enumerated the impositions suffered by her friend, and the latter sat listening to her with evident satisfaction, like a peasant who for the first time hears a speaker at a meeting shouting at him that he is oppressed, exploited, kept in subjection, and that the moment of liberation has arrived. Then, as soon as Signorina Vercelloni had finished speaking, Dora turned towards her brother and, with a stupid, elated expression on her face, explained how here she had a room all to herself and could go out whenever she wanted, even alone, even to the cinema or the café.

'It's as if I were the mistress of the house,' she concluded with an air of sagacity. 'In the morning I get up late, I have my coffee in bed ... I can smoke cigarettes and have a drink when I want to ... Maria takes me about in her car, she's given me clothes, she's extremely good to me. And besides, I can receive anyone I want to in my room, even at night...'

This last remark startled Marco; however he said nothing, and I reflected that, since he considered his sister to be more of an imbecile than a strumpet, he did not therefore wish to put ideas and suspicions of still unthought-of possibilities into that innocent head. Instead, he answered with great gentleness, clenching his big fists under the table, that if she came back home they would give her a room to herself and that she would be able, as here, to have her coffee in bed and get up late. But the girl shook her head obstinately. 'Up till now,' she replied, 'I haven't known what freedom was and how many advantages can come from it. But now I know, and I'm not going to let myself be persuaded. You and the others can say what you like, but you won't persuade me. I know now what it means to enjoy life'; and as she spoke, her wan, piteous face took on an expression of unmistakable, determined greed.

For a few moments there was silence. Signorina Vercelloni brooded over the girl with her calm black eyes like those of some fine animal; from the window, filled with the unreal greenness of the countryside, a ray of palest sunshine lit up the crockery on the table and the fair hair of Marco's sister. Marco shook his head angrily and bit his lips. The silence was again broken by the girl. 'I have a lovely life,' she said; 'why should I go back with you? Besides, even if I wanted to, I couldn't. Maria and I are due to leave for Paris in a few days.... At home, who would ever have thought of taking me to Paris? And really I think there's nothing so fine as to travel and to go and see a splendid town, full of shops and amusements, like Paris...' And she continued in the same tone, comparing Paris with her own native city and exalting the advantages of her new existence. Signorina Vercelloni explained that they were going to Paris for her customary buying of models. Marco sat listening; then: 'Would you be so kind,' he said, 'as to send Dora away? I should like to speak to you alone.'

His request was at once granted. 'Dora my dear,' said Signorina Vercelloni, 'will you leave us a moment? I have to speak to your brother.' The girl obeyed and rose to her feet. I then observed that she was not as thin in figure as in face but well made and almost buxom. She was wearing a very short dress which was raised up at the back by her over-large buttocks, on her feet she had plush slippers, and her big, exposed calves had something shameless about them. I was struck also by her somewhat unsteady walk as she went to the door, and reflected that perhaps drinking was one of the attractions of this good life which she said she was having. But my attention was drawn away from such notions by the violent tone in which Marco was speaking to the mistress of the house.

'You know very well,' he was saying, 'that my sister is almost insane and that if we had the money she would have already been placed in a home.... What's the point, then, of taking her away from her family, putting ideas into her head, making her believe that up till now she's been sacrificed, martyred? In my opinion it shows a lack of responsibility on your part, or worse...'

Signorina Vercelloni smiled and, taking a cigarette-case from her pocket, opened it and offered it to Marco. This gesture, for some reason, infuriated the giant who, with one blow of his hand, sent both case and cigarettes flying. 'Likely *I* should want to smoke,' he exclaimed angrily. She remained unruffled, but warned him that if he went on like that she would turn him out of the house. Then she picked up a cigarette which had fallen on the table, lit it and began explaining that she had been moved to act in this way because of the affection and pity which the girl had inspired in her. 'It's a real scandal,' she added, 'to keep a beautiful girl like her isolated under the pretext that she's mentally unbalanced. In point of fact she's perfectly sane; it's you and your family who, by continually telling her that she's stupid, have so intimidated her as to make her forget even how to speak. And anyhow, she's of age, and free to do as she likes.' There was a brief silence. 'I'm very fond of Dora,' she suddenly went on, in a quiet voice, 'and in no circumstances will I let her go back to a house where she would be ill-treated...' With difficulty curbing his resentment, Marco answered her that his family was too poor to send Dora on a journey all the way to Paris; but that his sister had never lacked anything; and that, furthermore, the only time they had sent her away alone on a holiday she had done so many foolish things as to undermine their good will once and for all. But Signorina Vercelloni did not seem convinced. 'What you call foolish things,' she said, 'are simply the normal life of anybody. Poor Dora told me the whole story: it seems that she fell in love with someone ... I see no great harm in that.'

The sound of a gramophone reached us at this moment from the adjoining room. Marco bent forward on his chair. 'In short,' he demanded, 'will you let my sister go or will you not?' Signorina Vercelloni lowered her eyes, shook the ash from her cigarette, and then, like a business man dealing with a question of finance, leant back in her chair and looked at Marco. 'No, in no circumstances,' she answered simply.

There was nothing more to be done. In the adjoining room the gramophone went on playing, and I seemed to see that room – the room 'all to herself' to which the girl had alluded – and the girl herself, fascinated by the mirage of a visit to Paris, dancing for joy at having escaped from the constraints of her family into the new atmosphere of an unfettered life. I thought also how well contrived everything was; an almost imbecile girl dominated by the gilded influence of this calm, self-assured Signorina Vercelloni; all those real advantages – Paris, the car, the coffee served in bed: the circle was closed, it was impossible to break it. Unlike Marco, who was serious and preoccupied, I felt cheerful and was almost smiling. Then my friend rose from his chair.

'D'you want to say good-bye to your sister?' inquired Signorina Vercelloni with the solicitude of a Mother Superior now sure of the vocation, hitherto uncertain, of one of her novices. But Marco gloomily answered no, and went out into the vestibule. Signorina Vercelloni did not accompany us; I saw her vanish into the darkness of the corridor. We went out. The workmen at the building-sites had resumed work; from the lofty heights of the wooden scaffolding hammer-blows echoed in the bleak white air of the winter afternoon. 'As far as I'm concerned it's as though my sister were dead,' said Marco all of a sudden. But I did not share his gloom. Rather did the vanity of his efforts make me smile, like one of those slight troubles about which one can never quite decide whether they bring pleasure or grief.

Bestselling Transatlantic Fiction in Panther Books

THE SOT-WEED FACTOR	John Barth	£1.50	☐
BEAUTIFUL LOSERS	Leonard Cohen	60p	☐
THE FAVOURITE GAME	Leonard Cohen	40p	☐
TARANTULA	Bob Dylan	50p	☐
MIDNIGHT COWBOY	James Leo Herlihy	35p	☐
LONESOME TRAVELLER	Jack Kerouac	35p	☐
DESOLATION ANGELS	Jack Kerouac	50p	☐
THE DHARMA BUMS	Jack Kerouac	40p	☐
BARBARY SHORE	Norman Mailer	40p	☐
AN AMERICAN DREAM	Norman Mailer	40p	☐
THE NAKED AND THE DEAD	Norman Mailer	60p	☐
THE BRAMBLE BUSH	Charles Mergendahl	40p	☐
TEN NORTH FREDERICK	John O'Hara	50p	☐
FROM THE TERRACE	John O'Hara	75p	☐
OURSELVES TO KNOW	John O'Hara	60p	☐
THE DICE MAN	Luke Rhinehart	95p	☐
COCKSURE	Mordecai Richler	60p	☐
ST URBAIN'S HORSEMAN	Mordecai Richler	50p	☐
THE CITY AND THE PILLAR	Gore Vidal	40p	☐
BLUE MOVIE	Terry Southern	60p	☐
SLAUGHTERHOUSE 5	Kurt Vonnegut Jr	50p	☐
MOTHER NIGHT	Kurt Vonnegut Jr	40p	☐
PLAYER PIANO	Kurt Vonnegut Jr	50p	☐
GOD BLESS YOU, MR ROSEWATER	Kurt Vonnegut Jr	50p	☐
WELCOME TO THE MONKEY HOUSE	Kurt Vonnegut Jr	40p	☐

Bestselling European Fiction in Panther Books

QUERELLE OF BREST	Jean Genet	60p	☐
OUR LADY OF THE FLOWERS	Jean Genet	50p	☐
FUNERAL RITES	Jean Genet	50p	☐
DEMIAN	Hermann Hesse	40p	☐
THE JOURNEY TO THE EAST	Hermann Hesse	40p	☐
LA BATARDE	Violette Leduc	60p	☐
THE TWO OF US	Alberto Moravia	50p	☐
THE LIE	Alberto Moravia	75p	☐
COMMAND AND I WILL OBEY YOU			
	Alberto Moravia	30p	☐
THE HOTEL ROOM	Agnar Mykle	40p	☐
THE DEFENCE	Vladimir Nabokov	40p	☐
THE GIFT	Vladimir Nabokov	50p	☐
THE EYE	Vladimir Nabokov	30p	☐
NABOKOV'S QUARTET	Vladimir Nabokov	30p	☐
INTIMACY	Jean-Paul Sartre	60p	☐
THE AIR CAGE	Per Wästberg	60p	☐

All these books are available at your local bookshop or newsagent, or can be ordered direct from the publisher. Just tick the titles you want and fill in the form below.

Name ....

Address ....

....

Write to Panther Cash Sales, PO Box 11, Falmouth, Cornwall TR10 9EN

Please enclose remittance to the value of the cover price plus:

UK: 18p for the first book plus 8p per copy for each additional book ordered to a maximum charge of 66p

BFPO and EIRE: 18p for the first book plus 8p per copy for the next 6 books, thereafter 3p per book

OVERSEAS: 20p for first book and 10p for each additional book

Granada Publishing reserve the right to show new retail prices on covers, which may differ from those previously advertised in the text or elsewhere.